AWAKENING

TO WAKE AND SLEEP NO MORE SERIES
BOOK ONE

BY NGOZI T. ROBINSON

I AM Publications

Awakening

I AM Publications
(617) 564-1060
contact@iampubs.com
www.iampubs.com

Cover Illustration by Karen Silberman

ISBN: 978-1-943382-08-8
First Edition, 2021

DEDICATION

To Ma, 1947 – 2002

PROLOGUE
THE MISTS

Cathy floated through a white mist, sensing nothing.

"Daddy?" Her voice faded as the mist swept by her, a raging, silent torrent.

"Child." Her father's voice answered, "So soon. This I did not see."

Cathy looked around but was surprised to see nothing. Even when she looked where her own body should be, she saw only mist.

"Where am I, Daddy?" Her voice faded as soon as she thought the words.

"While you are here, you shape yourself."

"The shapeless dimension," Cathy thought. She had always wanted to know this place, but travelling to afterlife dimensions had always been too dangerous for her.

Cathy allowed herself to remember her death, its circumstances. She remembered her physical life in the *I* dimension. She remembered.

"Daddy who is keeping the gate? I spun a block but it was weak. I think I was dying when I did it." Spotty details flooded in, "It won't last—She's not ready Daddy. She doesn't even know. I thought I had so much time."

"Cathy, come with me. You are to be a Watcher."

A Watcher. A Watcher in the Unmoved dimension. Cathy had wanted that for countless lives. She floated toward the formless source of her father's voice. She remembered.

"Daddy, who watches?"

"There is no one to watch the gate." Silence seemed to thunder.

1

"Sheila. Sheila can…"

"This is no longer your path." The mist seemed to grow denser, pulling her toward it. "Sheila is on her path. And she may yet take her place. Her fear may not bind her forever. But it is not for your energies to dwell there. That is her path."

"You seemed much more caring before." Cathy felt his acceptance flowing through her, becoming her. "I wish her well." She flowed toward her father's voice, the last vestiges of emotion flooding from her. "Father, the gate. Who watches?" It seemed to her she had not asked that question.

The mists stilled. She stopped. Cathy sensed her father's voice moving away.

"I see you are not to be a Watcher. Not yet, child. Your physical world holds you tight. Take care daughter. Some things are not to be trifled with from these dimensions. You are dead in the *I* dimension. And there are bonds on you. Do not damage the thing you are trying to save.

Know that I stand ready. Should Sheila ever open the door, I will be as I was for you, as my momma was for me." The hints of a smile, of pleasure, seemed to enter his voice. A voice that, more and more, seemed a million miles away.

"Goodbye Daddy."

Silence answered Cathy's farewell. And she was already turning away from her father's voice. She couldn't stay here forever. The shapeless dimension was not for dallying, and she had already spent so much time here.

There was much to do. And time passed differently here. She would not know the difference until she touched the *I* dimension. Her touch had to be light onto that world. Lighter than God's breath. As she rushed towards the edge of the shapeless dimension, she prayed that all was not lost. Everything depended on Sheila.

2

PART ONE
GONE

CHAPTER ONE
DEATH

Sheila was tired. In the last few days, she had slept an hour each night. Perhaps. And what little sleep she did have was restless, full of dreams of running down dark and empty halls, terrified of someone that she could not see chasing her. But that dream was nothing new. She was always running from something in her dreams.

Now there was nothing to do but rest. They had all gone. And nothing was left now but a huge mess, tons of food, and her own grief. Mom was gone, and she just didn't know how to act. Her life was incomplete, and she was alone. She was 28 and now an orphan.

She heard noise outside her room. Raines was trying to creep silently in an old house. The floorboards had given him away at least half a dozen times in the last few days. He had made it all the way to the bedroom and was staring at her, both timid and commanding at the same time. She supposed that was one of the reasons why she had married him.

"I liked what you said at the burial site. I felt like it really captured her, and I'm sure she was proud." Raines rubbed his eyes and took a deep breath, trying to hold off tears. He and Cathy had had their own special kinship, a fact that irked Sheila sometimes. But it was inevitable. Everyone could not help but to love Ma.

She tried to let his words wash over her unheard. He was not supposed to be here. He made her feel like she wanted to cry. She had been the one holding everything together. She could not afford to weep as she wanted to since…well, since this whole mess started.

she had never seen her mother so sad
her unshed tears shone and seemed to fill up the
*   whole world*
what had pushed her down that hill?!
her last moments filled with pain
a daughter looking on in helpless terror
searching frantically for a way to make this all go
*   away*
searching for a way to open up a pattern in reality
*   and go back in time*
just a few moments
a way to change places

She was glad Raines was there. She was suddenly aware of herself wrapped in his arms, wracked with tears she had not known were coming. Tears she had feared would never come. The last few days hammered in her mind, weights pulling her down as she drowned. She was tired.

They were in some secluded part of Carderock Falls at the crack of dawn to offer morning prayers. Sheila had been singing her heart out, competing with the birds for primacy. Who else was here to mind so early on a weekday? She twirled until she grew dizzy, and her laughter turned to breathlessness. This was her morning glory at its finest. Had it not been so cold, she would have been tempted to get naked. She loved feeling free as she danced before the Lord.

She looked back at her mom and saw no one. That

was just like Ma to get distracted or go off on a different trail. She decided she wouldn't let it dampen her spirits. As she backtracked to find where her mom had wandered off, she thought of how in the moment she must have been to have not noticed where Ma had gone. Ma usually liked to take Sheila on her diversions when they were together. They were both such free spirits, there was no fixed pattern to their ways. But when she noticed the disturbed earth near the edge of the trail that dropped into a deep gorge, her carefree thoughts turned to anxiety. She followed the skid lines to the bottom of the gorge, to her mother's broken and lifeless body.

Her ragged screams brought no one, so she finally had to stop. It was a waste of energy she didn't have. She hoisted her mother's light frame over her shoulder and stood. Her face was stuck in a horrified silent scream. She was carrying her mother's dead body.

Scrambling up rocks and, by overwhelming force of will and need alone, managing not to drop her mother, she finally reached the trail. It was hours after they had arrived, but it felt colder. She was freezing to her core. Looking around she still saw no one. She began walking to the car, thinking necessary thoughts. Would they blame her for this? Should she have left Mom at the bottom of the gorge, as evidence of an accident? They would ask her how she had fallen in a place she had been dozens of times, and she would not know! Fear, not grief, started to fill her.

She was making a mistake. There was a better way to do this. She just had to find it. Mom would say she had to allow the answer to reveal itself. She lay her mother down in front of a tree. As she straightened, she realized her body was shaking with tension. She turned away towards the waterfall. Its beauty was cruel. Nothing was coming to her. No mystical answer was coming. Her body felt like it was about to sink into the earth.

A lizard sped past her feet. She gasped. Why would a

lizard be here in the middle of winter? She shook her head. Everything was confusing and her ears were starting to ring with cold. She had lost her hat on the way up. There was no other way. Taking her mother to get help was the only solution. It was just harder. It made an impossible thing even more trying.

She wanted to run away from the hilltop shrieking. But it wouldn't solve anything and she would probably just fall and die too. That possibility held a faint glimmer of appeal. Ending it all would be wonderful. But then again, she might just break bones and be lying in pain and grief for hours. There was no other way. She picked up her mother and headed for the car. Somehow she seemed heavier, more dense than before. Inside she beat back tears and steeled herself for what was to come.

CHAPTER TWO
THE CALLS

Now, in the safety of Raines' arms, with not another soul in earshot and no more pressing arrangements to be made, she cried those tears she had been stuffing away since that day.

Nothing after that morning had been as impossible as that scramble up the hill and trek to the car. But it had come close. Park police had not questioned her too hard. She supposed they had seen the grief on her face and known there was no foul play. The ranger at the gate, Joanne, had let her sit inside the heated kiosk and drink coffee until the ambulance and park officers arrived. She must have downed eight cups, and she had still felt like she might faint at any moment. It was six at night and completely dark by the time she had left Carderock Falls. And on the drive home she knew sleep, much less rest, was an eternity away.

She hated the calling. Black people put big stock in spreading the word. Call and response. She had to let everyone know what had happened. It was their right. It was a ritual. And *everyone* was so many. Aunts, uncles, cousins, friends. Worst of all, two sisters, both a lifetime away from that morning. If she hadn't had been so completely exhausted, she would not have done it. But her mind had gone hours ago by necessity. She could not afford to feel or examine anything. Best to just do the thing that had to be done. Mourning would come later; it always did.

She gripped her phone so tightly that the thought occurred she might break it. She forced her hand to relax, and it ached. She put her clasped hands to her head and forced herself to take a few slow, deep breaths. "God," she strained at the name and was surprised at the anger that flared up. She blew out a breath. "It seems I'm angry at God," Sheila said to no one in particular. She tried again, "God, I know we're not right at the moment. But I need you now. Make this task less impossible somehow. You put me in this situation," she said bitterly. "Now get me through it." She waited a moment to see if any other words would come. "Amen."

"Aunt Rachel, there's been an accident. I need you to sit down. Is Uncle Joe there? He needs to pick up the phone too." By the time she made this call, she had developed a protocol. Get another person on the phone who she knew wouldn't erupt in tears. Someone who could hear all the information so she wouldn't have to repeat herself too many times. "Ma died today. She fell down a hill hiking and her injuries overwhelmed her. I was there. There was nothing anyone could have done. She didn't suffer." She was living a dulled existence. It was still hard. "I need you to come. Please fly down and I can pick you up. Just let me know the flight information and I'll be there." Aunt Rachel had wanted every last detail, and she wrung them out in between her sniffles and tears. Sheila was used to it. That didn't make it any easier.

When Sheila hung up the phone it was after one in the morning, and she still had the two hardest calls to make. Why had she left the hardest for last?

"Paribas et Banque National de Paris. Est-ce que je peux vous aider?"

"Bonjour. Je voudrais parler avec Corinne Orly." Her French was far too rusty.

"Corinne Orly? Ah Oui. Un moment s'il vous plaît."

"Merci beaucoup."

"Corrine Orly."

"Hi Corinne, it's Sheila. I need to talk…"

"Oh Sheeeiiila! Hi! It's been forever. Are you finally going to come see me? You have to make time Sheila. There's soo much I can show you. With your French you'll fit right in. If you remember any after all this time. Oh God it feels good to speak English! Tell me everything girl, leave nothing out. But do it in five minutes, I've got some managers in Tokyo to get in line. Well, don't you have anything to say?"

"Mom died today." It was unforgivable, to put it to her like that. But she honestly didn't know when she was going to get another chance to speak. Corinne kept a fast pace.

"What! Come on, I just talked to her. She's fine. I'm trying to convince her to come over here for the summer, so I was trying to get her to clear her schedule. And she said, 'why not now?' Doesn't that sound just like her? She likes to be in the wind girl…So what are you talking about? Don't be stupid. And see now, you've used up half of my five minutes talking about this. I ought to hang up on you right now. Why are you calling me during the week anyway? The rates are through the roof now. And you're lucky you caught me here. You couldn't have known I was in early today. My day doesn't start until 8 if I can manage it. Life is for living, not stupid jokes. You really need to grow up. I've got to go, you've used up your time. But call me next week when you get your act together. I love hearing from you. Takes me back to our summers on the farm when you used to gab, gab, gab. Oh! Time is getting away from me. I have got to talk to these managers before they leave town. Listen, call me next week ok? We have got to stay more in touch, you know. And tell Jasmin I said hi when you talk to her. I haven't been able to reach her for a while. It's like I'm having an affair with her answering machine or something. I can't keep calling halfway around the world and striking out. So you call her and tell her to call me! Humph. You'd think we weren't all sisters or something. Tell her hi and she better call me too!

10

Listen, I've got to go. Call me soon, ok? Bye—Je vous embrace ma petite puce!"

Sheila stared at the phone and let it sink in. She had managed about ten words in that call. And had she called her 'my little flea'? How had Ma ever let Corrine get like that? She would have to have Jasmin tell her, if she could get a word in edgewise. Looking at the low battery percentage on her phone, she got up to look for a charger. She had chosen to make her calls from the basement in seclusion. She felt like she weighed a million pounds as she dragged herself up the stairs and stood, staring in shock.

Raines had been home when she had gotten in from the park. She had sunk straight into his arms and was on the verge of letting her tears rush out of her. Without a word he pulled away. He was reading and it was always impossible to tear him away from a good book.

Six foot two with a muscular build, he always seemed to choose clothes that would accentuate that physique, hugging his body at all the right places to attract the eye, even though he denied that was his goal. His olive complexion and strong features spelled out gorgeous to her, and any other woman that saw him for that matter. She had to admit, her mouth had certainly watered a bit the first time she met him, though they had both been too proud to admit how attracted they had been to each other at first.

But what was really most noticeable about Raines was his confidence, he wore it like a suit he had been born in, just shrugged on naturally and exerted without effort. That and his hands, which were always roaming, gesturing, touching the objects and textures around him. Her little Lord Fauntleroy with ADD, as she had called him in the beginning to tease him, and still used occasionally when he really got on her nerves. What was she going to do with him?

"It's still kind of early, but I'm starving," Raines had said, eyes still on his book. "Do you feel like cooking something or should I…What's wrong?" He had finally looked at her.

"I couldn't reach you. I had a really hard day, and I couldn't reach you. Can I please…Ma died, and I have to call people and I couldn't reach you!" She wrestled away from him as he tried to hold her. "Don't touch me. Just leave me alone. Please."

She wasn't in the mood. Oh, he *would* be all wonderful now that he knew. But it was the first impression that mattered. He had pulled away. He did that all the time. But tonight she just couldn't let it slide. After a wooden recitation of what had happened that day, it seemed she was getting used to retelling her tragedy, she stormed out of the den to the basement and locked the door behind her.

That had been hours ago. Now, Raines was in the kitchen wearing *her* apron and had apparently cooked everything in sight. The house smelled amazing. He could cook something besides those frozen instant meals in bags when he put his mind to it.

"When my aunt died you cooked for me. I hope everything came out right. And I'm sorry about before. I should pay more attention to you. What can I do?" He was looking incredible with that apron hugging him. But she was still mad. He had bad timing. She couldn't afford to be soft now, to feel things. She would drown in her feelings if she dared let them out.

"I still need to call Jasmin. I called Corinne but she didn't believe me about Ma. Could you call her? Tell the operator it's a family emergency because she's in a meeting with some managers or something now. I'll put this food away if you wash all those pots." Before she had even stopped speaking she was pulling out Tupperware and plastic wrap. She had to keep moving. She had the feeling that if she stopped moving she would dissolve.

"I cooked this for you. Why are you putting it away?" He wrapped his hands around hers as she was wrapping a dish in aluminum foil. She jerked away. If she let him touch her she would break down. And there was still so much to do.

"It's the middle of the night. No one is eating now. Now just please call Corinne and then clean this up. I've got so much to do and I would appreciate your help." Sheila stopped for a moment and took a deep breath. She realized she sounded like his supervisor. "Thank you for cooking all this and not disturbing me."

"Oh I tried," traces of a smile started to paint his face, "but I saw the door was locked. I thought about breaking it down, but with you already mad at me...Well, I value my life, that's all. So I thought I would do something to make you feel good." He was putting on his best smile, and it was already starting to melt her. It wasn't fair that he was so charming, when he wanted to be. "I love you, and I'm here for you." He held out his hand and put on his puppy dog face.

She smiled and took his hand for a moment. It felt right. He looked so gratified. She went back to storing the food.

"So I'll make the call and bust these dishes. Then you have to talk to me. You're not alone, I can help you. We make a good team."

She nodded her head. He had wrapped his arms around her and was rubbing her back. She almost stopped to relax into the moment. But she felt everything slipping away. Pushing him away, she grabbed a charger from a drawer and walked towards the basement stairs. "Buzz me when you've reached Corinne." She locked the door and leaned up against it. Her head was killing her. All that coffee must be catching up with her. And there was still so much to do.

After an endless night that seemed at last to be over, Sheila was dragging herself to bed. She glanced at herself in the hallway mirror on the way upstairs and came to a stop. She couldn't remember when she had looked so bad. Her normally well made-up honey brown face was looking ashen and haggardly. Her usually engaging almond shaped eyes were glassy dark brown pupils staring blankly back at her. She normally approved of her somewhat angular features, but now everything seemed too pronounced; the nose too sharp, the lips too thin and straight—none of their normal mischief shining through—cheekbones too high, jaw lines too pointed and severe. Her straightened brown hair, which she took meticulous care in styling so that it looked like it was glowing with not a hair out of place, hung like straw down to her shoulders in disarray.

She grimaced a little when she took in her clothes. Her style bounced between flawless female professional and chic bohemian funk depending on her mood, so where she had found the drab sweatpants and discolored hoodie that hung loosely on her tall thin frame, she had no idea. They must be Raines'. She looked like a derelict.

"All bums must go to bed," she muttered as she tore herself away from the mirror and climbed the stairs.

CHAPTER THREE
PREPARATIONS

That Sunday turned out to be the easiest day of explaining she would have for many to come. Family and friends grilled her more than the police ever could have, squeezing out the details over and over again. Endless trips back and forth from the local airports. Why did so many of her mother's friends have to live out of town? Running up and down the stairs fetching things for her great aunts. She hated her stairs. Next time she would get a rambler so they could get whatever they wanted without having to call her. But her emotions were locked away deep inside, so the only way she could show she cared was to be there for everyone; making endless trips to the airport and up and down the stairs. That was the best she could do.

And of course there was Corinne. She called her every hour it seemed to dress her down for not telling her about Ma. "You tell me news like that yourself! What were you thinking having Raines call? Why didn't you just tell me when you talked to me? I don't know why…"

Sheila turned away from the counter at the florist shop where she had been trying to select a funeral arrangement to defend herself on the call.

"I did tell you. You didn't believe me. Then you wouldn't let me get a word in edgewise before you hung up the phone. And you have called me ten times already if you've called me once. What you are doing is calling me to complain, again. I am doing the best I can. You could call to ask what I need you to do, or even to ask me how I am or to talk about how you feel about Ma, not about the way you found out. I won't apologize for Raines telling you. You had to learn the truth and for some reason you wouldn't listen to me! Please don't call me again unless you have something new to say!" By the time Sheila finished she was screaming and shaking with emotion. Dammit. She had lost her temper again. It seemed to be on a hairspring trigger lately. Everyone in the florist shop was looking at her.

She depressed the end button on her phone and took a deep breath, exhaling slowly. "I'll take the calla lily arrangement in this picture please. And you can call Corinne Orly at this number this afternoon, she'll pay for them...I'm sorry for the disturbance. I'm hanging on by a thread here. I appreciate your patience." The florist was looking quite unforgiving. "Should I take my business somewhere else? I can do that if this is a problem."

The woman was starting to annoy her with that judgmental look. She would have to have Raines come down here and smooth this out. His killer smile and Spanish accent always won over cold prunes like this. "I'll have someone come down to handle the rest of the details. Thank you for your understanding." She hustled out of the store before the florist's sour disposition had a chance to spread.

Everyone was staying at her house. Hadn't they heard of hotels? Actually, they had tried but she had insisted on having them close. It was her caretaking nature she couldn't extinguish, even though she was being as hard and unyielding as she could to get through this trial. She was relegated to the floor of her study with Raines. Not that she ever got a chance to lie down. She had made a promise to herself. No stopping until it was over. Until everything was over. So as much as she began to tire of running up and down her stairs fifteen times a day, driving to the airport, handling

16

funereal details—everything from the selecting flowers to dealing with funeral home arrangements, picking out Ma's final resting outfit, arranging food for the repast, writing and submitting the obituary, and dealing with a million other things—she needed them fiercely. Sometimes she felt that the constant running was the only thing keeping her alive.

It was good and heartbreaking to see her little sister Jasmin. Since she had moved away they missed each other terribly. But they were always the most emotional, and when they met at the airport they had burst into tears and almost flopped onto the ground. From then on they were inseparable. Jasmin silently accompanied her on all her errands, even up and down the stairs getting food, fetching insulin from the fridge, and handling any manner of things for their elders. She hardly said anything. But she was always there. Sheila felt guilty, to be enjoying her sister's presence so much, given what was going on.

And it gave her a buffer to Raines. She just didn't want him around. That was another reason she ran around so much. If she laid down with him on that air mattress they had in her study, he would start rubbing her back and kissing her ear and telling her that everything would be all right. Then the tears would start. And she would die inside. Then how would everything get done?

Sheila did all she could to avoid Aunt Rachel, who bombarded her with silent accusatory looks almost constantly. Sheila had known Aunt Rachel would want to take over all the arrangements and make things the way she thought they should be, not how her sister would have wanted them. So, as with everything else, Sheila had all the major things taken care of by the time the plane landed. Sheila had left her a task: to complete the graphic design of the funeral program—but then hindered her from completing it by always giving her new or changing details about the order of events, names and such. She honestly hadn't meant to do it—the details *had* keep changing—but to be honest, she didn't exactly mind Aunt Rachel being in such a state of flux that she couldn't dig into other things.

And thus it went. Jasmin propped her up by always being around. Raines schmoozed away all the problems she couldn't fix and kept everyone else away from her as much as possible. And Mom was laid out in purple splendor at Brown's Funeral Home, waiting to be viewed.

Everyone else had gone in long ago. But she still sat outside in her car, hands gripped on the wheel until they ached and were white at the knuckles. She had even sent Jasmin away. If she went in there…would any amount of makeup and positioning designed to relay peaceful slumber be able to change things? How could it make things better? If she went into that viewing room, it was like admitting her mom was gone. She had busied herself with so many details that she could almost forget the cause of them. There would be nowhere to run once she went in that room.

So she sat there, hardly moving except to shake her head every time Raines or Jasmin came out the door to look questioningly at her. She listened to the radio, revised her to-do list, and even trimmed her nails. And, a half-hour or so later, when everyone had come back in the car, she turned on the ignition and followed in her Volvo after Raines in his jeep and took them home. She was doing the best she could.

Later that night she went back to the funeral home and knocked on the door until somebody answered. She saw her mom. She really did look splendid. Not a trace of the horror that had painted her face before. When she bent down to kiss her cheek, it was stone cold and rock hard. It was then Sheila realized she really was gone.

She sat there until the early morning hours. And her mother never said a word. She never would again. And what would Sheila do?

The Orlys were passionate, expressive people. So that meant they would have to go above and beyond for Cathy's funeral. That's why things in the program kept changing. First Jasmin wanted to dance. Then she wanted to say something moving. Corrine seemed to think she could say the invocation and prayer, despite the fact that high priests and celebrants from many of the faiths Cathy honored would all be there. She never let anything stop her. A million details danced a fine line between honoring her mother and outdoing every other funeral ever held.

The thing was, this *would* be different from other funerals they had seen; held in the non-denominational hall of her mother's spiritual institute with officiators from seven different faiths. Mom never wanted to limit herself. If a faith had a piece of spiritual wisdom she didn't know, she immersed herself wholeheartedly. Sheila had exerted herself the last few days in making sure as many of her mom's spiritual mentors were there as possible: Buddhist, Vedic, Christian, Islamic, Akhan, Yoroba, and Hindu. Each one involving trips across town to their temples, shrines, churches—where she had to defend herself against their attempts to touch her heart and let loose her pain—to secure their participation in the funeral and capture details about what they would need and how to proceed.

And she would have to keep a tight rein over some of their more secular traditions. Yes, they could deliver their verses in Arabic because the power of Allah's words were strongest this way. But there was no way they could bury her before sunset today because all of the family had not gotten in yet. Yes, depictions of the Goddess of Mercy would be present behind the dais along with other icons. And yes, she knew the God of War was not appropriate for this event, but she wanted his depiction to be there as a guard against anyone blocking her mother's transition. No, they could not sacrifice a goat at the hall before the ceremony. Yes, they could do so the day before and she and her sisters would attend but she would partake of no blood, not ever again. She did not abide by blood sacrifice, but there was power in the blood, and she knew her mother would have wanted it.

It was a lot, even Sheila had to admit. It would look like someone had exploded a pillow of faith, with feathers of different colors flying everywhere. What might be missing to the outsider would be the tender moments her mother had spent with the Buddhist Goddess of Mercy, the almost ecstatic joy she had derived from her Sufi Muslim studies, the quiet assurance she had drawn from the Bible's Psalms—the King James Version of course—and the naked power and piercing truths gained from her Akhan African rituals. It might look like a hot mess, Sheila resigned, but it would be true. And for her mom, wherever she was, it would have a sweet fragrance.

Her sisters would understand, but no one else in the family would. They always assumed everyone was Christian. They would all be shocked by Mama's ceremony. Another thing she just did not have time to think about. So much of her hard work went into this, yet everyone seemed to think they could just change any aspect of the program they wanted to at the drop of a hat. Even for the ceremony Sheila wished she had her mother's advice, her strength.

in my dreams
reaching toward the face in the mirror I cannot touch
plunging to escape into that reflection
of someone else

someone new
and free
and finally
free

Jasmin was curled up on the couch in the study reading. Sheila sat in front of the computer, trying to write something to send her mother off tomorrow. Something that would express all that she had not allowed herself to feel over the past few days. It was two in the morning and that cursor was still blinking at her from the top of a blank page.

"Sheila, what are we going to do now?" Jasmin took off her glasses and rubbed the bridge of her nose.

"I don't know Jas." Weariness oozed through her every word. She shut down her computer and started putting away all the books she had pulled out for inspiration. "If I don't have anything to say, then I don't have anything to say."

"It's ok." Jasmin was covering a huge yawn with her hand and stretching out her long legs.

"Where's Raines?" It finally registered to her that she hadn't seen him since dinner. Not that she had eaten. Her stomach had been in constant uproar the last few days and she had taken to drinking natural protein shakes. It was the only thing she could seem to keep down.

"I think he's in his studio still. I heard music from there when I passed earlier. Sheila, what's the deal with you two?"

"Nothing, I'm just tired, of everything. He's gotta understand."

"You married him. Now you act like you don't want him around. A man as fine as that, you owe it to the rest of the sistas and senoritas to let him go if you don't want him no more. Shoooot, I'd take him if you weren't my sister." She put on a tempted smile and stood up. "You better go get that man before he leaves."

"Raines isn't going anywhere. I've kicked him out too many times to think any different. He won't let me go no matter what." She didn't know whether that was good or bad. "I mean, he never even gets mad at me, and I know I do some messed up stuff. It's no fun fighting with him—he always takes it personally or refuses to listen…"

"Imagine! The man loves you. How dare he?" Jasmin was cracking up with laughter by the time she finished. "We should all have a life as miserable as yours."

"You don't know like I know. You just see a fine, handsome Chicano artist who seems to worship me. You don't see the way he treats me like a child who can't make responsible decisions, the hot and cold 'artistic' moods that terrorize this house, not to mention the drama with his family!"

"Are you listening to yourself right now? You can't be hearing what you're saying." Small tears were leaking out of Jasmin's eyes and she was holding her sides to keep the laughter in.

No one understood. But he *was* fine. She probably wouldn't understand either if she were on the outside looking in. Perhaps she was being a little hard on him at the moment, she relented. At least it was a change, to talk about something other than tomorrow. "It's late, Jas."

"We might as well stay up now. Only a few hours to go. Maybe I can get you to eat something." Amazingly, Jasmin suddenly looked very alert and awake.

"Ew, you'd just make me sicker than I already am. Your food is too hot to even smell!"

"I can make something good. Please? It beats those green protein shakes you've been forcing down. I know you must be hungry. You haven't eaten anything and kept it down the last few days."

22

"How do you know what I've eaten?"

"I'm around you all the time, remember? I see you take a plate of food and then put it in the refrigerator later. Do you even take a bite? This situation calls for some of Jas' jerk tofu." Already she was rubbing her hands together in anticipation.

Sheila just stared. She must be crazy. After all these years Jasmin still thought people liked that mess. "If Great Aunt Esther's rolls ain't tempting me, then you know I'm not going for one of your eccentric creations. Just go to bed."

"I will, when you eat something. And you might as well start with those rolls…and my jerk tofu." Jasmin walked towards the study door as if it were all decided. She had always been so good at getting people to do what she wanted. Sheila heaved herself out of the chair and followed.

For a few precious hours, they acted like tomorrow would never come. For that night they were teenagers again. Chatting away, messing up a perfectly clean kitchen that was already stuffed with food, trying to create something original. And in the end, all of it was inedible. They laughed at that too. As the sun rose, they packed away their laughter and prepared for tears, as if the previous night had never been.

Lord, can't you see me down here praying? You took her…and I'm not speaking to you right now except that I am. I need a miracle. Just get me through this day. I don't care that it is normal for a child to bury their parent: this is impossible. Can't you see I need you Lord? I'll never forgive you maybe, but I need you now. I need just a little more—of everything. Get me over this hump. Because I can't disappoint her. I cannot fail her in this.

CHAPTER FOUR
THE FUNERAL

Sheila rushed her sisters into her study. With the air bed that she and Raines had been sleeping on set up, it was a bit crowded for three people.

"Let's send up some timber before we leave," Sheila said. They all rubbed their hands at their heart centers. She kept going long after Jasmin and Corinne. Try as she might, she just couldn't seem to get her hands warm, to wake up her soul. She gave up. God would just have to take her as she was. They joined hands and stood in silence for a long time. None of them wanted to start this prayer, to say goodbye to Ma. The tears started flowing before any words were said. This was why she hated wearing makeup lately.

"Momma, we release you," Sheila cried out. "We don't want to, but you've run your race and now," she stumbled and searched for words. "Now you can take your rest. You did a good job with us. A good job with everything. There's nothing to worry about. You can let go." Sheila took another moment to gather herself. "Lord, into your hands we commend our mother's spirit. Help us say goodbye today in a manner befitting her and all that she meant to us. All that she meant to the world. Cover our wounds with your balm and let us rejoice in her true homegoing this day. Give us strength. Just help us hold it together and make Momma proud. Amen."

Corinne and Jasmin turned and hugged each other. Sheila felt alone.

"Raines!" She called near the top of her lungs. After a few moments he entered. Silently taking in the scene, he took her into his arms and Sheila had a good cry. Finally, the tears seemed to ease up for all of them. Sheila was stuffed up and

24

her head seemed too heavy for her body.

"I think we're just about ready," Sheila took Raines' offered handkerchief and dried her tears.

"Maybe you want to look in a mirror first, fix your face?" Raines offered. Sheila poked him with her elbow and cracked a smile.

"We know, we know. Well, I guess we've been told, ladies. Let's get it together." She and her sisters crowded into the first-floor bathroom and were even able to laugh a bit as they touched up their makeup.

They were ready.

Sheila was seized with a pained kind of sorrow. To her right, Raines sat wiping his eyes with a handkerchief and looking like he would start sobbing at any moment. He had loved Cathy too, she had to remember that. To her left sat Jasmin, tears quietly falling. She had looked so beautiful last night, trying to convince Sheila that what she had made was actually a delicacy. Now Jasmin looked like the kind of picture you would want to paint and frame forever, because surely that expression was too perfect, the sadness too pure to be real. Next to Jasmin was Corinne, looking shell-shocked. Sheila guessed it had finally hit home for her, that there was nothing she could do to fix or ignore this.

Aunt Rachel and Uncle Joe were beside Corinne. Aunt Rachel was making a wonderful effort at being stoic, though you could tell it was a façade. She had already ripped her handkerchief to shreds. Her hands were balled up so tight that the knuckles were white. Uncle Joe was looking concerned and rubbing her shoulders. He had always seemed like a stand-up guy. Great Aunts Esther, Diane, Mary, Sarah, Rose, Jean, and Ruth flanked them all on both sides. They were the picture of unyielding strength in the face of relentless pressure, belied only occasionally by brief looks of pain or grief that streaked across their faces.

Where did they get their strength? Sheila supposed it was just the natural consequence of growing up in a hard land, as they had. Having to walk five miles to school and scrub other people's floors and cook in their kitchens would make you tough. She wanted that strength, the power to be able to bend or break anything blocking your path. But instead she felt like a broken reed. Powerless against the elements.

She wondered how she looked, if her face gave away what was inside. Her face might show emotion beyond the peaceful exterior she was attempting to portray, but none would be able to tell what it meant. Her feelings had always been a mystery to others. She sat there in the deepest pain, unable to hear a word anyone was saying. Well, she could hear, but the words were just washing over her like background noise, they flew away before she could latch onto them. She had the awful feeling the imams, priests, monks, that all of them, were saying incredibly true, deeply moving, and even comforting words. But she was too far away to hear them.

She realized, finally, that the wall she had built to keep going was keeping her in, and no matter how frantically she banged up against it, she was trapped. She was safe from grief. But she was also locked away from love, companionship, support—release. So the rest of the service passed, and she came close to weeping in bitter pain. But not for her mother, for herself. In trying to be strong, she had turned herself into the most removed and inconsolable person in the world.

When they got to the graveyard and the People of the Dawn shaman had finished his blessing, no one was more surprised, except perhaps for her, when she stood up.

"I have something to say," her voice was ragged from the strain of not having said much for the last few hours and

26

holding that lump in her throat all through the service. Many looked surprised, some looked expectant. They had seen enough new things to their eyes and ears today. What was one more parting with their traditions? Her great aunts looked at her with the same expression, a united front.

"Say your peace girl." Great Aunt Ruth spoke with that commanding voice that could not be denied. Maybe that was what gave her the strength to go on. She had no idea what she was going to say, so she just opened her mouth.

"Momma was always this mysterious thing I could never quite reach. An enduring vision. So perfect I could not take my eyes away. So cruel because of its beauty. And I was just me. Try being the child of a goddess. She knew the moment when she had me. She said I was blessed. Now to her; to you mom, who I know is listening. I never got to tell you that I'm convinced, the one true reason I was blessed is because of you. You being my mom is the most special thing about me. It's how I know I am good. It's how I know I'm alive. Thank you for being a miracle in my life. And things won't be the same."

The words seemed to be done coming out of her mouth. So she did the only thing she could think of, sang that awful Kermit the Frog song her mother loved so much.

"Why are there so many songs about rainbows,
and what's on the other side?
Rainbows are visions, but only illusions,
and rainbows have nothing to hide.
So we've been told and some choose to believe it.
I know they're wrong, wait and see.
Someday we'll find it.
The rainbow connection.
The lovers, the dreamers, and me."

Tears streamed down her face and her voice cracked more than it held by the time she finished. She felt her entire body shaking as Raines helped her to her seat. He had suddenly just been there. She had thrown herself against that barrier between herself and her feelings with all she had. And maybe it had cracked a little. She didn't remember anything else that happened at the cemetery, except that all the aunts said she couldn't stay to watch them actually bury her mother. Apparently, it just wasn't done. But she wanted closure, and she felt that seeing that mahogany box packed down with dirt and covered over with grass would somehow provide that.

As little care as she had shown for tradition to that point, she was unwilling to fling herself at the grave and dare them to carry her away like some hopeless widow. So she forced her legs to move, one step after the other, until she was in the car. And she watched people stuff themselves with food at her house and laugh over funny memories of Mom as if any of it were appropriate, now that they had said goodbye.

How dare they all pretend that everything were suddenly alright again? Things would never be right again. They would only be a little less horrible. Someday. Perhaps. Some said that all life was suffering. That was putting it crudely. She guessed that maybe they were just all grieved out. And now it was time to laugh. For them. Maybe that was what gave her the strength to kick everyone out. Methodically. Not rushing them. But after walking folks to the door, one by one, two by two, and family by family, she was suddenly alone with Raines. It was time for her to grieve. And it was something she couldn't do in front of anyone else. Because how could they possibly feel what she felt?

She cried for what seemed like an eternity. And Raines rocked her gently, rubbing her back and hugging her. She thought she felt his tears too, sliding down her cheek where their faces met. So many tears. She didn't know what they could all be for. Her Mom, herself, a relationship lost, and an overwhelming feeling of helplessness and lost-ness.

She cried until she felt herself being lifted off the couch.

"You need sleep," Raines muttered as he climbed the stairs to their bedroom. Her sisters had been sleeping there. She shook her head against his chest.

"Fresh sheets. Fresh sheets." She hated sleeping on old sheets. It was one of her many obsessions with cleanliness. The bed had to be made and not have been slept in for her to rest comfortably.

"I know. Where do you think I've been for the last hour?" Raines, cracked a self-important grin. Oh no, he had done something. As they climbed the last steps she caught a whiff of her favorite scent, frankincense. Inside their room, candles burned and thick wisps of incense wafted around. He always complained that her atmosphere was two parts incense, one part oxygen. It was just the way she liked it. He set her down by the bed.

"I drew you a bath, and then you can sleep. There'll be nothing to bother you." He pushed the door open to the adjacent bathroom. She could smell cinnamon and cardamom coming from the bath waters as she tested the temperature. Just right. Soothing music was pouring out of the bedroom stereo. It sounded like her Buddhist chants music was playing.

"You done good Raines." She smiled, she guessed her fatigue must have shown on her face, because he bent down to kiss her and was suddenly taking off her clothes. She started to protest until she realized she was too tired even for that.

"Your sisters are crashing in your office tonight. I'm gonna sleep in my studio after I clean up a little so you can get some rest. Have a nice bath. Goodnight." He gave her another hug. Fragile, as if she might break. Maybe she looked even worse that she imagined.

"Stay with me, I'm done being lonely. I'll be nice, I promise." She had regressed to a baby, she thought. Where was her strength of will?

He smiled as if he had been waiting for those words. "OK, I'll lay your pajamas out, clean up a little bit, then come back." His smile went ear to ear.

"The blue ones, with the clouds on them. I wanna wear those."

"Of course," he chimed in almost before she was finished. She wondered if she were that predictable. She supposed she did wear those pajamas whenever she needed to feel better about the world. Nonetheless, she smiled as if he had said Christmas would come. And frowned just as deeply when he closed the door behind him. Suddenly, being alone wasn't the haven she had spent all week imagining it would be.

Still, she sank into the bath and enjoyed a long soak and a good scrub. The Buddhist monks seemed to be talking to her, though she had no idea what they were chanting. It was one of her favorite meditation and divining CDs. She dried herself off slowly on the bench in the bathroom. She was dizzy when she got out of the tub and almost fell. Walking to the bed, she barely managed to put on her pajamas without calling Raines for help. She would have called; except she was too tired to search for her phone. Everything was suddenly sore. Easing back onto the bed, she pulled the covers up to her chin and peered up into the ceiling. She couldn't see anything, but she was looking for something. "Good night," she said out loud to herself and she pulled the covers over her head. She lay still until she could feel the slight tension between herself and the covers every time her heart beat. It had been the way she got herself to sleep or go into a trance ever since she could remember. She was asleep before she could think to say her prayers.

The next day, she woke up groggy and with a throbbing headache. The shadows in the room told her it was the height of the day. Raines had opened the curtains to let in the light. She felt as if she had slept for an eternity. And yet nothing was any better.

PART TWO
AFTER

CHAPTER FIVE
NEXT

Groggily Sheila sat up and swung her legs over the edge of the bed. She yawned and stretched before climbing down. She had insisted on a ridiculously expensive bed that had three layers. They actually had to use a glorified stepladder to get in and out of it.

She looked out the window and surveyed the back yard. Nothing was stirring. Was anyone alive out there? Anywhere? She suddenly wished she hadn't sent everyone away last night. Now she missed voices, activity, laughter. She had slept well, but apparently had sweated buckets. She couldn't remember her dreams. She chose some upbeat Donny Hathaway to play as she took a shower and got dressed. He had been one of her mother's favorites, and now was one of hers.

She sat at her little vanity table in the corner of the bedroom and pulled out some of her stationary and a pen. She took a few moments to clear her head and think of what she wanted to write. 'Honey, I have taken you for granted lately, but you have been there for me like a champion. I have needed your strength and you have not disappointed me. You never do (unless we're fighting, and then of course everything is your fault).' She put a little smiley face next to that dinger. 'I want to say thank you and thank you and thank you. I've kept myself apart as my own way of holding things together. I'm not sure it was the best way, but it was mine this time. I hope you understand. I am trying to let my walls down, but I might not succeed in that for a long time. She was everything to me.' Sheila left it unsigned. Who else would write a nearly illegible note but her? She placed it on his nightstand before she had the chance to feel exposed and throw it away.

Finally, she opened her bedroom door. Though unable to face the world, she let her day begin. The first thing she noticed was...voices! Her sisters and aunts! She had somehow forgotten they were here. She ran down the stairs and stood at the entrance to the kitchen. Warm smells were wafting through the air as relatives talked, occasional bursts of laughter interrupting the quiet hum.

"Hey Sheila, get in here and taste this stew, tell me what's missing since you say you can cook. I ain't used to this vegetarian stuff." Corinne talked as if everything in the world, and between them, was right as rain. It was a relief that she no longer seemed angry.

Sheila cracked a broad smile. A smile that suddenly turned into a pained expression. And ended in tears before her aunts and sisters could get out of their chairs to reach her. She was glad they were there. Jasmin smoothed her hair after they had finally gotten her in a chair and stopped her tears. Activity in the kitchen picked back up.

"I love you Sheila. We none of us would have made it through without your strength. Thank you." Jasmin's whisper in her ear turned into a fierce hug that Sheila guessed they both needed.

"Girl, you must be hungry. I didn't see you eat a bite yesterday and you done slept half the day away." Tall and graceful, Great Aunt Sarah was headed toward her with a tray of goodies and talking fast. "Now dis is somethin' for you to snack on until dinner is ready. And you better eat too. Jasmin tole me about you sneakin' back down here wid your plate still full dese last few days and I won't have it." Sheila shot a glare at Jasmin who was giggling behind a dishtowel. Apparently tattling on Sheila was still funny after all these years. "So you sit right here and eat dis, where I can keep my eye on you." Great Aunt Sarah wagged her finger at her and seemed to be winding up to say some more. Sheila could see her arm fat jiggling, even in her sweater, and it tickled her, as

34

always. Equal parts tall and fat, Aunt Sarah was the only one in the family that matched her and her sisters' height. It had given them a bond with her when their height had besieged them in adolescence, helping them to feel a little less awkward and alone.

"Sis' leave dat chile alone. She ain't come down here for all dis fussin' and carryin' on." Great Aunt Belle gave her sister a warning glance. Aunt Belle was sitting at the table, her breast resting on the tabletop. Sheila never understood how a woman could be that buxom, but Aunt Belle had always had breasts that came around the corner before she did, as Ma used to say. As children, she and her sisters had found this beyond funny. Sheila made a motion with her eyes to Jasmin. Yup. Still funny and they both held in a laugh and tried not to look directly at the offending torso.

Aunt Sarah threw her hands up, "Well I ain't no fool. I know de girl ain't come down here for fussin' but she got to eat. She needs her strength. Dem green shakes can't be as good for her as a good ol' plate of fixins, I don't keer what she say."

Sheila felt like she needed normal right now, but maybe this was too normal. Another moment and she might have to throw her wall back up just to cope, and she had just spent last night starting to take it down.

"Aunt Sarah, Aunt Belle, pile that food up as high as it will go, I am starving. Those shakes might be nutritious, but nothing can hold a candle to your food. It's made with love."

Her Great Aunts Belle and Sarah both cracked smiles and got up, busying themselves with pulling out dishes and preheating the oven: the microwave would never do for heating up a real meal. Sheila had always been good at smoothing over family tensions, when she wanted to, once she had gotten old enough to understand these women and their lives were deeper than any well. She could smooth them over, but resolving them, she wondered if that was even possible.

Jasmin took the great aunts' accord to push her seemingly lifelong point. "And it's about time you gave up some of these family recipes. Uncover the big secrets! Rolls, corn pone, sweet potato pie, layer cake, fried fish; you have got to start giving up the keys to the kitchen." Corinne looked at Sheila and they both just shook their heads.

"Chile, I done told you dem time and time agin, I don't know what you keep askin' for. Jes takes practice is all. Keep at it you'll get it." Aunt Belle was whipping baking soda into day-old waffle batter to freshen it up with an old wooden spoon she had brought up with her. Her bosom was so big, it seemed like she should topple over but instead she stood ramrod straight. Her arms were moving faster than it seemed any hand blender could. Right now, she looked like a woman who could flatten you without even noticing. Sheila understood why you could never make a cake that tasted just like hers, not unless you had lived a life that built up arms like that, and kept a spoon so long you wouldn't cook with anything else.

But Jasmin would never accept that. Everything had to be replicable. "Yes you've given me the recipe but exactly how much is a 'smithering' and 'just a bit'? You *have* to be leaving something out of the peach cobbler recipe. It never tastes like yours, and I must have made it ten times if a one." Jasmin was just plain exasperated, "I mean, could you just show me the rolls again? I could videotape it and then I wouldn't miss anything! I could…"

"House your mouf girl." Everyone stopped, staring at Sheila. She cringed under the attention, chiding herself after she spoke. She was always saying things a 28-year-old had no business knowing. "Grandma said that's what her dad used to say when she was talking too much. I thought it would do for her," nodding toward Jasmin and trying to look naive.

Her Great Aunts Belle and Sarah looked at her,

calculating. But only for a moment. They went on with their work. Very little got in the way of cooking. "I tell you dat girl done been here before. Sounded jus' like Daddy talkin' out her mouf. I done seen a lot dese days I ain't expect to see." Belle shook her head as she tested the heat of the griddle with her fingertips. Just right, it seemed. She poured the batter.

"Oh yeah. I didn't think much could surprise you, Aunt Belle, all the things you've seen." Sheila was dying to know what she meant: Ma had always said the aunts were some of the most spiritual people she knew, when they wanted to be, they just didn't know it. Then again, maybe they did.

"Belle ain't no lie," Aunt Sarah agreed. "Strange business roun' here. Ain't never seen so many crows at a funeral. Not for one so young. She can't have dat many peoples waitin' on her. But dere it is. Ain't natural, didn't look right."

"And de dreams we been havin'," Belle confirmed. "Jes ain't right. Be glad to put dis to rest."

Dreams? Sheila had hardly slept at all since this whole thing started. But the times she had slept she couldn't remember dreaming about anything new.

"Jas, what dreams?" she muttered under her breath.

"Later," Jasmin whispered back in a voice the whole room could hear. She never was any good at being covert.

"Here now. Grits with cheese, waffles, dem fake sausages you like, corn pone, some of Sis Helen's eggplant, breakfast rolls, and a nice pot of coffee. Eat up now." Aunt Sarah laid the spread down in front of her and leaned on the table there as if she meant to watch her eat every bite.

Sheila looked at the plate and gulped. It was piled high enough for three starving men just in from working the fields! She hardly even felt hungry anymore. Well, she'd asked for it. She picked up the breakfast roll with grim determination and bit in. Soo good...Suddenly her appetite came pouring back. She had forgotten how good their food was. It seemed like she hadn't eaten in weeks. She moved on to the waffle, wanting to eat it while it was hot. She knew all this flour and starch was bad for her, but she couldn't stop herself.

She saw Aunt Sarah give a satisfied nod out of the corner of her eye, and Jasmin started back in on her quest for the family recipes, pressing Aunt Belle for the key to the waffles she had just made. Everyone else was going about their business in the kitchen it seemed, but for her, that plate was all that existed. It seemed there was a great emptiness inside her. And she hoped the food was making a dent, filling up some of that loneliness inside.

To her surprise, she finished just about everything on the plate, and felt pleasantly full, but the sadness in her seemed to have grown. She propped her feet up on the chair next to her and slouched down, staring into space. Ohhh, she had liked it more when she felt nothing. 'I guess this is just the way it's going to be for a while,' she thought to herself as she rubbed her suddenly round belly. At least she was around family. But she realized someone was missing.

"Where's Raines?"

"Don't know," Aunt Sarah said as she busied herself at the sink. "He came and got us dis mornin', den lit right out as soon as we were in de door…Don't you know where he is?" There was a bit of prying mischief in that question.

Thoughts swirled in Sheila's head. "Came and got you? You didn't stay here last night?"

Aunt Belle laughed, "Naw chile! Nice of you to notice, hmm. We was at Lorraine's. Raines ring us up, oh, 'bout seven dis mornin' and tole us to come on, he was gonna pick us up. Den little later he come 'round wid dat blue van and got us all over here. Tole us you was sleepin' and would come down when you want to. Den he left right out agin. Dat's de last we seen of him." She took Sheila's plate away and started wiping down the table.

38

Sheila looked around. Great Aunt Belle, Great Aunt Sarah, Corinne and Jasmin. "Who else is here?"

"Oh, Lorraine and sis' Ruth. Dem two been in de garden soon as dey found your gardnin' stuff all packed away. You waited too long to dig up yer bulbs. Don't know if dey kin save 'em. Took one of dem portable heaters from de basement and been out dere ever since. Don't know what dey dink dey doin', ground's hard as sheet rock." Aunt Belle and Aunt Sarah exchanged a look she couldn't figure out and just shook their heads. Sometimes Sheila thought she would never figure out just what the relationship was between all those sisters.

Belle went on, "And Rachel was here, off to herself mostly. She went back to Lorraine's I reckon. Joe ain't come wid her. Don't know what he had to do. And uh, sis' Mary and sis' Emily Sue still at Lorraine's, Leigh Ann's got an awful cold, and you know how Mary worry 'bout her chile. So dey home takin' care of her. Dey send deir love to you."

Sheila took it in. Six sisters, Lorraine, Ruth, Mary, Sarah, Belle, and Emily Sue. It would be seven but her grandmother died years ago. Three cousins, Rachel, Leigh Ann, and Josie. It would be four but they had just buried her mother. And three second cousins, three sisters, Jasmin, Corinne, and herself. Every chain was missing a link, because she felt like she was dead. What a broken family tree, she thought bleakly. She wanted to go back to bed and sleep for an eternity.

"What are we going to do now, Sheila?" Jasmin had always been good at that helpless voice. Maybe because she was youngest. Sheila felt as if suddenly all eyes were on her. Imagination, surely.

"Get her affairs settled. That's something I guess you, me, Corinne and Aunt Rachel have to do together." The pressure on her grew heavier.

"Sheila...Sheila I've got to leave tomorrow." Corinne finally spoke up. Sheila had been wondering when that was going to happen. She couldn't remember the last time she had been quiet for so long. Nearly an hour. "Well don't give me any flack about it. I've been gone three days. They just can't run without me there. I'm responsible for nearly every training program coordination in…"

"Corinne," Sheila interrupted. She had heard this many times before, as they all had. "You work in France. The family is always more important than the job in that culture. You said your supervisor told you to take all the time you needed and I believe he meant it. You work with a capable team of bright people. People you are more than happy to let take over when you enjoy your two months of vacation every year. I believe they can run without you there for a few more days. You need to stay, Corinne. You'll have to change whatever reservations you've made. You'll do just what you want in the end. But there's no running."

Sheila was shaking by the time she finished, her voice a little hoarse. Standing up to people always left her a wreck. Actually she surprised herself. She had rarely been able to challenge Corinne, and this made twice in one week. Though Sheila knew her last words had been for herself. There was no running. Not now, not ever. She had to get out of here. The air in the room was suddenly too thick to breathe. She was being pressed down by some invisible weight.

"Tell Aunt Rachel the four of us will go over to momma's house this evening, to get started on things. Both of you work together on a list of the things you can think of that have to be done. I've got to get some rest. I'll be in my room. Jas, wake me at six if I'm not up already. Ok then." She was headed for the stairs and to her bedroom before she even finished speaking. But the weight didn't get any lighter, the air no more breathable. She leaned on the banister like a crutch.

In her mind, a part of her wondered how she sounded like she knew what she was doing, like she was in charge, when all that was inside was a frantic ball of indecision. It

40

had been like that these last days. All the things that had to be done had fallen on her. At least that's how it seemed. She was tired of making decisions. And tonight, they were going to ask more of her.

She felt like she had been asleep forever when she had woken up that afternoon. But she had still been tired. Behind her an eternity, before her an eternity. And this rest she was about to try to get, she had a feeling it would make nothing any better.

She pulled the covers over her head and tried to breathe. As she searched for sleep, she dreamed she was an innocent little girl whose mom was still with her

CHAPTER SIX
NIGHTMARES

she stood at the edge of a great precipice
motionless
seeing all
her future lay before her
past the edge
where no one could go
where everyone died
here was where reason ended
someone had died
here
her wings unfolded
she ran toward insanity
and flew
she lived

"*Baby girl.*" The voice wasn't even a whisper.

Sheila woke to a darkened room as if she had gotten the shock of her life. She lay on her back and tried to catch her breath. Her heart beat out of her chest it seemed. And she was alone.

Slowly her breath evened out, and her heartbeat became more regular. She tried to think. What had woken her so suddenly? What had made her so afraid? She saw something by the window, a sort of white shimmering mist. Just light and shadow she guessed.

Only...the room was dark except for that mist, which seemed to be giving off a faint light of its own. And...it seemed to be floating out the window. But the window was closed, so how could it...She shot bolt upright, racing through the fear and questions in her mind, desperately searching for an affirmation...Archangel Michael.

"Lord Michael to the left, Lord Michael to the right, Lord Michael in front, Lord Michael behind, Lord Michael above, Lord Michael below, Lord Michael, Lord Michael wherever I go." She repeated the affirmation until she was sure she was protected, until her fear eased up a little. Then she went flying out of that room as fast as her legs would carry her, never looking back. She didn't stop running until she slammed into Jasmin halfway down the stairs.

"It's dark," Sheila panted for breath, "I told you to wake me." She grabbed the banister and sat down on a step, holding her head between her hands. 'Breathe. Just breathe,' she thought.

"Thanks for running into me! I'll have you know I was just on my way to wake you. After your outburst this afternoon I thought you could use a little extra time for an attitude adjustment. But I see it wasn't time enough." Jasmin looked at Sheila, who was still fighting to take an even, relaxed breath. "What's wrong?"

"There's something in my room," Sheila's voice trembled and cracked. "I tried to make it go away but it wouldn't." Sheila filled her lungs to busting then exhaled. That seemed to help, a little. "I just want some rest."

"Something like what?" Jasmin's face filled with concern.

"A mist, glowing, I don't know. It was by the window and it was...moving through the glass. I had the feeling that it had been in the room before I woke up. I...do you think it's still there?"

"I don't know. But let's get Corinne and go get it out." She stood up and started heading back downstairs, an aura of decidedness about her.

How did she do that? Be so fearless when she didn't

even know what she was facing? "No," Sheila leaned forward to catch the back of her shirt. "I'm sure its gone by now. We can just leave it be."

"No we can't. We have to figure out what's going on and make it right! Ma wouldn't want you running."

That hit like a giant triphammer. Sheila was just…stunned.

"Sheila I'm sorry," Jasmin rushed, "I didn't mean that." But one can never apologize enough for speaking the truth.

"Oh, shut up!" Sheila snapped. She wanted to run, but there was nowhere to go. "Oh, Jasmin," Her head fell to her knees and a kind of pained grief washed over her. Tears, again.

"You're not the only one that misses her. It's time you stopped acting like you were." Jasmin spoke quietly as she rubbed Sheila's arm.

Sheila lifted her head to look at her. So innocent looking, yet she had been imbued with the powerful quality of always telling the truth. Quite irksome and outrageous at times.

"I have been strong for all of you. Who do you think got Ma buried? Who put together all the arrangements, put up everybody in my house without a second thought? Who arranged the program, secured all the holy people, found clothes for her to wear, got a funeral home? How dare you accuse me of, of…I've done everything I can for everybody, and you come at me like this! How about some support, some understanding? Everyone in this house has been stealing my strength. And then, the moment *I* need some, you tell me I'm grieving too much? That it's not fair to the rest of you for me to miss her soo? You don't know! You lived halfway across the country and saw her several times a year for a few days at a time. I had her in my life almost every day. She was my everything. I can *never* grieve for her too much!"

Sheila's eyes were streaming with tears. She was

screaming at what had to be the top of her lungs and was towering over Jasmin on the stairs. She collapsed back on her step, shaking with emotion.

Before she could recover, a blinding pain flashed across the side of her face. Jasmin had slapped her, hard.

"How dare you compare?" As always Jasmin's voice was quiet and composed. "How dare you compare? Well? I'm asking you. I won't yell a bunch of rhetorical questions. I want to know what gives you the right or ability to compare how important Ma was to all of us, and how much we miss her?" Jasmin settled back on her step and waited, her face showing streaks of hurt and pain.

Sheila hated herself just then. Jasmin never suffered weak moments like she did. She was always honest and open. She wished she would have just yelled back so they could have had a good fight. But Jas wouldn't take the bait. She never did. She wanted to talk. How did she do it?

Jasmin almost always had the air of a delicate beautiful flower that any strong wind could wipe away. But she never faltered, and she was always so honest with what she was and what she thought. And because she was so real, she wasn't afraid to experience life. That made her tough, full of inner strength.

Ma had given her that quality. Just like she had given Corinne a gift, the gift of fearlessness. That girl did whatever she wanted. She wasn't afraid of the unknown. She had picked up and moved to Paris without a second thought. And learned French as she went along. She put herself through school there and then worked the system until she got a job, which led to a better job and so on, until she had gotten what she wanted. She let nothing stand in the way of her dreams, no matter how outlandish the dream or overwhelming the obstacle. At least she had her faults. She couldn't seem to hear what anyone else was saying. She seemed to live with herself, for herself, most of the time. She was a little less perfect because of that. So Sheila could at least reach her pedestal.

Sheila had nothing to speak of in the way of extraordinary qualities. They all had inherited gifts from Ma except her. She was just herself. Perpetually afraid and self-critical. Overly stubborn and unyielding, undisciplined and uncertain. Why hadn't she any strength in her like the others? Why had Ma died with the weakest one of them? She thought she had been being strong for the family these last several days, but she had really just been running. And now Jasmin was calling her to task. She wished she had never come out of her room.

"I, I...Oh, you're so perfect! How can you get on me for not being so great the last few days? I'm sorry!" Sheila's words slipped out in a mixture of indignation, pleading, and earnestness. It all sounded kind of mangled.

"Is that the best you can do? You hurt me, and anyone else who heard your screaming though the house. I think I liked you better when you weren't getting any sleep. Much less disagreeable then. Yes, I think so." The faintest traces of a smile painted Jasmin's eyes, then her lips, until finally a smile bloomed on her face, even though tears still ran down her cheeks.

"I know I'm not the nicest person right now," Sheila said sheepishly. "I'm struggling. I told myself I had to be heartless to get through the funeral. Now the funeral's over. And I'm still horrible. What if I can't change back? What if Ma was the only thing that made me bearable?" Sheila's eyes shone with tears of doubt.

"Ma raised us. She poured all that she was into us. Life may dampen it at times, but some fires cannot be extinguished." Jasmin always said the absolutely perfect thing.

They hugged a long time on the stairs. As if time had stopped for a moment. Finally, they pulled away to dry their tears, laughing as if the most frightful yelling and slapping that had just taken place had never been. Or perhaps *because*

46

it had just been.

"I guess we'd better go over to the house." Sheila stood up and straightened out her clothes.

"Oh no you don't. Not so fast." Jasmin's smiled hardened. "Upstairs."

"Upstairs." Sheila didn't think she would be able to get out of it. But she had tried. "I'll get the Florida water and some sage, you get Corinne. And—tell her I'm sorry."

"Oh you know her, she already knows you're sorry." They shared a smile before scattering in different directions.

Sheila stood at the door of her shrine room a moment before entering. She realized she hadn't gone in since she came home from the Falls and everything had changed. She wondered why. Normally she spent the auspicious times of day in her meditation room when she could. After work, just before midnight, and morning and midday when she was here. But, when she needed it most, she had seemed to have forgotten this room even existed.

Sheila pushed the door open. It stuck a little. Inside was completely dark except for the moonlight coming through half open blinds. Every candle on every alter and shrine was dark. Shadows from statues stretched long against the walls and hardwood floors. She felt ashamed for not coming in here earlier. And only now when God-knows-what was in her room did she enter. And now not even to pray or ask for help, but for Florida water, a cleansing liquid that helped banish negative spirits and energies from people and places.

There was a bottle on all four shrines. Buddhist, featuring the Goddess of Mercy, God of War and Monkey God alongside the Buddha. Her ancestral shrine with its…oh, her ancestral shrine! She suddenly remembered that while she had been preoccupied making sure the funeral arrangements were correct, sticking her hand into almost everything and controlling it, she had done none of the spiritual things that were required to bless and release her

47

mother's spirit into the next dimension. Sheila let out a deep sigh. So many things left undone. She felt incapable and afraid, an utter failure. Part of her was glad her mother wasn't here to see her forgetting all of this. A very, very small part.

She willed herself to put those thoughts aside and walked into the room. Her Vedic shrine stood dark, as well as her Yoruba shrine. In addition to those, there were some more casual altars. The People of the Grey Dawn, a tradition she had learned from her Indian cousins in Virginia, Taoist, and Hindu. A hodgepodge of deities she had found and related to. Christianity was reflected in a bookcase and workstation, filled with interesting books that some might not call Christian at all, but actually were.

Oh, Florida water! She couldn't deal with all of this now. She grabbed the Florida water and walked out. She hadn't turned the lights on, but in those few moments she had taken in every detail.

So much to do. She rushed towards her room and found Corinne and Jasmin standing there. The auras surrounding them were intense and bright. Corrine grabbed Sheila's hands and rubbed them. She could be so perfect at times.

"Well dears," Corinne said briskly, "let's do what we came to."

They took turns using the Florida water, rubbing it briskly between their palms and then outlining their entire bodies with it, sometimes directing their energy also towards each other. This was the best way to clear negative energy and empower themselves, but it felt like forever since Sheila had done it. She tried to push her fear out of her mind and concentrate on the white light flooding her being; preparing herself. They all stood at the door and looked at it. Jasmin looked at Sheila. Corinne looked at Sheila. That was her cue. It was her room. She stepped toward the door and pushed it open. Uncertain of what lay ahead—in so many ways.

48

Sheila flipped the light switch at the entrance, walking determinedly inside, to see…nothing. She felt a fool. There was nothing there! Why had she even thought there would be anything here after all this time? Only now did it register how much time had passed since charging out of the room.

"Well, there are laws against crying wolf you know. I cut short an overseas call for this, for nothing. Why I think…"

Sheila shut Corinne's voice out of her mind as she turned on another light and moved deeper into the room. Now that there was nothing to be afraid of she could investigate what had happened, what she *knew* had happened despite Corinne's moaning.

Walking over to the window where the mist had left, her thoughts were confirmed: it was shut tight. How could anything have flowed out of this window? She didn't even feel a draft. And outside of the window she saw no fog, mist, or any other thing resembling what she had seen earlier. What was going on? All she wanted was some peace. Space to breath.

"Come on then. Let's clear the room. Since you gave up so much to support us, Corrine." Jasmin's voice was spiked with just a little sarcasm. She was funny. The sound of her voice jolted Sheila out of her ruminations. Wordlessly they all moved around the room, praying, bathing the room with sprays of Florida water, and directing energy from their hands into areas of the room. Finally, the energy in Sheila's bedroom was cleared and purified. And her own mood was better.

"Let's go," Sheila said in a weary and resigned voice. Without another word they all exited the room, called Aunt Rachel and told her to meet them at the house, found their coats, piled into Sheila's car and headed home.

Home…
I will admit that I am failure
There will I be embraced in the arms of my mother
When I die I will be home

PART THREE
NEVER HOME AGAIN

CHAPTER SEVEN
HOME

They pulled up to the house with reluctance, at least on Sheila's part. She had no intention of going into that house, ever again. But she knew she had to. The mood had eased a little on the ride over. They had started talking. More accurately, Corinne had started talking, and the rest of them listened. She really was interesting and entertaining. Most of what she said you wanted to hear. Her years in France had clearly not shown her the art of conversation, though. She was a one-way mouthpiece. By the time they arrived at the house, things were much more relaxed and easy going. Except for this frantic anxiety inside her desperately trying to escape. She felt like that cartoon rabbit the hunter was trying to push into the pot, that was doing everything it could to stay alive.

"Do you want to wait for Aunt Rachel, before we go in?" Jasmin's voice was hesitant. No one knew what to do.

"I haven't been here for a long time." Corrine sounded weary. "Things have been so busy. I can't really remember what it looks like. And I will not sit out here all night just because I'm afraid." And with that she was out of the car and striding toward the front door. When she realized she didn't have the key, she stood waiting impatiently. Out of the car, up the front steps, and turning the key slowly in the lock. Sheila felt like she had dragged herself all the way.

The entrance was a set of heavy double doors. Mom had taken Sheila's advice, or her persistent nagging, in picking out the doors. A door said so much about who you were and what you wanted to say about yourself. They had gone to antique stores, estate sales, and everywhere else she could think of in search of the perfect door. Finally, Sheila had found an artist her mother had known from before she was born to create it. They had argued cats and dogs over the carvings.

At last they had decided: on one door a woman streaked upwards with a determined look, on the other a rippling lake reflected the Sanskrit symbol for truth. In the background a large yin yang symbol framed the images. She had waited months after the doors were finished for her mom to go on vacation. It took an entire day to hang the doors, lay sealing strips on the frame to keep the cold out, and get the balancing just right. When she picked up her mom and drove her to her new front doors, Ma had almost burst from happiness. That evening they had eaten dinner on the front lawn facing the house, enjoying the view.

Seeing these doors always brought her such happiness. Even now she found the edges of her lips curling up in a smile. As she pushed open the door, she thought happy thoughts. The first time in a long time.

She flicked on the light and stepped aside to let in Corrine and Jasmin. She remembered that Aunt Rachel would be here soon and turned on the porch light, leaving the front door unlocked.

Sheila put her things down on the bench in the foyer and headed for the kitchen. When she was nervous and restless, she needed to eat. There had to be something that hadn't spoiled yet. In no time, she was shoveling popcorn into her mouth in between bites of Twizzlers. Happiness. A happiness that also reminded her she hadn't exercised all week.

If she didn't know better, it could seem like Ma was simply out of town. The whole house was clearly awaiting her return. Sheila could almost be lulled into believing it from the contented silence the home exuded. She hummed as she chewed her Twizzlers and busied herself with the thought of how nice it would be if Ma just walked through the front doors, chastising Sheila for eating her popcorn

Jasmin and Corrine had been wandering around the house. It had been at least a year for both of them. Headlights streaming in the windows at the front of the house let them know Aunt Rachel was here. Sheila made her way to the front door and saw Corinne and Jasmin coming out of the study to join her. They opened the front door and stood expectantly as Aunt Rachel came inside.

"Hey my niecies, I'm here!" Aunt Rachel was full of bustling, loud energy that instantly changed the dynamic. "Well, isn't this house beautiful. She changed the living room," Aunt Rachel was already hallway down the corridor, taking in every room in a heartbeat and moving on. Where her aunt was headed, Sheila already knew. "Oh, she took my picture down. I wouldn't have gotten it for her if she wasn't gonna use it, jeez! That cost big bucks. Get people things and they don't appreciate it. I don't understand it."

"I thought you were more observant. Your picture is hanging in the great room—there's even a light over it. You need to give up the victimhood. Nobody's wronged you. Least of all Momma. Go on to the study and wait for Sheila to get Momma's papers. I know that's where you're headed." Jasmin's voice managed to be stone serious with even an edge of judgement, her face perfectly arranged as she spoke. Then she gave a shell-shocked Aunt Rachel a sincere hug and walked past her into the kitchen.

Jasmin may have taken it all in stride, but she was definitely the only one. Sheila fought tooth and nail to keep a straight face. She almost hooted with disbelief. She turned on her heels and scurried up the stairs. Just in time to hide a huge grin as she doubled over at the top stairs with hysterical—but silent—laughter.

Corinne just stared, finally saying, "Well…let's go then," and guided a still shocked aunt into the study. That was almost as big a surprise as Jasmin's act; Corinne at a loss for words. It took a long time for Sheila took pull it together enough to go back downstairs and head into the study. On the way down Jasmin emerged from the living room, took one look at Sheila's barely composed face, and just shook her head.

They walked into the study together. Jasmin sat down in Mom's favorite reclining chair and settled in. Sheila felt their focus pressing in on her. They were waiting. She walked toward the desk and sat down at the chair behind it. Digging through her purse she got out her keys. A smaller set was attached to the larger ring, the keys to Ma's stuff. House keys, car keys, keys to the various locks she had on chests and to a couple of small shacks out back, and a key to her wall safe.

Swinging her chair around to face the bookcase behind the desk, she reached down and felt under the bottom shelf's edge. Finding the lock, she put in the tiny key and turned it, then pulled on the edge. The entire bottom two shelves swung outward to reveal what Ma and she had each thought was the most ridiculous and novel hidden safe. They had had to have it. She remembered when they had gotten it installed. They laughed for days over it, locking up nachos, stuffed animals and tv remote controls in the safe until they had finally settled down, and put only important papers inside, and not giving it much thought after that. Looking at that wall safe made her think, 'Gee, we must be upper class now.'

Sheila quickly spun the combination wheel on the safe, her mother's birthday, her birthday, followed by their personal numerological destiny numbers. She almost wanted to laugh. Taking such a materialistic, third dimension item like a safe, and using fourth dimension principles such as destiny numbers to get into it. Ma had always thought that weird kind of fusion was funny. But she didn't laugh, for she could feel three pairs of eyes boring into the back of her chair as she leaned down to collect Ma's papers off the top shelf of the safe.

Sheila turned around with a small stack of documents

and set them down on the desk. Sorting through them she found a will, to her surprise, legal and notarized. She knew Ma had prepared an informal one a few years back but not that she had had one completed by her lawyer. If Mom were still alive, she would have chided her for keeping secrets. It always bothered her when she found out Ma had parts of her life she knew nothing about. But Ma had always been her own person, fiercely independent, so it kept happening.

"Ok, Ma has a legally binding will here. I had no idea there was anything but an informal one she had prepared, so I guess the lawyer will have to formally execute the will." Sheila felt tired. She hated being in charge. So why did she always angle herself so that she had to be?

"I guess there's no reason why we can't read it now, just to get a sense of what she wanted." The air felt heavy, she could barely get enough into her lungs. She scanned through the perfunctory opening of the will to find the real beginning. "Ok, uh 'I leave all bank accounts, stocks and futures investments as outlined in Appendix A to my sister Rachel. I leave my private home and land holdings as outlined in Appendix B to my daughter Jasmin. I leave my art studio, all its contents, and all royalties from previously sold works as outlined in Appendix C to my daughter Corinne. I leave all the contents of my home, my Institute for Life business and all its related aspects as outlined in Appendix D to my daughter Sheila….um, it goes on to give specific things to relatives and friends, but nothing else substantial. I could continue reading if you want, though I don't think there's anything else that applies to us."

"That's enough," Jasmin said decisively. It seemed like the room let out a collective sigh.

"How much money did Cathy have?" Aunt Rachel had finally found her voice. "I mean, what exactly is the value of what she left me?"

Sheila stared at her, frozen for a moment before flipping toward the back of the will to an appendix.

"Well, it looks like various accounts, some tied up, total around $127K. And there's stock and futures and currency investments that were valued at the time this was put together at about $82K. So that's about $200 thousand. Is it enough?" Sheila risked throwing in the damning question at the end. She was getting more and more annoyed by the moment. Yet she regretted the sting of her words as soon as they were out of her mouth.

"What? Well I'm only asking. I mean I may have to lend some to you girls to make mortgage payments or something. Though you should probably sell. No sense in carrying on a debt. Then we could all share in the profits and that would be fair." Aunt Rachel was smoothing out her clothes as she talked. She did that when she wanted to leave.

"Ma owned everything free and clear. And her studio, rental properties, and Institute were all in the black the last time we met with the accountant. I'm sure the lawyer can lay it all out to us more clearly." Sheila was so proud of her mom. It had taken her a while, but she had gotten the things in her life she had wanted, things that brought her joy. She never did anything halfway when she decided to do it. "Besides, her will is legal like I said. There's no changing it."

That shut Aunt Rachel up. Sheila guessed she had assumed Mom was swimming in debt to have all that she had. Quite the contrary, and every bit of it earned. She wished Mom were here to keep on enjoying her life and all she had.

Only now at this very moment had she given any thought to her mother's business. How was the Institute going to run without her? Ma was its heart, she *was* the Institute. Why had she left it to Sheila? Better with anyone else but her.

She shook her thoughts off and turned around, putting the papers neatly back in the safe and shutting it. "I'm sure the lawyer will be calling us all soon." She had started speaking before she turned around, and when she finally did, found no one else preparing to leave. They were all tucked in as if the movie was just about to start.

"Sheila," Corinne started, hesitant for once, "We've all got to get back now." Corinne looked at her with wide eyes and an apprehensive face.

"Back where? To the house?" Sheila had been ready to go home anyway. So why were they all still sitting here?

"No, back to our homes. We've been here for days now. And we dropped everything to come. Now we've got to get back." Corinne's voice sounded very nearly sympathetic. Did they all think she was so fragile? Well she was.

"Oh," Sheila said in a small voice. "I know you have to go…I mean, I see." Now she would be all alone. How could they leave? They were supposed to stay together. What would she do when they left? Her mind was spinning. "When are you leaving?" Her voice was as squeaky as a mouse and barely audible.

"Tomorrow." All three of their voices lapped over each other. Sheila felt her heart squeezing like a sponge in an angry fist. They were all leaving.

"My company's booked me on an afternoon flight out of New York so I was going to hop a late morning shuttle up there. Aunt Rachel needs to get back, so we were going to leave for the airport together around 10, after traffic dies down a bit. Jasmin's got responsibilities that can't wait any longer…She's got an 8:30 flight back and Raines said he'd take her in to the airport at 6 tomorrow." The room waited, barely breathing.

Just as she had been doing since she was a kid, she shut her eyes tight, becoming invisible and escaping from a pain she could not bear. Right now she felt as if she had no family at all. How was she going to grieve without them? How was she going to live? She felt arms and bodies suddenly surrounding her, supporting her, as she burst into tears for what had to be at least the third time today. She was certainly making up for those cold and stoic days before. And it seemed the pain was just starting to come on. The realization that the center of her life was now missing was just dawning on her.

Sheila pulled Jasmin aside after they left Ma's study. "The dreams. What dreams were Great Aunts Sarah and Belle talking about?" Sheila demanded.

"Oh," Jasmin said. She took a breath and avoided her gaze.

"This isn't like you," Sheila was genuinely confused. Jasmin always looked so deep into your eyes until it was like she was piercing your soul. "Tell me."

She finally raised her eyes to look at Sheila. "They've been dreaming of Momma."

"OK," Sheila was waiting for something out of the ordinary.

"It's the same dream. Four of the aunts have had it." A look of pain filled Jasmin's eyes. "In it she's screaming. And she's shaking you within an inch of your life."

Sheila stepped back as if she had been pushed. "No. No, no, no," she shook her head fiercely. "That's not right. Ma would never scream at me, at *anyone*."

"There's more," Jasmin said reluctantly. "They've been having the dream since *before* she passed. Even called to tell her about it, they said."

"What in the blue blazes is this about?" Sheila wondered aloud. "What do you make of it?"

Jasmin threw up her hands and blew out an exasperated breath. "No idea."

Sheila thought on it as hard as her stunned brain would allow. Everything about it was wrong—the timing, the content, the recipients. Had Ma been mad at her, and had she somehow not known? The thought broke her heart. The last time her great aunts had seen her mom, she had been screaming in their dreams. That just wasn't right. No wonder her aunts thought there was something strange at work. She couldn't say she disagreed.

they piled into their cars and headed back
not home, just to her house
they dragged all their suitcases into the den
threw them open and took all night trying to pack
*   what had never really been unpacked*
they made plans
promises that almost sounded like they would be kept
to keep in touch
more
it was still dark when Jasmin left
to tears and soul-draining hugs
the words 'don't go'
spoken far too late to matter

It always seemed too early when Sheila woke up. But for the first time in a while, she wasn't alone. Raines' limbs were sprawled out on their huge bed but he still barely touched her. She had objected to a California King-sized bed as an intimacy killer. She often slept in it and never felt him beside her. It was just too big. Right now he seemed an ocean away, and the world a harshly lit demanding master.

But it was 9:30 and she had to get up. Corinne and Aunt Rachel would be leaving soon. Traitors, all of them. Malevolent thoughts skimmed across her mind, settling nowhere. Restless. It was easier to blame them for leaving than to admit she had no idea how she would survive without them, even Aunt Rachel.

As she looked around bleary eyed. Raines stirred, turning over to look at her.

"I love you." He moved closer, wrapping his arms around her and rubbing her back. She always enjoyed that.

She snuggled into him and almost went back to sleep, until she caught herself starting to snore and heard him laughing at it.

"I'm up. I'm up!" She wrestled away from him as his laughter grew louder. "Nice to know you haven't changed," a grin spread across her face. She supposed it was funny.

She looked at him. Considering. She had been too hard on him…lately. Maybe just a little. He was a good man, more than decent. But he couldn't help her with this. And now that her sisters were gone and going, no one could.

She remembered when her grandma had died. All her great aunts had said they would be her grandmother. But it hadn't worked out that way. You only had one grandma, and there was no pretending that you had another. She had no mother now.

She rolled over in the bed, suddenly washed over with grief. Raines got out of bed, already dressed from taking Jasmin to the airport earlier. She had to hand it to him, he was never one to fight impossible battles. She could be sure she would be left alone now, to just lie there and languish.

"You might not remember, but John was at the funeral. So were Aggie, Rick and Massad." Raines spoke as he pulled on a hoodie, "And last night while you were out John called." He sat on her side of the bed and put his hand on her waist. "Honey, he wants to know when you're coming back to work."

Sheila's head emerged from under a mountain of covers. She just looked at him. "You can't be serious," she groaned, head falling back onto a pillow.

"I'm just letting you know what he said. You know they can't run that place without you. Or at least that's what you always tell me," he smiled.

Sheila pulled the covers back over her head and moaned. She had been so sure he was going to leave her alone today. So much for safe bets. Something tugged the covers away from her face. He was still there.

"How long has it been?"

"A week."

"Really? It seems like…" her voice trailed off as she remembered screaming into the emptiness of the Falls. Everyone just wanted life to go on. As if it ever could. "I guess I'll go in the day after tomorrow." Sheila rolled out of bed, leaning over on the edge.

"Ok. I'm going downstairs to work. Let me know if you need me." He leaned over and kissed her temples and hugged her. "I love you." Raines shut the door behind him. She could hear his footsteps barreling down the stairs.

"I need you." Sheila's voice wasn't even a whisper.

CHAPTER EIGHT
WORK

She sat in her car on level P3 of the building's garage. She had been sitting there for about 10 minutes. At least that's what the clock said. She had no sense of time. But sooner or later she had to go in. She hadn't gotten dressed and driven in to work just to sit there.

She had realized that it wasn't going to get any easier anytime soon. So she might as well get on with it. Staying home wasn't helping.

"Lord, help me to feel your love in my heart stronger than my pain and grief. Look down on me with kindness and help me to do a good job at work. Let me keep it together today and be effective and useful. Guide my actions according to Your Will. Let not my will but Thy Will be done in all things. Open the door and clear the way for me in all good things this day and every day. Remove all negativity from within, around, and about me. Free me from the pain and limits of the third dimension so that I may feel and know You as my True Source and Supply. I am not flesh and blood, I am a spark from the Divine. So be it and so it is."

Sheila raised her head from the steering wheel. Her eyes were full of tears. She looked like crap, but she felt better. God, she thought as she cleaned herself up in the driver's visor mirror, it felt good to pray. It always changed things.

Five minutes later, the elevator doors opened on her floor and she stepped out, not knowing what to expect and for once unsure in her work domain. But she had to trust in her prayer, either you believed, or you didn't. With that thought to pluck up her courage and faith, she headed to her office a bit more at ease.

She had hoped to be deep in her office with doors shut by the time folks were in. But she must have spent more time quaking in her car than she had thought. The place was bustling. She could never understand why these people started work before nine. She was in the middle of a busy lobby that suddenly seemed to slow and revolve around her as she emerged from the elevator. Was it her imagination? This was one thing she knew how to do—cope. But if even one person gave her condolences right now, she didn't know what she would do. Firing her would be better than giving a sympathetic pat on the arm. She was still too raw. She didn't have it together. She didn't know when she would.

Sheila almost streaked to her office. Trying to avoid the inevitable. She shut her doors behind her gasping, as if she had run a race.

Sheila settled against the door and took in her office. Now *this* was her realm, where she had control. Except for the flowers, those were new. Well, not new, but new to her. They looked a few days old. They had obviously expected her to come back sooner. She just shook her head, and caught a glimpse of her intake box on the corner of her desk. Piled impossibly high with papers, she approached it with a toxic mix of shock and disbelief. How was it possible? She picked up a single piece of paper from the pile, turning it over in her hands.

"They must have killed a million trees for this." It was almost funny. No wonder John had been calling to see when she was coming back. The place really *couldn't* get along without her. Either that or they were punishing her for trying to promote a healthy office culture, making her sorry she ever created this position, forcing a change in their world.

'Well at least the game ain't changed,' she thought. And with that she opened her door back up and hung the "In Process" sign under her name and title: "Sheila Orly Montoya—Corporate Ombudsman & Director of Organizational Development." It still meant a lot to her. She

64

had made a place for herself here, Fourteen floors up from the real world. Actually, John had made a place for her here, but she held it. And that was worth something.

She turned to face her intake desk as if confronting an enemy. With a rueful smile she shook her head and picked a pile; "scheduled arbitrations." She carried it over to her workstation and got started.

By lunch she had worked her way through both scheduled and pending arbitrations and was well into filed bias grievances. She had compartmentalized and streamlined this office and everything around her. It was her way. Her office was immaculately neat and efficient, but still warm. She loved it. She never wanted to meet in anyone else's office. Who would? Hers was perfect.

Ma had seen to that. Sheila looked around and saw the many things that pointed to her mother in the office. Ma had given her permission to let her real self shine through in the decoration. And the result had been spectacular, in her obviously humble opinion. It was a welcoming, refreshing, uplifting blend of everything she loved. African-American, Christian, Buddhist, African, Taoist, Islamic, and even Hindu influences were all present without overpowering or alienating visitors—well, most visitors. Plants, running water, a Zen garden, even a fish. All Feng Shui-ed, blessed, and cleansed to the hilt.

She had found out very early on that the figure of Shiva was not going to work out in plain sight. She thought it was painfully relevant. The God of destruction of the old to make way for the new, that was what her office was all about. But people just looked at it and looked at her like she belonged in an asylum. So she had put it atop her highest bookcase. No one could see it, but it was there. Its energy was present.

Sheila chuckled. That's the way it was with Universal Laws of God, they were always in effect and you were subject to them, whether you knew they existed and agreed to them or not. That's what made her work easy. Truth was Truth. And if ever she found herself in seemingly impossible situations, she just remembered that, and she was elevated to a place where the third, perfect option was crystal clear. Sometimes it took a while, and sometimes the parties didn't choose the third option, but she was always honoring the God Presence within her. She was always on point.

And that's what made people put up with her egotistical and eclectic self. That's what made people put up with the Koran she kept on her shelf and was occasionally seen reading. A big deal since 9-11. That's why Christians, Jews and agnostics alike came to the office party she had for Buddha's birthday. And why the president paid for it. They all saw that she was being obedient to God, whether they were conscious of it or not. The God in her made the God in others shine brighter. And here, in this small corner of the corporate world, God was creating a holy space.

A place where, whenever possible, her supervisor was either taking credit for or downplaying her dedicated work. She had saved this company $3 million in lawsuit fees since she had been here. At least. Damn John. So many people loved her. Sheila wished she could love herself. She wished she could unlock the key to that puzzle and see in herself what others saw.

She sighed, rubbed her eyes and swiveled away from her desk. It was 1:15 already and she was done for now. She buzzed for Jerry, her assistant, to come inside. Jerry stuck in first his head, then the rest of his body before shutting the door behind him. He was a funny fellow, and not the fastest assistant at the company. But he was a bulldog, what she told him to do he did full out, she never had to repeat herself, and he seemed loyal.

"Jerry thanks for this morning. Nice and quiet. I wasn't up for visitors or conversations."

"Sure." Oh yeah, and he never said much.

"Let's see if we can keep the streak going this

66

afternoon. No call, no visits."

"Mmm hmm."

"Ok so please take this," she gestured toward the two small piles on her desk, "and enter them into the system, reconcile my schedule, then file. I'm out of water so if you could get another jug in here," Jerry nodded as he scribbled on his pad, "And let's talk about 3 to debrief about the time I've been away and make sure we're on the same page with the schedule. Um…am I forgetting anything?" Jerry usually caught what her scatterbrain missed.

"Lunch. Are you eating? Rick said he would wait until 2 if you wanted company."

Rick. That would have to wait until later.

"And John. I think he's really put out by the locked door." He gestured toward the door on his right adjoining her office with John's. "He wants to see you. He's a bit puffed up." Jerry had an honest dislike for the man, and she sometimes thought the sole basis for his dislike was hers. She didn't know what to make of that.

"No one sees me today but you. Put it on me and that huge pile of work I've got to get through," she said, gesturing to her inbox.

Jerry smiled, "Got it."

"OK, lunch," and Rick. Later was now. "Can you ask Rick to pick me up something like veggie juice and a soup and meet me in…um, which breakout room near here's empty?"

"The Maple Room, uh, and Beech until 3."

"Ok Maple for a quick bite. I'll see if I can get there without having to talk to anybody."

"Don't know about that. You had five visitors and seven calls this morning."

"Agh," she wasn't going to be able to dodge people forever. "Ok, start scheduling people for tomorrow. Everyone in one day, I don't want it dragged out. And schedule John for breakfast around 7:30 tomorrow."

"Breakfast?" Jerry looked up from his notes. He knew she rarely mixed business and food.

"I'll eat before I come in and just have tea or something. So then, let's push lunch with Rick to 2. If you could get everyone scheduled in the next half-hour, then I should be able to get to Maple for lunch unharmed." Jerry cracked a smile as he wrote. "Then after our 3 o'clock you close out. Go home early, you've earned it. And you'll need your strength to get through the coming week."

Jerry looked like she had just given him a lollipop. She didn't know how she had found someone as easy to please as him to work with.

"Let's hustle now, and hot water for tea is the priority. Be sure to let me know when it's time to meet Rick for lunch."

"Yes ma'am." Jerry slid out of the door as if trying to keep prying eyes out. It couldn't be as bad as he said, that so many people wanted to see her. Why would they want to see her? Right now she felt like the most un-special girl in the world. She stayed locked in that thought until Jerry buzzed her for lunch. At least it was better than grief. She shook herself out of it.

Five minutes later the buzzer sounded again. Sheila heaved herself out of her chair and headed toward the door. Half a minute later she was closing the door to the Maple Room. It was small but had a view. As she stared out towards the river, she realized how long it had been since she had really looked at nature, honored it. She had been so full of pride, pain and grief lately that she had found it nearly impossible to honor anything outside of her own wounded-ness.

"Hello." Rick stared at her from his seat at the table, hesitant. "I got you some food and drink...Is there anything else?"

He was feeling her out to see if she would break. No, he was trying to be proper. Always trying. Sheila stared back at him, blinking. She smiled and sat in a chair beside him. "First course please," in a mockingly proper and petulant voice.

"Ah yes. We have a small endive salad with balsamic vinaigrette." Rick scraped half of his salad onto an empty plate in front of her.

She stuck her tongue out at him before staring at the salad. He knew she hated salad. Sheila chewed and made unpleasant faces as Rick talked about the latest adventures at the company. Eventually the salad was finished and she could listen better. For the next half hour Rick regaled her with his recent escapades—always stepping into something anyone else would know not to—and always surprised at the results.

"One day you're going to go back to your own planet, and everything will make sense," Sheila snickered over her pear.

"Ah, only if you come too."

Rick's eyes sparkled. So pretty to look at. She'd always suspected there was something more behind them, but had never found any evidence to support that. Still, she forgot sometimes.

"How are you?" Rick converted to all sincerity and seriousness.

Sheila suddenly stood and began collecting her garbage for the trash. "Ohh...not now, ok?" She flashed him a completely artificial smile. "Thanks for lunch. Nice break...and we should do it again. Sometime next week, ok?" The door shut behind her and Rick was left off balance. Well, that was how she liked to play, only on her terms.

Sheila leaned back from her desk and rubbed her eyes. Outside her window it was dark already. She had lost track of time. She had let Jerry go some time ago. Their 3 o'clock meeting had been enlightening, they often were. Jerry seemed to have as great a passion for gossip as she. Within an hour she was caught up on all the office maneuverings and power plays, with room for a few totally frivolous but hilarious tales of embarrassment.

Sheila swiveled around to face her window, staring out at the office lights in the building across from her. What was the point of having a window if you just got to look out into somebody else's office? Her mind was already off that persistent question and onto her immediate problem. What was she going to do about tomorrow? If she had her way she'd continue to work closeted up here indefinitely. She disliked politicking; it required far too much energy that was better spent actually doing her job.

Breakfast with John. What had she been thinking? Well she had to get it over with, and sooner was better than later. She grabbed her appointment book from the desk and turned back to the window. Working through tomorrow's meetings one by one, she planned out her strategies, mapping them out on the notepad in her binder. She read back through her notes, committing them to memory. Tomorrow morning she'd review them once more and later file them in her home office. That, her mom had taught her. Always make notes of your strategies and summarize the results of your meetings, no matter how brief or informal, and store them off-site. It often added an hour to her days, but had more than once justified the time spent.

So, at 6:47pm she was finally wrapping up her first day back. By seven that evening, her office was neatly tucked away, and her attaché case was packed with a few items to take home. Stopping at the bookcase near the door, she pulled out a notebook filled with cards for various occasions in plastic sleeves. Flipping through them, she pulled out a thank you card and wrote, "You're the best" inside and folded $10 from her wallet in the card. Sliding the card in its envelope, she scrawled "Jerry" on the front and sealed it. John had spoken to her repeatedly about the way she treated Jerry, that it was simply unacceptable and unprofessional and caused problems since the other assistants were not treated as well. They could fire her if they wanted, but he was her staff and she would treat him with a high level of respect and appreciation. And she had said as much. All of which made treating Jerry well even more fun.

Grabbing her things, she shut off her lights, closed her door and took the "In Process" sign off her door and laid it down on Jerry's desk along with the card. There'd be no escape tomorrow. Soon enough she was on the highway headed home, thinking all the grievous thoughts she had had the luxury of avoiding at work.

"There's no escape from now," she echoed as she drew closer and closer to her fate. A home her mother would never visit again. Closer and closer to absolute loneliness.

PART FOUR
FATED

CHAPTER NINE
OXYGEN

Sheila sprang up, gasping, terrified.

"What, what?!" Raines sat up looking around.

Her heart was beating too fast. She couldn't get enough air in her lungs. This moment was never going to pass. And it was excruciating.

Raines was standing on her side of the bed, lifting her up and onto the floor. He rested her legs on the edge of the bed and ran to open a window, letting in cold air. "Breathe, just breathe."

Sheila wanted to roll on her side, curl into a ball, and shrink into nothing. But she breathed. She lay there—breathing. 'Oh God, oh God, oh God.' Her mind was frantically searching for a prayer, an affirmation, mantra, anything she could latch onto that would put the Truth above her fear. To find a way out of this panic attack. All she could grasp onto was a steady "Ohm," playing over and over in her head. Outside of herself she became aware of Raines, breathing deeply in and out. He looked as bad as she felt.

Slowly her heartbeat began to moderate itself. Her breathing evened out and slowed. And finally, she was free. Sheila just lay there, breathing.

Raines leaned over her. "Hey, you had me scared." He looked it. She hated how her spate of recent panic attacks was affecting not only herself, but him as well.

"Yeah well, the rumors of my death are greatly exaggerated," Sheila said in a raspy voice and let out a meek laugh, still staring at the ceiling. She felt so weak, exhausted. "Sleepy."

Raines picked her up with a heave and tucked her in bed. He lay on his side and rubbed her arm. "Need anything?"

"What?" Sheila was already half asleep. "Oh, no. I'm good baby. Night."

Sheila was drifting. Floating in nothingness surrounded by a thin white mist. It seemed…familiar somehow.

"*Let it go. Let it go,*" a voice boomed from everywhere and nowhere, from the very air itself.

Funny. Mom used to say that, about letting go. She dreamed of letting go. But Mom never realized she couldn't do that. She would never be able to be all that she could be.

"*Let it go.*"

With that her entire body seized up. She had heard that voice before. She had had this dream before. It was the last thing she remembered before waking up, heart pounding out of control.

Sheila woke up in a sweat to gently rising chimes. Five am; time to start the day. Past time really. But she lay there, worn out as if she had lived three lifetimes already. Entranced. 'Let go of your fears, huh?' She let herself remember last night, the dream, and her reaction to it all. 'All you are is fear.' Damn, the truth always intruded. She didn't want to believe it, but there it was. Eventually she got up to begin her day, to move on.

"*Baby Girl.*" A voice she couldn't be hearing was calling to her. The incense floating in the room seemed to thicken. Sheila squeezed her eyes shut even tighter and tried to focus on her breath. She was going to meditate and find some peace if it killed her, she demanded. Having hardly even prayed, let alone sat for meditation, since Ma passed, Sheila was determined to meditate today.

Everywhere, folks seemed to be rushing her to go

back to normal. And while she knew there would be no going back, she didn't want to stay where she was either. She was going to have to drag herself out of Hell, one deep breath at a time.

"*Baby Girl.*" It sounded like Ma; it used her mom's pet name for her. But she knew it wasn't Ma. Of all the people to pass on, she knew her mother would not be one to get caught in this realm. No, her mom was too enlightened to stay in the third dimension after her passing. Anyone but Ma.

Sheila had to keep a tight rein on herself. She ached for her mother so badly that she was hearing her voice. But she refused to build a figment of Ma in her imagination. That wouldn't do mom any justice. And it might possibly drive her insane.

So, she would ignore her mind's feeble attempts to soothe her. She was just going to have to feel this pain. And perhaps one day it would fade a little. But there were no shortcuts. That Sheila knew for sure. As she slowly inhaled a long, deep breath, she continued to search for inner peace.

CHAPTER TEN
I QUIT

Sheila sat at a table by the window. The Grand Hyatt restaurant was on the top floor of the hotel and she liked the view. Still too cold to sit outside, though. She preferred that. She was finishing up a long mantra under her breath. It always made her feel centered, like she had a place in the universe. She visualized herself filled with Light, surrounded by a shield of Light, unapproachable by anything not of the Light.

"God be praised, most merciful and benevolent and ever-present. I Am Light and I go to meet Light. So be it and so it is. I Am that I Am." She took slow deep breaths after whispering these words.

Moments like this, she felt the only Truth was God's Light and Law, that she was bathed in that Light and in accord with that Law. She felt sorry for anyone who tried to step to her with negativity when she was like this. And up walked John.

"Welcome back, kiddo," he sat down and was all smiles.

"John, good morning." 'Let's see how this plays out,' she thought.

"Good morning, may I take your order?" an inquisitive waiter intervened.

"Oh, yes. I'll have three eggs scrambled and two pancakes with blueberry syrup, hot."

"Very good sir. Ma'am?"

"Just another tea please. Oh, and perhaps a cheese plate. Yes. Thank you."

"Right away." The waiter moved to another table.

It was busy this time of day. Working breakfasts were

the new thing, she heard. John cleared his throat, bringing her attention back to the table. He looked sincere and serious.

"How are you doing?"

Damn. Two for two. Everything he said was not helping. She wondered what he would say next. I mean, what kind of question was that? How could people ask the bereaved that? They didn't really want to know. They couldn't. How was she supposed to respond? He didn't honestly think he could stomach the answer, did he?

"I'm managing." Well, it was true, in a way. She ran a finger around the rim of her teacup, now growing cold. She hoped this part would be over soon.

"I'm glad." John smiled, but his smile didn't look relieved. It looked feigned, Sheila noted. "Because you have a lot of work to do. The conference is around the corner and we need to get our presentation together. I've been working on a lot of ideas and I need you to put them together and do a run-through. I'm hoping this will stave off the wolves a little longer. Your office is barely keeping its head above water and I don't know if I can keep protecting you. So we really need to roll up our sleeves and give everything in these next few weeks." He gave her that smile again.

"Oh yes," John rubbed his hand together and looked anxious as the waiter set down his food.

"Eggs, pancakes, and syrup—hot. I'll be right back with your tea," the waiter reported.

"Thank you." John was already starting in on his food. "So you can see,"—he was talking with a mouth full of food—"why I'm so glad to have you back and doing well."

Co-opting her work, threatening her job, prodding her for more. All in a day's work for him. So this was how it was going down. She had thought it might. She was tired of him. She joked with Raines all the time about "John's ulcer;" which was what they called her tension stomach aches.

Suddenly an idea took hold of her that she had only jokingly fantasized about. And before she could talk herself out of it she had decided and was reciting a quick prayer of preparation in her mind, 'Lord bless me. Remove all obstacles. Open the door and clear the way. All things in your name. So be it and so it is.'

"I'm so glad to hear you say that, John. It makes what I have to say a lot easier…Thank you and can I get some more honey?" Sheila focused on preparing her newly arrived tea as she went on. "I mean, if you had said you and the company were standing behind me and intended to keep me and my department around then I don't know what I would have done. But this way, it seems like the best for everyone."

She peeped over the edge of her cup as she sipped her tea. She could see she had his attention. He looked dumbfounded. Inside she was howling with laughter…and scared witless.

"I mean, it's no secret that you and I have had some serious differences of opinion about human resources issues at the company. And I'm tired of it, especially now. And you have the absolute right to run the department and all its activities exactly the way you want. I really believe that. I just wish your way was closer to my way." She put on her best puppy dog look.

"I'm sure I'll come up with something. And goodness knows Raines wouldn't mind having me around more." That last part was a lie she was sure.

"So," she continued briskly, "Let's concentrate on getting the presentation off without a hitch. And then I can give you thirty days to get affairs of the office in order." She was suddenly exhausted beyond belief. Sheila took a deep breath and leaned forward.

"John, please consider this my resignation." She sighed and fell back in her chair. Not so much internal laughter now that the reality of her decision set in. But it was right, it had to be. Any decision she made when she was in the Light always was. It was the doubt and fear that surged through her afterwards that was the killer. Why had she gotten herself into this? She didn't want to quit her job. Did she? 'God help me.'

"Sheila you can't be serious. I won't accept your resignation. All of this is unnecessary I'm sure. Let's just talk about it." John had shaken out of his stupor and was back to his old self. And that was enough to flare Sheila back up.

"Really John, this is ridiculous. I can lose my job but I can't quit?"

"But I want to keep you here. I was working overtime to make sure you stayed."

Lies, but she rarely called others out when there was another way, at least in her work life. Probably why she was such a good negotiator. She let others save face and left their delusions barely ruffled.

"It's not about you, John. It's about me and what I want and need right now. What I've needed for a while now. I'm truly sorry for what this may mean to others, but I have to do what I believe is best for me. And I ask you to respect that decision." How could he respect her decision when she barely did herself, she wondered. She cupped her tea with both hands and slowly gulped it down. Still nice and hot. Soothing.

"Well, Sheila, I really disagree with this whole thing, but I can see now is not the time. I have to run to another meeting anyway. I'll talk to you later. I want to see you at noon. You're not quitting." He stood up and pulled some money from his billfold.

"Can't. I have a meeting." Sheila smiled pleasantly.

"I expect you to cancel it." The forceful tone of his voice gave away his desperation.

"John calm down," and before he could protest that he was calm she raised her hand and continued, "And the VP of R&D doesn't like his appointments broken. I'll have Jerry schedule something for you and me when we're both free." Unflappable as always, or at least as usual.

John tensed. "David? Why are you seeing him?"

"He asked. I've got meetings scheduled all day."

Poor John. You could see his wounded pride clear as day. He was so easy to read at times.

"Well, schedule something then. I've got to run. This isn't over." And with that he set some money down on the table and left.

So predictable! It was amazing how the man listened to nothing. He came here with his own agenda to put her into turmoil over the fear of losing her job, less than two weeks after...after Ma. She looked at his plate, eggs and pancakes piled high. He had planned to eat that. There was no other meeting. Humph. Well, soon enough it wouldn't be her problem. Oh God, what had she done?

"And how is everything?" the waiter asked smoothly.

"Mmm. Take that away please," she gestured toward John's food, "and I'd like some more hot water and lemon. And the bill please."

"Yes Ma'am."

She needed the privacy of her office to fall out and question herself thoroughly. She knew she had made that decision in the Spirit and Spirit was never wrong, but surely this had to be some sort of exception. This was so serious. Her head was starting to ache already. She paid her bill and spent ten minutes hailing cabs before one stopped.

A black woman, well dressed in front of a first-rate hotel, and she still couldn't catch a cab with ease. No surprises there. But that's not to say it didn't hurt. Sometimes she felt like nothing had changed. She could feel it in her bones. Still reeling from a history of slavery. And today she had acted like she was free, deciding what she would and would not take. But John had known she must have been out of her mind.

God how she wanted to be free. She wondered if she ever would be. She had achieved so many of the things she wanted, almost all of them. But she wasn't free. Not in her bones, not in life. And things as simple as a cab ride could remind her.

Then everything that she had, all the things she had accomplished, they melted away. Who was she to quit her job? Who was she to expect equality in anything? She was for the goal of reparations but she doubted blacks and other non-white races would ever get what they truly, desperately needed. Equity.

"Just drive around a while. I'll pay."

The cabby looked back at her warily. Sheila's cheeks were moist with tears just wiped away. She must have earned his sympathy. He took twenty minutes to make a trip usually finished in five. And by then she had re-packed all her feelings about race in America and her "place" back under her slick and professional veneer. Back to her normal self.

Later, in her office, after much pacing and hair pulling, she came to one inevitable conclusion. There was no point in believing in God if she wasn't going to believe in the works of God. Her quitting had come from the God-Presence within her. She knew that. So she had to abide by it. Else she may as well not believe at all. Faith was so hard to come by. She sat back in her chair full of disgust and resignation. How dare God put her in this position? Of all the reckless, pointless decisions! She was sure she would regret this. Only she knew she never would. God's plans were always best. Far better than her own, however clever. She just hated giving up control. Hated being powerless. Still, there was no fighting the Truth. So she gave in, on this point.

Three quiet raps on the door announced Jerry arriving for the morning. Ah, repercussions and consequences. Exactly how was she supposed to go about this "quitting"? And what would it mean for the people around her. Jerry…and Raines. Raines was a whole 'nother ball of wax. Something she would have to deal with separately. But the work aspects she had to deal with now.

Turning on her computer she drafted a letter of resignation. With only 20 minutes before her first scheduled meeting she wanted to get this in the hopper so she could inform everyone she was leaving as she met with them. This would cut off efforts by John to pretend she wasn't quitting. Finally, the wording was acceptable and she printed out 4 copies and signed them. She buzzed for Jerry to come in.

"Jerry, please sit down."

He smiled in greeting and took a seat next to hers.

"Look, at breakfast this morning…I quit." She couldn't believe she was repeating it out loud.

"What? Are you serious?" Jerry looked shocked for the first time she had known him.

"Yes. I had no idea it was going to turn out that way, but that is my decision. I don't know what's going to happen to you. The company can reassign you, but knowing how well you were treated with me they might give you a less than desirable assignment as retribution. If you want to leave the company, I'm happy to give you a glowing recommendation, and if you want me to make a few calls I can do that too."

"What about you?" Jerry asked.

"I'm just going to do consulting on my own for now. After taking a breather of course."

"Won't you need an assistant?"

"I don't know. I haven't really had time to think about it."

"How 'bout I come with you?"

Jerry, he really was loyal. "Jerry, that's a nice thought but with me just starting out there's no way I could maintain you at a salary like what you have here, not to mention benefits and insurance. And the work wouldn't be steady. But I can't tell you how much it means to me that you'd offer to stand in the fire with me." She felt like someone really special just then.

"Now wait a minute. Let's think about it. You've never done consulting before so of course you're going to need some help. What if I can facilitate your work, getting contracts, in a way that I can pay for myself? Would you be willing to train me and let me get more involved?"

"I guess, but…"

"Well what if we just try it out for a few months? After I've helped you set up shop? I could consider it an apprenticeship. Then you wouldn't have to go it alone. And neither would I. Think about how much I could help you. I could start your networking now. We'd be off to a running start by the time you walked out the door." Jerry smiled in enthusiasm and anticipation.

Efficient and intelligent, of course. But Sheila had never suspected Jerry was ambitious.

"Well, seems like a good opportunity for both of us, if you're willing to take the risk. I mean, are you going to be able to pay your rent and eat?"

"I have enough savings to support me for almost six months."

"I didn't know you were independently wealthy." Sheila joked.

"Every bonus and tip you've given me I invested. Now I have something to show for all that."

Sheila's jaw dropped. Surprise, surprise.

"I think I'm pretty lucky, and I say yes." Sheila shook hands with a very happy man.

"This all doesn't happen until thirty days after the conference. We're ramping up for the big presentation and then there'll be time to wrap things up. And I don't want anyone saying you're using company time on my personal agenda, so use your discretion. Put these in John's and the president's mailboxes, and let's just focus on today. Schedule time for another meeting with John for me today. And let's talk tomorrow sometime about the future."

"OK boss." Jerry picked up the letters of resignation and bounced to the door.

This, she hadn't expected. At all.

It was almost nine and her first meeting of the day

started soon. All that strategy she had mapped out for today's meetings, gone. What was she supposed to say now? 'I'm quitting so whatever it is hold onto it until the next person gets here—if there is a next person—otherwise give it to John?' She didn't imagine that would go over well. She fished out a tea bag from a canister in her drawer and walked over to the water cooler in her room to fill her cup with hot water. Maybe some chamomile would give her inspiration. Maybe not.

And Jerry wanting to go with her, what was that all about? Did he think she was a captain of industry or something? She imagined the way ahead would be hard. There were so many organizational development consultants out there. Having to carry one more person, well, it only seemed to make it even more difficult. She hoped he was right to be so optimistic. But she didn't think so.

CHAPTER ELEVEN
FALLOUT

Five minutes before her first meeting and she still had no idea what she was going to say. Well, best put herself out there. Just tell them where things stood and that she really wasn't sure about anything except that she was leaving soon. Risky, but it was clear she wasn't going to be developing any other brilliant ideas before it was time to act.

Five minutes. Just enough time to get in a few good mantras. She was way too unsettled to meditate, and this might reel her in from her frenetic thoughts.

"I call upon my personal angel to intercede for me in this situation to give me strength, calm, and guidance—and whatever else I need but can't think to ask for. So be it." That invocation made her feel better. Usually.

And now it was time to look in the mirror and make sure she was ready to receive. Make sure she looked like a woman who was confident and happy about her decision, not one whose deepest fear right now was that she was making a huge mistake.

"Julie, hi." She pressed a sincere handshake on her first meeting of the day and guided her to a chair, making sure to maintain eye contact.

"It is such a pleasure to see you! And I'm so glad you're my first meeting. This will set me on the right foot."

"Well. You seem much happier than I thought you would. Some people saw you come in yesterday and said that wasn't the case." Julie eyed Sheila, her suspicion barely showing.

"Oh, I'm getting better and better every day." Sheila rolled her eyes in her mind. She couldn't wait to get on with it.

"So Julie, I've been out of the loop for a while. Tell me what's on the agenda for us today. And then I have some tremendous news for you." Sheila's eyes sparkled. She tried her best to be completely in this moment, not in the ones before or ones to come.

"I understand Jules Sert has filed a grievance against me for pulling him off a case he was working. I want to know what's going on." Julie, VP of litigation, tapped her notebook impatiently.

"Oh?" Sheila said coyly. "Well, as you can see," gesturing to her intake table, "I have quite a way to go before I get through the whole pile. I'm not sure that I've come across that one yet." She was sure she had. "What shall I do?" She looked studiously at Julie, as if seeking advice.

"Tear it up and tell him to learn some professionalism," Julie started indignantly. "I will not have him sullying my good name and costing me time and energy because his feelings were hurt. I don't suppose you would know but litigation is in a critical stage right now. I simply cannot afford this."

"I can only imagine the pressures you are under. How you do it I don't know. Don't worry about this for now. I'll have to locate his filed grievance and figure out how best to deal with it. Hopefully I'll be able to take the matter in hand before I leave. So focus on your other responsibilities right now. I'm happy to take care of this for you." Sheila looked at Julie, waiting for it to register.

"Look, I'm going to give you a piece of professional advice." Oh, this was going to be good. "Do your job. No one who's really trying to get ahead with a career can afford to let their grief control them. I know you lost your mother, but taking another leave of absence right now is uncalled for. Not everyone is as loyal to you as I am. You can't afford another holiday."

She didn't know why she hated John so much, he was clearly cut from the same cloth as the rest of them.

Sometimes she was frightened to be around these folks.

"Oh I totally agree. But I'm not taking a leave of absence. I'm quitting. Going out on my own for a bit. Less workload. More variety. Seems like the best thing right now. Especially since my job is in such peril."

"Quitting?" The word came out like an exhausted sigh. Julie just sat there for a minute. "Who told you your job was in peril?" Julie asked keenly.

Sheila had to give it up to Julie. You dropped the slightest clue, and she was on it. "John, of course. He tries to protect me as much as he can, but he has better things to do with his time. And even you so much as said it just now. I've got to tell you, I don't like living on the edge. And if it weren't for people like you and John, I would have been thrown off the cliff a long time ago. So I'd like to leave, on my own terms. Now more than ever." Sheila sat back in her chair. This meeting was over.

"So listen," she added off handedly, "I'll get on top of this thing with Jules and let you know when I've taken care of it. Thanks for letting me know about it." Her smile was sincere but tired. She really had spent a lot of energy on this seemingly casual conversation. Now she was just ready for Julie to leave.

"How long are you here?" Julie's voice sounded perplexed, stumped.

"A few weeks. I'll see John through the HR presentation at the conference and then take a couple of weeks to tie things up. Should be enough to take care of most of the things currently on my plate, including your situation." Sheila stood up, prompting Julie to stand, and guided her towards the door.

"Listen," hand resting on the doorknob, "I really wanted to tell you first. You've always looked out for me and I appreciate it. I'll keep you updated on how things work out. Thanks for your support. And I'll certainly take care of you as much as I can." Her hand turned the knob and opened the door.

"Yes, I'd appreciate it if we could meet again soon."
Julie, still confused, was obviously going to have to get her
next moves together.

"Of course. Jerry, can you schedule Julie for another
meeting whenever it works out for our schedules?" He
opened her calendar on the computer and nodded. "Great. I'll
see you soon Julie." She patted her on the arm and smiled.
"And thanks for your advice. Jerry, I'll leave her to you
now."

And with that, Sheila turned back into her office, shut
the door and slumped against it. Softly, so no one would
hear. She heaved herself off the door and into a chair. She
felt about five years old in a room full of adults. She had a lot
to learn about the business world. She had thought John was
a lone detractor. But it was she, not he, that was out of place.
Why didn't she just join a commune somewhere?

And so the rest of the day went, almost to the letter.
"Friends" and "colleagues" giving her advice, painting her
into corners, and her pulling the ultimate trump card by
announcing her resignation and rushing them out the door,
but always petting their egos in a way that suggested she
owed everything to them.

And finally, at the 5:30 mark of a very long day, it
was time for her second meeting with John. She hadn't had
time to plan out her approach, and here he came barreling
through the door.

"It's all over the office. You're telling everyone!" He
looked ready to burst. But Sheila was too tired to find
anything funny now. "I really can't have this in my
department. How dare you spread this, knowing I wanted to
talk to you further about it? I've just about had it with you. I
thought we were a team. We started this organizational
development innovation here together. You know how much
I depend on you. This department cannot survive without
your valuable help. This is a stab in the back." John stood

over her, looking stern and foreboding.

"Nevertheless, this is the way it is. And the thing to do now is prepare for the future, the certain future. Tomorrow we can start preparing for your conference presentation. And in another day or two I should have a draft transition plan ready to share with you for review." Sheila paused, swiveling in her chair and eyeing him. "And I must say, it is nice to hear how valued and valuable I am." Her voice was clearly sarcastic.

"Sheila, you're a hard woman." John sighed. It seemed his day had been nearly as hard as hers. After the initial bluster, he didn't appear to have any fight left in him. She had expected a protracted evening battle. But he seemed resigned to her resignation. That took some of the fun out of it. But she would take it.

"Go home John, you look tired," Sheila said honestly and caringly. She couldn't help the motherliness within her from coming out sometimes.

"Yeah. That's fine." John stood, seemingly at a loose end for a moment, then headed for the door. "See you tomorrow."

Sheila blinked. When had she acquired the power in this relationship? He must be dead on his feet. She saw him to the adjoining door between their offices.

"You take it easy now, OK?" She patted him on the shoulder. "See you." She looked out after him until he was well into his office and shut the door. His behavior was perplexing.

Sheila turned around, stunned. His behavior might be odd but hers was not. She was acting like a slave without her master. As soon as he had stopped riding her, she was trying to get him back to his old self. What was scary was that it had been instinctive. She had done it without thinking. Sheila had to admit, given what had just happened, that she was at least partly responsible for the situation with John. She had been giving her power over to him, believing that he had all the power between the two of him, but hoping that perhaps he would be nice enough to give hers back. Just like Lincoln supposedly "gave" certain slaves their freedom.

She had heard some author on the radio once talking about how African Americans had "post-traumatic slavery disorder." She remembered thinking then, 'Ah, that's the name for it!' She thought it affected the way she felt about her hair, interracial relationships, and her skin tone. But it also affected the core of her work life. Damn, it was insidious. Times like this she wondered what it would be like to be white and carefree. She didn't really imagine John and Jerry had it carefree, but theirs had to be better lots than hers.

Ah, well. "Jerry," she held down the intercom button, "I'm going home." Times like these, she felt she couldn't take another minute of this place. But it was really from herself she was running.

She collected her things, for a change not taking any work home with her, and tidied up her office. Soon she was ready to leave, and closed her office door with a heavy sigh. Now there was Raines to deal with. And he was a man for whom developing a strategy was useless. Why had she picked a man who could see right through her? On the way home she fretted over what to say to him and what he would say back. By the time she pulled into the driveway, she was in a right state.

"This is going to go *great*," she muttered as she opened the front door.

CHAPTER TWELVE
COUPLES FIGHT

Sheila set down her things at the bench by the door and took a deep breath. She headed over to the door to Raines' basement studio and headed down. She walked down and sat on the bottom landing, watching Raines watch his canvas.

"Hi," she drew her knees up to her and rested her head on them.

"Mmmm." Raines cocked his head and squinted at the unfinished picture.

"Umm, I need to talk with you when you get a moment. So I'll be upstairs. Have you eaten? I could fix you a little something." Maybe she was trying too hard to please. He'd see right through this.

Raines set a cover over the painting with an exhausted sigh. "What? What did you say?" He turned around to look at her.

Oh dear. He was frustrated.

"I need to talk to you…when it's a good time for talking." Sometimes he made her feel like a little girl, scared to wake the sleeping giant.

"Well, it might as well be now. I'm out of ideas for my opening. I spent all week on this painting. Then this morning I realized it is completely ordinary. All the other pieces have gone to the gallery. Just one more I need and this is what comes to me. I've only got one week. That will have to be enough time. I know I've got something left in there." He pounded his stomach. "Just gotta get it out." He stared at the cloth-covered canvas in searching defiance.

"Hear! Hear!" Sheila cheered from the steps. She loved this passionate side of him, even if she thought the theme for this latest showing, *Women on the Edge*, was downright depressing. And she swore every woman looked like her. Was he trying to say something?

"So what's up with you?" Suddenly he was near her, arms wrapped around her and kissing her hair. "I missed you." He looked at her with his best puppy dog eyes.

She unwrapped herself from him and moved up a couple of steps to meet him at eye level.

"Ok. I quit my job today," she blurted out, then held her breath, watching Raines reaction.

"What happened?!" He sounded like he was shocked, concerned, and urgent all at once. "You love that job. You spend enough time at it."

"I love the job, but I don't love what I have to do just to do my job. John put all this pressure on me and I just decided I didn't need it anymore." She couldn't tell him the Spirit had guided her to quit—a reality she could hardly believe herself. That would not go over well.

"Oh, *you* didn't need it anymore. I'm just so glad you considered me and us when you made this decision. I can't believe you just up and did this! No warning. No clue." He was pacing back and forth, on the verge of becoming irate. To understand Raines, the one thing you had to know was that he *hated* change.

"I had no clue myself! It is just something that happened. I mean…"

"Just happened?" he interrupted. "How does quitting your job just happen? I wonder about you sometimes. You are so irresponsible! This is just great. Now I guess I'm supposed to support you while you find another job." Raines sat on a stool, suddenly exhausted, or fed up.

There was only so much she could take. He had put her back up now.

"Don't dare call me irresponsible. You don't know anything about what happened, and already you're jumping on me. You're reacting, not responding. And *you*, support *me*? I have never not pulled my weight around here. Don't worry about me if that's all you're gonna worry about. It's always money and expectations with you." Sheila was on a good tear by now. "I need some understanding and support. Not this! Man, give me a chance, please. Can you listen to me?" Pleading filled her voice.

"Fine. What happened." His voice was as blasé as it could possibly be.

She would have to take what she could get here.

"John has been threatening me and bullying me since he got me that job. And when we met for breakfast this morning, he did it again. Since Ma...I mean I just couldn't take it one more time. I quit. I'm gonna go out and do some consulting on my own for a while. Jerry, my assistant wants to come with me, kind of in training I think. Then I'll see."

Sheila looked at him. Trying to hide her deep irritation. Halfway through he had started laughing to himself and had seemed to stop listening.

"Is there something funny here?" she asked.

"I see what this is about now."

"I just told you." Patience was wearing very thin.

"No, what it's *really* about." Raines laughed out loud. "This is about you and how you won't bend your neck to anybody for anything. You got tired of John and you decided you were going to do him one better. Yeah, you're probably better off working for yourself, because you think you're the most superior person alive. My God woman! How can you stand yourself?" Raines looked like he was about to cry with laughter. "I'm glad you didn't say love, honor, and *obey* in your vows to me. I'd know my days were numbered." Raines whooped and rose from his chair, suddenly pulling the cover from his canvas. "Now *that* was the inspiration I needed. This painting isn't about desperation at all; it's about hysteria, wild insanity. Untamed and over the top." He ran over to her at the stairs and gave her a big kiss. "Thank you! I'm unblocked!" He turned around and started mixing paints.

Sheila sat there, shell-shocked. O how he 'got her pressure up,' as her Great Aunt Ruth would say. She had asked God for someone who would call her on her shit, and this is what God had put in her path. She hated getting what she asked for at times like this.

She should have been more specific, describing how her perfect mate would *gently* and lovingly call out her faults. But she hadn't. And now she had Raines. He didn't even listen to her half the time. He could be insensitive to the point of rudeness. Yet he knew her. And seemed to be there when it really mattered somehow. Nothing more infuriating, enigmatic than him.

She walked over to the couch and stretched out, listening to him hum and talk to himself as he painted until she fell asleep. When she woke later, she was in her bed and Raines was wrapped around her like it was going out of style. Sheila nestled into him. Yeah, she hated him almost as passionately as she loved him, she thought. A moment later she was back among her dreams.

PART FIVE
RUNNING

CHAPTER THIRTEEN
SWEAT

She was alone. And afraid. Her breath formed a mist in front of her. Not this dream again. She walked ahead into nothingness. Her footsteps made a loud clanging. Like she was walking on a steel grate, though she could not see. Mist suddenly surrounded her and she was afraid to move forward. So she stood there.

"Mom," her voice called out. "If it's you, can't you let me know?"

A ripple moved through the mist. She heard footsteps coming from somewhere, she couldn't tell where. They sounded heavy, slow. She was terrified.

She suddenly realized she was sitting and stood up, banging her head on the ceiling. She hated dreams. There wasn't enough room for her to even sit upright.

The footsteps stopped. Either the floor was moving up or the ceiling was coming down, but soon she was on her hands and knees, slowly being pressed into a flat pancake.

She started to scream. Someone had to hear. This couldn't be happening! She was spread eagle, pressed tight between grates beneath and above her. Her head was about to be split open like a melon.

The walls stopped pressing in. They pinned her down like prey. The footsteps slowly walked on the grate atop her.

Ah yes. She remembered this dream.

Out of the corner of her eye she could see some shape. She heard heavy breathing. Was it hers? Something sliced into her left shoulder and she let out a howl and struggled to move between the grates.

She heard an amused laugh from above her. Her clothes felt wet, soaked through. Soon her struggling became faint, then stopped. She noticed she had stopped screaming. It was getting harder to breathe. Then the breathing stopped. She blinked, looking ahead into darkness. And then there was only the nothingness.

She woke up crying and Raines drew her closer into him, kissing her forehead and rubbing her back.

Since Mama died, she hadn't remembered having this dream. She had thought she was free. 'There's no such thing as free,' she thought. Slowly she fell back asleep in Raines' arms and dreamed of dreamlessness.

Sheila laid her head down on her desk and sighed, her whole body caving in. She had lived a thousand lifetimes since the week before last. And she seemed no closer to anything. She turned her head to face the clock on her computer screen. 12:45. She could not believe it. Past midnight and she was still at this place! At least the presentation was finally finished.

That John. If he changed his mind once he changed it a thousand times. He was an "idea man." At least that's how he put it. She had other names for him and how he came up with vague concepts and expected her to mold them into his ideal vision only to change his mind later. She got so mad thinking about all he had put her through she wanted to scream.

She needed to go downstairs to the gym and work out some of this aggression. She had gotten more fit than she had ever planned since announcing her resignation. And it was all due to the frustrations this job—that quitting this job—had put in her path.

And she had to give it to Raines. He had certainly been there for her. But always with a shameless grin relaying he thought the whole thing was hilarious. Jerry had helped too. She had always thought he was just a tad slower than other assistants, but he had shown her he had a lot in the reserves. He already had worked before and after hours to secure three clients for their budding consulting business. The first gig started in only eight weeks. And he had pitched in beautifully getting the technical aspects of her presentation with John together.

But gawd if she wasn't tired. Despite all that help, she still had so much to do. So much energy to expend, so many explanations to make, and a lot of politicking to do. In the process she had discovered a lot.

Apparently, everyone here thought the only reason she was still employed was due to their tutelage and protection. She was like the collectively adopted rescue puppy of the company. The white man's burden. Incredible.

And now, the result was that she had to endure countless moments of being drawn to the side and given advice she didn't need from people with only passing knowledge of her, all the while having to pretend she valued their words and concern as hallowed things. She was tired!

She turned off the computer and dragged herself around the office while tidying up. Finally, sighing in resignation over a clean-up job only half done, she grabbed her gym bag and headed out the door, purposely leaving her attaché case sitting in the chair by the door. There would be no work at the home office tonight or tomorrow morning.

In the gym, she burned off a lot of anger and pain, until she was left with only a nervous sense of utter exhaustion. She showered and changed. When she looked in the mirror, she saw a ghost looking back at her. She went back up to her office, fluffed the cushions on her couch and collapsed onto them after setting an alarm for 7:30—little more than five hours from now. She even forgot to turn the lights off. It didn't bother her a bit.

CHAPTER FOURTEEN
RAINES HOME ALONE

Back home, Raines was in a frantic state. It wasn't like her not to call. When he had emerged from his basement studio at about 4am and she wasn't there he had begun dialing all her numbers. She had answered none of them. He had checked the voicemail, text and email. No messages.

What should he do? Where was she? He was so worried about her lately. Since her mother died, she hadn't slept through the night once. Always waking suddenly like she had had the fright of her life, or worse, in tears. And when he asked about it she reacted as if he was giving her a hard time. Quitting her job was a horrible mistake, but he knew there was no talking to her about that.

So he just painted, and tried not to be an asshole. She rarely got in before ten since going back to work, and had in general withdrawn into her shell. He knew this behavior. But it had never been so intense and lasted so long. And he was scared. Sometimes he looked at her and felt he could hear what she was thinking, that she wished he would go away and not come back—ever. So he just painted, and tried to be nice without getting on her nerves—which of course was impossible.

And now she hadn't come home. Where was she?! It was five in the morning, where was she? He was losing his mind. And he knew when she finally showed up she would blow off his concern as ridiculous. That made him mad. He didn't need this in his life. Any of it. He had had a show last week and she hadn't said boo to him about it. It was nice when she would come down to the basement and lay on the couch watching him paint until she fell asleep. He liked just knowing she was there. But why couldn't his life be important? And why couldn't they talk about Ma? Every time he tried to bring up her mother she made tracks, sometimes literally running away from him.

She had always been so spiritual. Not that that was his thing, though he always looked up to how she had something in her life that was her center and brought her peace. But she seemed totally shut down since her mother's death. Nothing brought her peace for long. He was even praying for her. It didn't seem to be helping.

And they hadn't had sex in forever. That had always been one of the highlights of their relationship. He was no Wilt Chamberlain, but he had had his share of women before her. She was the best sex he had ever had. And he was going crazy these last weeks without it. She seemed not even to notice and brushed off his advances as if swatting a fly. Yet she still wanted to be held and cuddled. Women.

That's why he had proposed. The mystery, the feeling that there would always be something new with her—and the feeling that she would think less of him if he didn't. Her esteem was a powerful thing. It motivated him to take chances and be brave in ways he never would otherwise, just to see that look in her eyes. Sometimes, she treated him like a king. And he felt like there was no better feeling in the world. Those moments had been fewer and fewer lately. And since Ma died, he felt more like a eunuch father caring for an invalid than a man, a husband, never mind a king.

He loved her. But he sure didn't feel loved, or even cared about lately. She used to wake up earlier than she needed to just to make him little snacks for his day, or hide love notes and sexy pictures in the last place he expected. Sometimes she even wrote sarcastic commentaries to go with his paintings. He had included a few in his shows. The girl had wit. The best was when she woke up early to give him a blow job. She was good.

He was in love with her joy. In the summer, sometimes he woke up and looked out the window to find her dancing naked in the back yard like a little fairy. The way she laughed until she cried at the lame jokes she would make up for herself, wondering why he didn't get it. The way she loved to dress him just so she could undress him. He missed *her*. And now he didn't even have her around physically. This wasn't right.

He was doing his best to carry her through this rough patch, but he didn't know how much longer he could hold his tongue. And where was she?! As the man he was supposed to protect her, keep her safe from harm. And here he was. He had lost his wife. Oh, how his brother would laugh.

He pulled out a bottle of tequila from the kitchen bar and sat down with a shot glass. As he went to work on the bottle he thought, less and less carefully the more he drank, about all the things he would say to her whenever she deigned to show up. It kept him from worrying about whether she was dead or alive.

Sheila was dreaming two dreams at the same time. In one, the more interesting one, she was making love in a cave to a man she had never met. He was rushing her. She had no time to catch her breath. Then it was over. The scene repeated itself endlessly. In the other, her mother was calling her, screaming her name, but she had no idea where the voice was coming from. And something was wrong with her voice. She couldn't say anything in return. She was afraid to. Both dreams terrified her. And when her alarm blared at 7:30, waking her up drenched in sweat, she was relieved beyond words to be rid of them both.

Hurriedly she tidied up the couch, went to the gym to take another shower, and caught a cab to a shop that opened early to pick out some clothes for the day. By quarter to nine she was strolling into the office as if she had just arrived for the day. And in a way, she had.

The light on her phone was already flashing furiously. Who could have called alrea…Oh God. Sheila sank into her chair and thought about how much trouble she was in. Raines! He would *kill* her. There was no way around it. She was dead. That Latin temper was going to come out and he would kill her. Simple as that.

She picked up the phone receiver. Her hand was dead calm. How could that be? She should be shaking like a leaf head to toe. She pressed memory 2. Memory 1 was Mom's number. The other day she had called it and was halfway through leaving a message before she remembered…the other day she had forgotten everything, and it burned another hole of shame right through her even to recall it.

"Hello." A rough voice answered the phone. Haggard.

"I'm so sorry babe," pleading filled her voice. "I'm sorry, I was soo tire…"

"Are you ok?" A slurred and rash voice on the other end of the line demanded.

"Yes, I'm here at work. I…"

"OK, call me when you're coming home. I want to talk to you…I'm glad you're safe." The phone went dead.

CHAPTER FIFTEEN
APOLOGY

She sat there shocked. He had hung up on her. He hadn't even been listening to her, only enough to know that she was alive and safe. She was scared to death. He was past the point of no return with her. He had sounded like a different man. He wanted to "talk" to her. He had hung up on her. She was in for it so bad when she got home. Here was a reason to run away from home. And he sounded drunk. At nine in the morning he sounded drunk. Had he been drinking all night? She grabbed her purse, rifling through it in search of her cell phone. Six voicemails, thirteen missed calls, eight texts, all from him. Her face sank into an expression of utter dread.

Memory 1. She sat without breathing while she waited for Ma to pick up the line. Damn! She felt like throwing the phone across the room, but instead, a shaking hand placed it back on the hook. She was alone. Who was going to save her? 'Let me die now because it couldn't possible get any worse,' she thought.

Jerry knocked three times then stuck his head in, buoyant and cheery as ever. She remembered hearing the door shut softly before she started rocking back and forth in her chair and crying all over her new outfit. Inconsolable.

She pressed the intercom, "Jerry, cancel today and call a car service to get me home soon...I'm not feeling very well at all." She pressed the buzzer and took a deep ragged breath in.

She took out a notepad and wrote, 'Raines, I am so sorry. Maybe I haven't been treating you so great lately, but what I did last night was absolutely horrible. I know how much you worry, and I should have called. I know when I get home, I probably won't say anything right. I hope you don't hate me. I hope we don't say things we regret. I love you very much, but it's been hard for me these last weeks. Hoping you understand. Please don't hate me. I need your support, even though I guess I'm not giving any back right now. I'm sorry for so many things. And if I get home and things only get worse between us, I hope you'll read this later and it will soften your heart. I'm a dead woman's child. I don't know how to be anything else but that right now. I called her today. But no one answered. It's not the first time. I can't be who you want me to be. I'm amazed I can even function at all. Maybe I need help. All my sisters have left me. No one calls. Who loves me but you? And now I've even fucked that up. Forgive, forgive, forgive. I think I might actually die right now if you don't. Help me. Please. Love, Sheila'

Sheila leaned back from her words and took them in. Unreal. She tore the pages from the pad and crumpled them up, throwing them in the trash. She retrieved the strips of torn paper from the trash and smoothed them back out. She walked to a corner of her office and fed them through the shredder. If she could have, she would have burned them too, but that would have set off alarms. She wanted those words to die a thousand deaths. They were too true. And no one, not even she herself, would face them.

She heard the click of her intercom. "The Barwood Cab car's downstairs. And now's a good time to leave, there's a couple of big meetings going on and it's kind of dead out here." Jerry's voice was anxious.

"Thanks." Sheila mouthed to herself. She was suddenly dead on her feet. She grabbed her purse and gym bag and headed straight for the elevator, which she took downstairs and into the back of the cab without a word to anyone.

On the way home she slept, too tired to care about how much trouble she was in. She awoke bleary eyed in front of her house.

"Fee's taken care of. This is the place, right?" Sheila nodded as she opened the door and slid out. "You have a nice day now. Feel better." The cabby waited until she went inside. She heard him pull out of the driveway.

She leaned against the inside of the door, closing it shut. Sheila sighed. The future was now. She was scared to call his name. "Raines," she whispered. "Raines," a little louder this time. No answer. If he was as drunk as he sounded—and it took a lot to get that man drunk—then he was probably sleeping by now.

She looked first in the basement and then in their bedroom, where she found him, laid out in his clothes on top of the covers. She went and sat down beside him. He was snoring. She put her hand on his chest and he reached for it, taking it in his own as he moved toward her. She lay down beside him and he curled around her.

"You're home." Raines' voice was groggy.

She nodded her head.

"You miss Ma?"

Sheila nodded her head.

"I'm soo mad at you."

"Me too. I hate myself." Her voice came out a whimper and was followed by tears and shaking.

"Shhh," Raines wrapped his arms around her and held tight. "Don't say that. You're my idol...sometimes. If you fall down how will I make it?" He kissed the back of her neck. "We'll get through this. Together, ok?"

She couldn't decide whether it sounded like an order or request. She nodded her head.

"I need you." His voice sounded desperate. "I need you to be nice to me too. To treat me like I matter. Like I'm your husband."

Sheila turned around in his arms to face him. She nodded her head and kissed him. "Forgive me. I'm an ass! And you're so wonderful. I didn't mean it. I'll be better. Give me a chance to be better."

"Oh boo." He hugged her even tighter. She thought she would burst.

Sheila untangled her arms from around his neck, held his face and kissed him. It seemed like forever since she had done that. Raines pulled away and looked at her. Searching. She wasn't sure what she saw in those eyes, besides her own reflection of tears and uncertainty.

He pulled her toward him and kissed her like he had been waiting fifty years to have her. Suddenly she remembered him. The first night they met. He had made her laugh like it was going out of style. She loved that about him. He would make a fool out of himself in a minute just to make her smile. She remembered all the nights lately she had awoken frantic from nightmares. He had been there, kissing her temples, rubbing her back and telling her it was ok, that he was there for her. All the times she had shied away from him when he had reached out for her since Ma died.

She was filled with shame and longing and love at the same time. She hadn't been fair to him. And it was so easy to love him. So why not love him?

The very first time they had made love, Raines had just lain there afterwards and stared at her.

"You are...*something*."

After all these years, he still wouldn't say what he meant by that. She chose to take it as a complement. He had always seemed the more experienced one to her. So she tried to surprise him. She thought she made her own mystery. And as spontaneous and adventurous as she seemed to him, it was really quite planned. She even had a sex and romance journal hidden away in her home office. She wondered what he thought of her after all this time.

Minutes later—it *had* been a long time since they had had sex—Raines was holding her tight wearing a big grin and fast asleep. She looked down towards the foot of the bed. He still had his socks on. They didn't even match. There was nothing funnier to her than a naked man with socks on. She laughed to herself and turned on her side, snuggling into Raines' chest. She hadn't felt this relaxed and happy in forever. This time it didn't take a nightmare for her to fall asleep in his arms.

She woke up to a familiar feeling. Raines was kissing her waist and groping her.

She swatted at him. "Go away!" Sheila teased.

"That was good. That was great. Let's do it again!" Raines was showering her with kisses everywhere. Everywhere.

"I'm still sleeping, damnit." Sheila sat up, grabbed her pillow and whacked him good on the head. Before she knew it they were rolling around on the bed wrestling, laughing, yelling, and kissing in-between.

It was longer than a few minutes this time. It was like she was rediscovering pleasure, sex, orgasms. Why had she not been doing this before? Suddenly she could think of no reason why she had been so cold to him lately. He was a god to her now. At that moment she felt somehow connected to herself in a way she hadn't for a long time. She felt clear and unhindered. She could hardly keep a thought in her head. It felt wonderful.

"I love you." He sounded like a little kid sometimes. "Thank you thank you thank you thank you." His voice sang with relief.

"Mmmm." She put her arms around him. "What do you want to eat?"

"Oh yeah?" Raines' grin got even bigger. "Oh yeah, that's what I'm talkin' 'bout! Biscuits, fried chicken, mashed potatoes, salad. And later, beef stew." He was rubbing his hand together in anticipation.

"You want me to fix red meat? You ain't worked it like *that* you know. I was thinking omelet and some hash browns. Beef stew? Hah!" Sheila pretended to be put out and started putting on her clothes.

"Wait, wait, wait," He grabbed her shirt and threw it across the room. "I can earn the beef stew." He pulled her from the edge of the bed towards him, full of mischief.

"Baby. You wanna earn my stew." Sheila had no idea how she had gotten so good at making beef stew, but he swore by it. "You *know* what you have to do." She lay back on the bed and chuckled.

"Nice to see you haven't changed…you freak." Raines rolled over and threw his legs over the side of the bed. He flashed her that gorgeous smile she loved so much. "Your bath will be ready in ten minutes."

One of her cherished fantasies was for him, well really for any man but since she was married, she supposed it had to be him, to draw her a bath, bathe her, dry her off, oil her down and lay her in the bed. It didn't get any better than that in her book. Well maybe it tied with a good foot rub. He certainly was going to earn beef stew, fried chicken, and whatever else he wanted. She stretched out in the bed, pulled the covers over her and let her mind wonder over the last few hours. She remembered happiness.

The bath had been as wonderful as she had hoped it would be. And she had the best nap afterwards. When she woke up it was late afternoon and she really didn't feel like cooking anything. But the thought of all Raines had just done for her, that and his excited face once he saw that she was awake, got her out of the bed pretty quickly.

A couple of hours later they were sitting at the kitchen table. Raines was digging into his fried chicken dinner and she had a plate of sweet and sour tofu with vegetables and rice. She hated fixing two separate dinners. But sometimes Raines just had to have his meat and she would rather he got it from home than Burger King. And he certainly deserved it tonight. He usually did.

"I missed your cooking." She believed it. He was wolfing it down. Ten minutes and two plates later he was leaning back and rubbing his belly.

"Mmm mmm! I deserved that?"

"Uh huh. And then some." Sheila was bubbling over with warm feelings. "And I just love you and I haven't been showing it, but you've been so good to me despite it all. The beef stew's on the stove. Be ready for a midnight snack if you want it." She rubbed his knee under the table.

"Tell me something." Sheila kissed him and lay her head on his shoulder. Loving him was certainly a better way to ignore her grief than working to death.

Raines stiffened a little. "My show's opening in New York next week. The opening in LA last week went well…I wish you had been there. It was my first show since we've been together where you weren't there. People asked where you were…I missed you. You keep me from worrying too much or taking the comments too seriously." He kept eye contact with her as he spoke. And his hurt was clear.

Sheila blinked and stared back at him. How had she blown off his gallery opening? To be honest she hadn't even noticed he was gone. How long had he been gone last week? Two days? Three?

She sat back in her chair and sighed, looking down at her hands in her lap. "I'm an ass." Her calming effect on him was the only thing that made him tolerable at his openings. No wonder people had asked after her. He must have been a basket case. "So you were a man on the edge opening the *Women on the Edge* collection? I hope that wasn't lost on everyone." She smiled her most endearing apologetic smile and took his hands in hers. "You and me from now on. A second chance for this messed up wife of yours. How about it?"

A huge smile and a soft expression overtook Raines' face. "Uh huh." He pulled her toward him, and they sat hugging for a long moment. Then she heard him crunching on another piece of chicken!

"Raines! Where do you even put it all? We're supposed to be having a sensitive moment here!" she poked him in the chest.

"Spoils of war baby," he said, waving the drumstick, conspicuously missing one bite, in his hand. She had to laugh. There was no getting him to be serious sometimes. That was probably a good thing, but sometimes she couldn't decide.

"Um, wassup with your friends?" Raines asked around bites of chicken.

It was Sheila's turn to stiffen up. "Huh?" She started clearing the table.

"Your girlfriends have been calling every day or something. They even call me, just to see if you're still alive and ok. I think they're about to pull an intervention on your ass. Should be fun," Raines smiled.

"So, if you are gonna call them do it now, 'cause I do not need Rick calling me one more time asking about you. That fool is asking for it."

Raines hated Rick. He only tolerated him because she demanded it. He seemed convinced Rick was always trying to seduce her. The idea was so funny that she had fallen out from laughter at the thought of it. She just didn't see Rick that way. But that didn't convince him. Well, she supposed she had her insecurities about the company he kept. So how could she throw stones?

"And what do you say when they call?"

"I tell them you're alive, but I don't know if you're ok. I don't think you are. I'm worried about you. I was on the verge of inviting them over here myself. I wasn't having any effect, besides annoying you. Maybe they could have better luck."

Raines was giving her that "explain yourself" look. There was no dodging him when he decided to have it out. "So, if it's you and me from now on, then tell me what's going on in your head. Why haven't you been home before ten since you went back to work? Why haven't you been to Ma's house since your sisters were here? How come you

110

never talk about her? What has been scaring you every night in your dreams? Why did you really quit your job? And why does Rick have to call me to find out how you are when you work at the same place? Why don't you pray anymore? Have you *been* in your shrine room since Ma died?"

As he had been speaking, he had gotten up and walked over to her by the sink. He put her hands on his chest, lifted her chin and peered into her eyes. "I'm here for you. I'm only me, but I'm here." He sounded sincere. Sincerely worried to death.

"I miss her Raines." Tears started flowing from her eyes. Her voice choked up and got uneven. "And no one can feel as lost as me. Oh, I'm drowning." Her knees gave way and he caught her before she fell onto their nice terra cotta-style tile.

"Baby I'm sorry. I miss her too."

Sheila looked at him. She was feeling exposed. That made her combative. "No one knows my pain. No one." She was shaking with tears.

"Does God know?" He was such a smart aleck.

Sheila wiped her eyes with the handkerchief Raines had given her from his pocket. In the back of her mind, she wondered what he was doing carrying a handkerchief in his pocket. He had never done that before.

"He can't know." Sheila said, turning away from him. "Else He wouldn't have done this to me." Sheila started to shake and continued in a low voice, "I hate Him. I hate Him. God and I won't be right for a long time." She spun back around and started in on Raines. "Well, you asked. For better or worse. There it is. This is stuff you don't want to hear…Oh and it was all going so well! The working to death and annoying you. It was allowing me to live. Now here you come. Have I prayed? How can I? I can hardly get up the will to breathe every day! I am a miracle. The fact that my heart has not broken yet from pain is God's sick joke on me. If I were dead at least I could start over, not knowing I was an orphan. I could take a breath free and clear. I would be free.

"How could you *not* know that I've been in Hell since she died. I held her broken body in my arms!" Sheila's words were choking with tears. But she hadn't turned away. In her eyes she was begging for help. And deep inside her some part of her hoped he heard her.

Sheila took some deep breaths and wiped her tears. "Oh, it's all too much!" She attempted a laugh. "But you make it better…a little." Sheila smiled, sort of.

Raines stood there looking shocked. "I didn't know you were feeling like this. I'm sorry." He rubbed her forearms. She had taught him a few spiritual and metaphysical things when they had started getting serious. This one, she recognized, was an easy way to change a person's mood, shift their focus to be more energetic.

"I'm sorry too!" Sheila leaned forward into his arms.

"What should we do?" He asked.

"Good question. Don't suppose you know the answer too?" Sheila looked exhausted. She suddenly felt very tired.

"Well," He took a deep breath, "you always tell *me* to be brave. That God has given me all the tools I need to do the job." He peered into her eyes. "Maybe the same applies to you."

God had really blessed her good putting him in her path. But he didn't leave her any wiggle room sometimes. The Truth hurt.

"Maybe." Sheila looked down and suddenly seemed very interested in the floor tiles.

"It's time to go to her house." Raines grabbed her hands and she pulled them away and looked at him like he had just betrayed her. "She would want you to take care of her things. You have things to tend to. You gotta do right by her."

He was pressing every button right now. But she was simply too tired to jump down his throat like she should have. 'Do right by her?' What did that even mean?

"OK," she caved. It seemed inevitable anyway. And with him she had to pick her battles. "I don't wanna do it. But I will...tomorrow. After work then." She slapped her hands together to break up the energy and rubbed them briskly at her heart center. That was better.

Sheila heaved herself off the kitchen bench and looked at him. "Is there anything else, or can I have some peace now?" She smiled

"Thank you. For everything." He looked up at her smiling, thinking about how he couldn't even remember why he had been so angry with her just this morning. He felt really lucky right now...he wanted to paint.

Raines jumped up full of energy. "I'm inspired! Come downstairs with me and fall asleep on the coach. You know I love it when you're there." His eyes were sparkling with excitement. Damn he was fine. She forgot sometimes.

"OK. Carry me." She held out her arms and closed her eyes like she was a little girl. She felt herself lifted up moments later. She kept her eyes closed for a long time. Mama's house tomorrow. It would be like remembering she was gone all over again. Oh God...

CHAPTER SIXTEEN
HOME AGAIN

Saturday. 2:15. She had been sitting outside Mama's house for days. That's what it felt like anyway. She had gone into work for about six hours today to make up for missing yesterday.

Boy was she sorry she had told Raines how bad she felt. Now he treated her like she was on suicide watch or something. He had driven her to work and sat on her office couch, sketching and reading while she worked. Trying nonchalantly to peer over at her every now and again.

Then again, maybe he had just gone with her to work to make sure she would keep her word and come here afterwards. He was sneaky like that. Now he was sitting quietly. The kind of quiet when you're dying to make noise but don't dare.

He missed Ma too. This had to be hard for him. But right now that wasn't making it any easier for her. She had to go into this house. And waiting out here wasn't making it any easier either.

"Call Jasmin would you?" She had to do something to get her courage up. She was aware of Raines' voice, of hearing one side of a two-sided conversation, but her focus was on the doors to the house. How many times had they gone through them together? She wondered how in the world she had been able to walk through them that day with Jasmin, Corinne and Aunt Rachel. She must have been comatose, because now that she was sentient, it seemed like the most impossible task in the world. Had God really given her the tools for something like this? How was it possible?

"Sheila? Sheeeeeeilaaa? Helloooooooo?" Raines had pressed the phone against her ear. Jasmin's voice filled her head.

"Mmm." Sheila grabbed the phone from him. "I'm here. Hi Jas."

"Hi." Jasmin's voice was very loving and tentative. "I guess you know I haven't called. I wish I knew why. I think I'm afraid...of everything really. All I do is cry, and go to work, and come home, and cry, and wake up exhausted and hurt. Life's horrible for me now, and I didn't want to depress you. I didn't want you to make me feel worse than I already did. I'm sorry. I'm here for you, though I don't know what good that is these days. I didn't mean to make you feel alone. I'm here, always."

Sheila looked at Raines. What had he said to Jasmin? Whatever it was, her words were exactly what she needed to hear. That maybe, just maybe, she wasn't the only one suffering to the core of her soul since Ma passed. Jasmin was always so brave. Some of it might just have rubbed off on her.

"I love you. I'm out here in front of Ma's...and I'm scared." She started to cry. "I'm scared she won't be inside." She felt Raines rubbing her back. She was leaned forward with her head on the steering wheel, trying to dissolve into a ball of nothing.

"Go inside. Tell me what the house looks like. I want to remember. Make me feel like I'm there." Jasmin's voice was compelling. It always was when she told you to do something.

"You mean you want to feel as bad as me? 'Cause I'm here. It shore ain't no crystal staircase." Sheila let out a little laugh and leaned back in her seat.

"Go 'head." Jasmin's voice was quiet on the other end.

Sheila let out a big sigh. "Raines, open the door."

He gave her a conflicted look from the passenger seat.

"Right," she heaved herself out of the car and headed towards the house. She would have to do this herself.

"Tell me what's going on."

"Damn keys," Sheila fumbled through her purse. "Ok," she stuck the key in the lock and turned, leaning in on the door as it opened. Sheila turned around to close the door. Raines was standing at the foot of the stairs outside.

"I'll be here, ok?"

Sheila nodded and closed the door. Inside she put her purse down on the bench by the door. She found the earpiece to her phone so she could talk to Jasmin hands-free.

"Ok Jas." She let out a deep breath and allowed herself to take in the room.

It looked normal. That surprised and offended her. Nothing should be as it was.

"The house looks good. Smells a little stale. The last room I wanna go in is that kitchen."

"I don't know what to say. But I'm listening." Jasmin's voice, usually so sure, sounded very small on the other end.

"What do I do now Jas?" Sheila found herself sitting on the bench by the door. She knew that she had had to come here. That it was important. But now that she was here, she felt aimless and lost.

"Well. You're the daughter closest to her home. Maybe since I moved you've been the closest to her. You need to go through her things and get them in order. Decide what to do with her clothes, her shrines. Everything you are looking at is yours now. She left the contents of her home to you."

Everything Jasmin said hit her hard. She had thought somehow that if she could just get through the funeral that she would have no more decisions to make. That she could just grieve. But things so rarely went as she planned in her personal life. Work was something she could control. That's probably why she had been working herself to death since going back. She was queen there. Nothing ever out of place. No problem too overwhelming. She knew she could win.

116

Everything here was hers? How was she supposed to take her mother's things? True, she often wanted whatever her mother had, and they had raised their voices many a time over things she had taken "on loan" and never really returned. But *everything*? Oh, there was just no stopping life.

"Thanks Jas. Thanks for getting me in here—through the door, anyway." Now that Ma was gone, she was convinced Jasmin was the best thing smoking.

"Anytime. Raines told me you quit your job. I'd love to hear some more about that. Maybe you can come out here and visit me sometime."

"I'd like that. But like you said, I got stuff to tend to here. I'll call you next week. And if I don't call you promise you'll call me."

"Deal. I love you. Are you praying for me? I'm praying for you!" Jasmin was more jovial now.

"Of course," she lied. "Talk to you soon. Thank you for loving me." The last bit came out a bit mangled. But it came out.

"Peace my sister." Sheila could feel Jasmin's smile. She couldn't help but return it.

"Peace." She hit end on her phone, took out her earpiece and threw the whole contraption into her bag. Sheila opened the front door and saw Raines sitting on the front porch. He popped up when he saw her.

"Well come on," she nodded toward the house and headed back inside, leaving the door open.

For the next few hours, they went through the house, throwing away the things that had spoiled, talking about what to do with everything, and even sharing a few memories. It was as normal as it could be. Raines put some music on and turned the volume up on his phone, and for a few minutes, they even danced in the kitchen like nothing was wrong. She laughed with him, and she felt sparkly again for a time.

As they drove home Sheila felt like she hadn't really accomplished anything, because she still didn't know what to

117

do. She would be much more comfortable when she got back to work. Sheila wondered what she would do when she stopped working, after her notice was over. How would she run then? But 'then' was such a long way away. Why worry about it now?

"*Baby Girl.*" Her force of will swatted the voice away.

Of course, John had something to say about her missing work on Friday. He expressed his disappointment by not talking to her for all of Monday. What he didn't realize was that she preferred it this way. She mused about how to irritate him into giving her the silent treatment for the rest of her time. Jerry and she worked hard that day. Fine-tuning was always the most agonizing task to her. But at 7:30 that evening, finally, with four days to spare, the presentation was finalized.

"Alright!" Jerry leaned back in his chair and stretched out his arms. Sheila leaned back on the desk to the right of his.

"Ok," Sheila laid down the blue line of their materials for the presentation. "These are ready to go. Messenger them to the publisher's tomorrow. Don't come in until noon. You've earned a bit of a break. Plus I have something else I'd like you to work on. I emailed it to your home address." Sheila rubbed her eyes. "Man I'm tired!"

"If I may say, I think you've earned a break as well. You've been burning the candle at both ends for a while now." Jerry peered at her cautiously.

"Not you too! Oh well, you all may have a point. I promise I'll go home after I clean up my office. It looks like a tornado hit it. Ok?" She had an approval-seeking, slightly mocking tone.

118

"You know they're planning something big for you. You'll have some kind of goodbye party in two weeks."

"I hope you're telling them not to get me any crappy gifts. Just tell them I want a nice cake, fruit and good music. That'll work.

"Now, in these next four days I have a lot of mediations. This is as good a time as any to begin your learning process. You can sit in on the initial grievance intakes I have tomorrow afternoon and the mediation I have on Thursday. Then Friday I have a follow-up interview to do with…um, Clarke and Leens. That ought to be something for you to get your feet wet."

Jerry had leaned forward and was listening closely. He grabbed a notepad off of the desk and took down his notes.

"Mmm hmm. Sounds good. Sounds good."

He was excited and trying not to be, she could tell. It made her smile.

"Well let me clean up and get home. Goodnight Jerry, and thanks."

He beamed a smile in return. She half-hazardly threw things into piles in her office in order to see the bottom of her desk. Neatness had gone out the window today. After things were at least nominally in order, she sat down on her sofa. Tomorrow would be her first mediation and interviews since she had come back. She had scheduled them as far away as possible, to give herself time to get back on her feet. Now she felt a nervousness she hadn't felt in a long while. She hoped it was like riding a bike. Shaking herself out of her fears, she collected her things and headed home.

PART SIX
GODLESS

CHAPTER SEVENTEEN
PLYING THE TRADE

Sheila had had enough.

"Ok I'm going to stop this back and forth. There is no place for infighting in this organization—and certainly not in my office—no matter how valid both of your perspectives are. This is an unhealthy pattern of communication, and we are going to have to find a better way to discuss this issue. Let's stop and close our eyes and take ten slow deep breaths and clear our heads." Her clients were staring at her like she had lost her mind. "I insist."

Sheila pushed her seat back a bit, closed her eyes and began breathing, and prayed for help. 'Lord give me strength and show me how to be a vessel of your work. Lay your hands on Janet and Roger to open their minds and create opportunity. Keep me humble so I don't break their frickin' necks. Lord give me strength.' Seven, eight, nine, ten. She opened her eyes and smiled.

"I am committed to finding a positive way for everyone here to be heard and to come to an understanding conducive to you both having a workable relationship. To that end, I want to recap what I have heard here so far and we're going to have to take this all from a different angle." She was determined to finish this today. She would not adjourn. Sheila flipped back through the papers on her lap. Not having a table at this arbitration had been a huge mistake. She had wanted to take them out of their comfort zones, true. But who knew they would be such hideous beasts outside of the zone?

Sheila stood up abruptly and walked over to her butcher-block paper. She flipped back a few pages and read her writing. She turned to face the two thorns in her side. Her expression was stern and just this side of sore.

"Janet. Do you really think it is acceptable to tell *anyone* they don't have the balls for their job?"

"That is not what I said. Roger is just…"

"The answer is no, Janet." Sheila walked towards her seat until she was almost looming over Janet. She could not let her get the upper hand in this meeting again. "The answer is no." She stepped back and sat in her chair and held up her hands to stop Janet from bursting out. "I'm saving your job. Our lawyers will tell you flatly the answer is no. They won't even listen to what you have to say. On its face the answer is no. If you think that the principle of what you did was so right that you are willing to face the very real consequences of sticking by it, then there is nothing more that I, or this company can do for you. Can you live with that?"

She had begun speaking slower, softer, doing everything she could to deliver these harsh words in as unthreatening a tone and manner as possible. Janet's head swiveled from Sheila to Roger in exasperation. Roger's face was blank. Sheila suspected he was working hard not to grin from ear to ear. She hated being the bad guy, but she had thirty-five more minutes to finish this, and they had been getting nowhere. Maybe this was why people were afraid of her.

"Lose my job? You must be kidding! I didn't do anything wrong!" Janet looked like she was about to explode in her chair. She crossed her arms and tossed back her head as if she were untouchable.

"I'm not kidding. I happen to think you did something that is very wrong in this company in this day and age, but you know I'm not here to take sides. I'm just telling you the way things stand. Either the complaint that Roger has, the part of what happened that you agreed with, is the kind of thing that never happens with you, or it is something that has happened and may happen again. If it's a rare instance then we can settle it now, I believe, while easily protecting both of

122

your positions. If it is indicative of ongoing behavior then we will have to work much harder to create a situation where you can continue to keep your job, not just through this incident, but through your career here. May seem unfair. May *be* unfair. But there it is." Sheila leaned back in her chair and let her palms face upward. "You tell me." She stood up and turned to face her whiteboard. She had to give Janet a little time to think without feeling watched by her. In blue she wrote the word Resolution at the top and underlined it. She smiled. Everything was going to be alright. 'God please let everything be alright.' She turned with an expectant, excited smile on her face.

"So how are we doing?" Her voice was upbeat.

"Fine." Janet's voice sounded defeated and disgusted.

"Good," Sheila's voice was warm and happy. She had to counter Janet's negative energy. "So let's finish up here by coming to a common understanding of how you will treat each other in the future and write it down. Then you will both sign this pledge as well as the complaint settlement forms." Sheila felt for the switch on the side of the easel and flipped the power on. It would record the board and print out copies. She could hear Jerry, tucked silently in a corner, shuffling through his papers, probably locating the settlement forms. She had to smile. This was the part she loved. "Let's get started."

Thirty-five minutes, and no small amount of browbeating later, she pressed the print button on her easel capture machine. She heard the soft squeal of it turning out pages.

"Jerry, can I get those settlement papers now." She moved halfway across the room to meet him. Even he looked tired. She sat back down in her chair and handed them clipboards containing their pledge of behavior for their initialing, and their settlement of complaint forms for their signatures. She took in Janet and Roger. They looked exhausted. It had been a damn long hour and a half. The last part was always the hardest because people believed it would be the easiest. They signed their paperwork, and she took back the clipboards, quickly reviewing.

She leaned forward and split her eye contact between them.

"I know it hasn't been easy. Neither of you wanted to be in this position, and certainly not cooped up in here with me all this time. But you've done something here that shows that you both, and your department, are committed to justice in the way you treat each other. And maybe at some point, perhaps not now, you'll be proud. Thank you." Sheila stood up from her chair and stuck out her hand to Roger. He got the cue and stood up to shake her hand. She walked him to the door. "I *strongly* encourage you to get out of the office for a bit just to clear your head and get some fresh air. If I could I'd make it a law. No work immediately after settling complaints! But hey, I just work here." She opened the door and shepherded him out. "Let me know if you need *anything,* Roger."

Sheila went back into her office. She glanced at Jerry. "Jerry, can you file the paperwork now please." She stood quietly and watched as he collected his things and brushed past her to his desk outside. Then she closed the door and turned to Janet.

"I am so sorry. Who knew it was going to go like that?" She walked over to her desk chair and plopped down in it.

"You didn't seem like you were *soo sorry* before." Janet leered at her.

"Now you know it's not my fault you think its 1970 and you can treat workers like that. Back then you'd be a queen of industry or something. Now, stuff like this is a civil suit prosecutor's dream. You better stick to that pledge, as you know I only have four more weeks here. Next time John won't save your ashes from the fire. He'll let it slide until Roger hires a lawyer and you're knee-deep in formal charges.

124

I'm just telling you true now." Sheila's voice sounded casual and off-hand, but she hoped Janet was getting the very important and deliberate message of her words.

"Queen of industry. This is just the way I was treated all through law school, clerking, and those other jobs I worked that got me to here. Now I'm on top and he's where I used to be, but the same treatment is not ok."

"Exactly. The same treatment you got, that you think nothing of, it's not ok now, not without repercussions. It's a whole new world. Too many people passing the bar. Just itching to sue folks. You know this." Sheila smiled and threw up her hands. She hoped Janet was getting it.

"Yeah, well…I've got work to do." Janet rose from her seat and collected her things.

"Nah, go out, have a bite to eat. Don't think about this place for the next hour."

"Take time off before the big conference? Then I really would lose my job."

Sheila thought about that. 'Oh well, I tried.' Sheila walked her to the door with a few parting words and, finally, she had the office to herself. She felt like heaving onto her couch but instead she pulled out a small folding stepladder and climbed up it, peaking over the top of her bookcase to where she had placed her statue of Shiva, the Hindu god of transformation, to put it deceptively simply. "Are you doing your job up here?" She shook her first two fingers at the statue. "I felt awfully alone down there. I need you to go to work on these people now. I ain't got much longer to stay here and I need all the help I can get."

Telling her subordinate that she was beginning to wonder whether he had the balls for this job! She had never heard anything so ridiculous. Janet didn't have balls. What did balls even have to do with it? These people were crazy. And she knew Janet really meant what she said, that she stood by her acts. Sheila had given her plenty of ways out if she had just been trying to save face after doing something

125

she knew on reflection was wrong. But she had protested until the end.

It's just as well Sheila was leaving now. The threatening them with dismissal only worked but so many times. Then it became seen for what it was, an idle threat. And with a person like Janet, if they got any more lawyers with backbone working in her department, she would be in and out of this office as if they had revolving doors.

While she had her stepladder out, she filled her canister with water and watered her plants, slowly unwinding and debriefing in her head from the session. Two more this afternoon. With people she thought might actually hate each other. She put away her ladder and canister and called Jerry into her office, showing him to a seat. Finally, she crashed down on the couch and kicked off her shoes.

"So, what did you think?" That was open-ended enough. This had been the first session he had observed past the intake level, and she wanted to get as wide a degree of feedback as possible. For the next half hour, they reviewed the techniques she used, questions and observations he had, and potential ways he could play a greater role in future sessions.

"You're very observant, Jerry, and it's great to see you are attuned to people's microaggressions. You could do very well in a wider role in this field and I want to help set you up for success." She touched her fingers together in her favorite plotting position and attempted her very best mastermind voice. "We'll rule the world, together!"

Jerry, who was used to her humor, chuckled and she gave a full-throated laugh. These walls had been missing that sound from her lately. They would do well together, she decided. She left him with the assignment to type up the debriefing notes and draft follow-up letters to the clients. If her—if *their*—consulting business was going to work, this was just the beginning of duties he would have to take on.

CHAPTER EIGHTEEN
OOEY GOOEY

With an hour before her next mediation, she shooed Jerry out of the office and set herself to returning phone calls and emails for a half hour. She was just tidying up her office and opening the notes on her next session when the phone rang. Her home number showed up on the caller id and she picked it up before it rolled over to Jerry.

"Hello dear." She tried to sound sexy and alluring, but worried she just sounded like an old smoker.

"Well, hellooo...There's the sexy voice I needed to hear!" He always seemed to flatter the part of her about which she was most insecure. She loved that.

"What's up doc?" She smiled and leaned on her desk. He was just the voice *she* needed to hear. God, he *always* sounded sexy. How did he do that?

"Tomorrow. New York. Be there." He did a good job of sounding tough and intimidating.

"Yes sir." She put on a fake timid voice. "How are we going? Gimme the details. I told John I'd be gone Friday afternoon, but you know he wanted to know the appointed hour."

"Well, the trucks are coming tonight to pick up my pieces. I was up there Monday to go over the hanging locations, so that's taken care of. I'll only need to double-check it before the opening. I figured we could take the train up. I thought I'd rent a sleeper car. I know it's only a few hours but I think we can think of a way to put that top bunk to the test. I haven't made love on a train in forever."

Sheila's body temperature was spiking. "Now you stop it right there. I have to mediate in twenty minutes! I can't have you getting me all discombobulated like this." She tried to wipe the blush of her face.

"Ok, ok. Train leaves at 1:17 from Union Station. I'll bring your bag with me and you just meet me there, quarter to one let's say. Don't be late." He hated lateness. He could be late all he wanted. But if you were late—hanging offense.

"Ok boo...and Raines, get the sleeper car. Definitely." She started to blush all over again.

All she heard was a delighted laughing on the other end. He had a pretty cute giggle.

"Bye."

"Ok, see you tonight." Raines had finally composed himself.

"No, not tonight remember. I'm spending the night at Ma's." It hurt so much to say her name sometimes. "Got some things to do there."

"Oh. Yeah...You sure you don't want me there?"

"I have to do it alone. But thanks. You've really been helping me these last few days. Got me to this point." Sheila suddenly felt nervous and anxious.

"Ok, um, how will you pack if you're not coming home?"

"Bag's in the study, I did it this morning before work sleepy head. Don't forget it ok?"

"Ok. Call me if you need anything. I love you."

God. Sometimes he said that like it was really meant to be said.

"I love you too. Don't stop saying it."

For the next minute he showered her with pet nicknames and promises of undying affection. She was a veritable pool of jelly by the time he finished.

"Hasta manyana Sheila."

"Ok. Bye-bye."

She hung up the phone and laid her head on her desk and smiled dreamily from ear to ear. He made her so happy to be alive sometimes. She felt like the luckiest woman anywhere right now.

She let that warm gooey feeling bubble over inside her for a few more minutes. She sat up from her desk, picked up her notes and paced the room reviewing them. She had work to do and she had to get her sea legs back.

In the back of her mind, she thought about tonight. She had told herself she would go to Ma's and figure out what to do with all of her shrines, to ask God for direction. It was like…it was like a daughter doing a mother's job. And she didn't have the strength. Ma had always talked about what it meant to have an unfailing heart. It meant that even though you were afraid, you did what you had to do anyway. Right then and there she asked God to renew her unfailing heart, and she actually felt better, more equipped and stronger than when she started. She didn't know how, but she knew she would get through this.

CHAPTER NINETEEN
THE SHRINE ROOM

At eight o'clock that evening, as she finally finished wrapping up her day, she mused where that feeling of strength she had earlier had gone. She always tried to work later to make up for time off, since it wasn't like the office suddenly stopped when she was out, so she could keep up with everything. This weekend would be a nice change of pace from working herself to death. Raines *had* been really nice to her lately. She had let down her guard, if only a very little bit, and they had been clicking. It would be nice to support him and get sucked into his world for a few days. And she really wanted to see how the crowd reacted to his opening. *Women on the Edge* was a gutsy collection from him. She still wanted him to challenge *himself* in his work, not just his audience. But this collection had verve on every level. He had even let her rename one of his pieces from Hysteria to Hilarity. That he had been that flexible surprised her. So, she was gladly dropping everything to support him.

But between now and this weekend was tonight. And there was no getting around it. She searched her office and found there was nothing else she could busy herself with to pass the time. Collecting her things, she set them on the couch by the door, and pulled out her thank you cards in their binder on the shelf. She found one that said "You're a real trooper" which pictured a guy about to jump out of an airplane, scared witless. She fished out the crispest $20 she could find from her wallet and stuck it inside, adding, "To add to your collection—I'm sure you'll need it!" Sealing the card, she placed it in Jerry's inbox, picked up her bags, and headed for Ma's.

Any other time—before—she would have opened the

door to find inspirational music playing and delicious smells wafting through the house. Now, there was a disturbing silence and the smell of something stale. She and Raines must have missed something from their collection of all the perishables in the house. She set down her purse and headed upstairs. No time like the present.

Outside the door to Ma's shrine room, she removed her shoes, watch, and cell phone. Using the Florida water on the small half-moon table she poured a generous amount in her hands and rubbed them briskly together at her heart center, letting her mind go blank. Picturing white purifying light, she brushed her hands over her body, brushing off the funk and replacing it with Light. She put her hand on the door. "Speak oh Lord so thy servant can hear, speak oh Lord so thy servant can hear, speak oh Lord so thy servant can hear." As she turned the knob, she was flooded with memories.

"Ma, that's the craziest thing I ever heard." She had just told Sheila in excited tones how she wanted to spend New Year's Eve. "I like to pray, but all night? Surely you just mean for a few hours. I could do that."

"No baby girl, I mean all night," she said exuberantly. "I figured we could start about eight or nine at night and go until sunrise."

Sheila looked at her like she had lost her mind. She crossed her arms and softened her expression. It was hard to withstand Ma's joy. "Convince me."

They had spent the afternoon laughing and making plans. She had supposed she should be happy and perhaps even honored Ma wanted to spend the time alone at home with her. She had assumed she would be opening up the Institute for a special ceremony or something.

But instead, they had moved a low coffee table into the shrine room. The set themselves up with lots of blankets, pillows, snacks, and music. They had spent the night laughing, praying, talking, singing, and noshing a bit. And yes, they had stayed up until the sun rose. Those were the days.

The first thing that surprised her was how dark it was. In this room of the house, you never needed to turn on the light. There were always so many candles lit that it seemed like daylight. Now it was pitch black. She fumbled for a light switch at the edge of the door and switched it on. Pink light bathed the room. Sheila looked up. Where in the world had Ma found pink light bulbs?

The next moment Sheila found herself face down on the floor, arms outstretched. Sheila turned her head to the side and couldn't help but smiling. Every knee shall bow, every tongue shall confess. It didn't say nothin' in there about dropping her like a sack of potatoes.

"I confess there is no God but God. I confess there is none greater than God. I confess God is my God." That ought to do, she thought.

She felt the pressure on her ease up and she sat on her knees, bowing three times and giving glory to God. She thought about how long it had been since she had done that. Ma was still alive then. In all humility on her hands and knees she crawled forward to the middle of the room and sat down. Finally, she could begin to take everything in.

This was where the stale smell was coming from, that much was for sure. Every shrine was littered with offering plates. In her Grandma's day, it was called 'leaving something for the pot:" the extra plate at the table, or food intentionally left in the pan. Offerings to the ancestors and

deities like Shango and Allegba. Remembered truths from
the time before they were slaves. Great Aunt Mary and some
of the others still did it. That's why when they came in this
room they had nothing to say. Well, almost nothing.

Sure, the modern Christian railed against it like it was
devil worship. But the old-school relatives and friends, they
knew the language being spoken. While having it so much on
the surface, not hidden or obscured merely as tradition, was a
bit discomforting, they *knew*. Even that which they had never
seen they knew. That was the power of God for those who
seek Him. Praise God, she was starting to feel happy in this
room. She had to take care she didn't get possessed, or 'catch
the Spirit' as they said in church, with no one here to look out
for her. She tried to put a lid on her exuberance and focus on
the task at hand. What to do with these shrines?

She stood up and walked over to a large trash can in
the corner. Going from shrine to shrine she collected all the
plates of food and candy and emptied them in the bin along
with empty candles. In the end the bin was full. She placed it
outside the door and set down her pile of saucers, bowls,
cups and glasses next to it. She walked over to a large
bookcase in the corner of the room and opened the cabinet
below it. There had to be fifty candles there if there was one.

And all the shelves above held countless offerings.
Candies and chocolates from around the world. Jasmin rice
for the Goddess of Mercy, red rice for the God of War.
Cornmeal, peas, honey, tobacco. It was like a well-stocked
spiritual offerings general store. Above that, incense, smudge
sticks, cowry shells, Florida water, white cloths, special
cleansing soaps, materials for Ma's spiritual baths, essential
oils, High John the Conqueror oil, dragon's blood resin. All
for clearing negative energy and setting the space for God's
blessing to flow.

Above that, where she was standing now, the
principle text for every religion that spoke truth. Torah,
Qabalah, Quran, Holy Bible, Eightfold Path, Taoist and

Vishnu Texts, Hindu, the list went on and on. Ma always said she needed the whole Truth, not just a piece. She thanked God she grew up with Ma. She wouldn't have had it any other way, even given the way things had turned out.

With that dampening thought, she set to honoring the shrines.

She selected candles for each shrine and began cleansing and setting the energy for each one. She placed them on the shrines then selected incense for the shrines. She would have to wait to place offerings until she could clean the saucers and bowls that had been there before. Now, she had to tell these shrines what they already knew. Ma was dead.

She started with the Buddhist shrine. She knelt before it and lit the candles and incense. She took in the shrine. On the highest level stood the God of War, looking terrible and fierce. He was the energy you wanted when you needed to go to battle and be protected from all harm. Perched high above, of course he seemed to be staring right at her, saying, "What child?"

The focus of this shrine was definitely Quan Yin, the Goddess of Mercy. Sheila had adopted all goddesses whose energies were that of the Divine Mother, but particularly Quan Yin, very early on. She so often seemed in desperate need of mercy and compassion. It was a perfect fit to her. She was a beautiful statue. Resplendent and powerfully graceful. She seemed to be saying, "Speak child."

Below her on the bottom level were seven different representations of the Buddha. He had so many faces, so many energies and truths. Skinny ancient man bent over his stick, fat laughing man steeped in mirth, somber elder with powerful eyes. On the left of them stood the Monkey God, always fighting the battles of the powerless, when he wasn't mired in mischief. They all saw through her.

Behind the shrine the whole thing was framed with a giant gold hoop, with a circular antique blue mirror in it.

134

Perfect for divining. She had seen many visions of her future and ways to overcome challenges gazing in that mirror. She wondered what it might reveal to her now, though she dared not look.

Looking around she realized that every one of the energies on these shrines talked to her. It was like that when you carried the Spirit of God in you and begged him to be present in your life, not just in church and through books. God spoke to her all the time. In ways she could understand, words her mind could hear. And at these shrines, representing the Divine presence in so many of its manifestations, she spoke with God. She interacted with the One Source. That was the true gift her mother had given her.

She bowed low and long before Quan Yin three times. Then she began to speak her heart.

"She's gone. What do I do?" Before she knew it she was prostrate on the floor weeping tears she thought she'd emptied long ago. It felt like someone was smoothing her hair. This was what she had needed. The love of God. God loved her more than Raines loved her, more than her sisters, more than even Ma loved her, more than she loved herself—combined. It was also frightening, 'cause there was nowhere to hide. She could lie to Raines, herself, the rest of the world, but God knew. And when you went before Him, there was no pretending. No holding back.

Now all her pain, anger, loss, fear, and feelings unnamed and unknown were overwhelming her. And she felt like she would die. But here, surging through the compassion and mercy of Quan Yin, God was saving her from dying of a broken heart. God was saving her from shrinking into nothingness from fear. God was saving her from hating Him. She held on for dear life, feeling as tossed and lost as a canoe in an ocean storm. But she knew she was not alone. And she knew, no matter how close to death she felt right now, that somehow, because of the love and singular power of God, she would survive.

She didn't know how long she lay there. But she actually noticed a pool of her tears on the floor. She had to be seeing things. With a big heave, she turned over on her back and wiped her face. Looking up, she saw pink lights shining down on her, and she felt comforted. All of the candles on the shrines were lit. She hadn't remembered doing that, but she could feel all the spirits in the room awake, though they hadn't been when she first came in, and they comforted her. Life would be fine if she could never leave this room, she thought.

CHAPTER TWENTY
GRANDAD

Sitting up, she found herself facing the ancestral shine. Her grandfather's cup of coffee and cigar lying there as if he would be back any moment. He had always loved coffee and cigars, at least that's what Ma had said. She could barely remember him. Now she would have to put her mother up on this shrine as well. But not yet. Her grandfather's energy still dominated this place. She could feel it radiating out, pulling her in. Without thinking she moved closer to the shrine, picked up the cigar, lit it and started smoking. She had never smoked before. She had never had the faintest desire. In many dreams and meditations, her grandfather had appeared to her as a guide over treacherous ways. Often she had come to this shrine when knee-deep in sorrow, put some honey on her tongue, and been comforted by his spirit. In all that time she had never felt the impulse to smoke his cigar or drink his coffee.

"Well Granddad, it's just you and me now." Sheila hugged her knees up to her chest. "So what should we do now?" She waited, expecting an answer but received nothing. "Speak oh teacher so thy student can hear."

"Hear my voice Y-Y." A voice boomed from everywhere and nowhere.

Sheila jumped out of her skin. She was losing her mind. When she said she spoke to God and the blessed spirits, she meant internally—she heard words in her heart or was simply blessed by understanding in her soul. But just then, she had heard an actual audible *voice*. And Y-Y? The only person who had ever called her that was grand…Her brain just froze. It *could not be*. Her grandfather had just spoken to her. It couldn't be.

"Who is this speaking to me?"

She heard laughter. A man's voice. "You don't remember me. But everything you do I have seen. And what you *will* do I know. And you've come a long way, child, but you have a ways longer to go."

There was no mistaking that voice. Though he had died while she was a child, she remembered her grandfather. But she had to be sure. Mama had told her that energies, when asked a question three times, *had* to answer truth the third time. A lie could not persist.

"Who is this speaking to me?" She was paralyzed with fear and wonderment.

"William Howard Robinson," the voice thundered back.

"Who is this speaking to me?"

"Your grandfather chile." The voice seemed to smile.

"Who is this speaking to me?" She threw in a fourth repetition for good measure.

"Look in the mirror."

Looking around the only mirror she saw was behind Quan Yin. She stood up, slowly. In the mirror it was like looking through a window. On the other side was her grandfather, exactly as she remembered him, as if he had never aged. But his physical appearance *hadn't* aged, she supposed, since he was no longer living.

He looked exactly as he did all those years ago, when as a kid she would sit at his and Grandma's kitchen table, swinging her legs and laughing with him at their shared secrets. He always let her take a sip of his coffee when no one was looking. She inevitably made a face at the horrible taste, which made her grandad laugh. Good times.

"How is this possible?" She believed in visions, but to have it happen…Seeing was entirely different from believing. And now that she saw, she realized she had never really believed. Yet another thing on which her faith fell short.

"It is good to speak with you. I have appeared as a guide in your meditations, spoken to your heart, and helped keep you from harm. All because you needed me. Now you are needed."

His last words hammered her. She plopped down on the floor. It was all too much to be believed. And now here he was, like a regular person talking to her, telling her that she was needed. She put her hand to her head and shook her head, hoping to wake up. Was it a nightmare? Was it a dream? She just wanted to wake up. Right now!

"Hear my words and take heed!" Her grandfather's voice was hard and compelling. "You have a duty to perform. A responsibility that falls only to you. And it is time."

Sheila shook her head from side-to-side. Why couldn't she wake up? She was beginning to think she would never wake up.

"Granddad please! I can't take this." She wanted to ask him to go away but she was afraid he would. She had never really known him, and Ma loved him so much. What if this was her one chance? It was a good thing she had cried herself out before. This had all the makings of another tearful fit. She wondered if she was going crazy or if she were seeing the Truth right now.

She opened her eyes to peek at the mirror. He was looking right at her, right through her. Waiting.

"Yes?" She supposed there was no fighting it.

"You are being called to your mother's post. And there is work to be done. Right now." All the smiles and warm tone seemed to have leapt out of him to parts unknown.

"What? I don't understand what you mean."

"Of course not."

Sheila's back stiffened. Was he giving her lip? Oh, this just kept getting better and better. Sheila's shoulders slumped and she gave up.

"If this is your attempt to just beat me down, I've gotta tell you I'm pretty much there." Her voice was resigned.

"The first thing you need to know, child, is that I don't attempt to do anything. I *do* it. Secondly, I have never beaten anyone down. You will show me the respect you should, even when you are at your worst."

Oh, he admitted she was at her worst, did he? That got her back up good. She hated being told she was out of order, especially when she was.

"I'm here. I'm listening, with respect." She supposed that if this was all real—which she was getting the horrifying suspicion that it was—that at the very least he deserved her respect, admiration, fear, and love.

"Our family has held a special place in your dimension since time immemorial. One from every generation since the beginning. I taught your mother, and she was supposed to teach you. Now it falls on me to tell you that you are being called to serve. You are the chosen one of your generation to fill this task."

'What task?!' Her brain was screaming, but she supposed interrupting at the top of her lungs would certainly not be respectful. She waited, increasingly on pins and needles with every word.

"I was a gate keeper for the third dimension. This was your mother's life, and now it will be yours. What you should have had decades to adjust to and learn, you must accept and become now. I have been waiting for you to come. Welcome home."

CHAPTER TWENTY-ONE
REFUSAL

Sheila reeled. She opened her mouth, but nothing came out, nothing came in. She stood there, frozen. She walked over to the corner and sat down in a chair. Leaning over she rested her elbows on her knees and thought out loud.

"Mother used to talk about dimensions, but when I pressed her about it, she would never get specific. I know we live our physical lives in the third dimension—the world of human flesh and man-made power.

"We try to elevate our consciousness to the fourth dimension: a consciousness based on the Truth that God is the Source. I know about the fifth dimension: chaos and trickery and madness rules there. Mom sometimes mentioned the tenth dimension, but she would never say what she meant.

"And we talked about the heavenly dimensions— places where souls from the third and other dimensions at different stages of opening up reside. But I never learned their names. So, I suppose if there are heaven dimensions there must be hell dimensions—where souls glorifying power of the flesh and not acknowledging God as the true power suffer. Ma said that's where my dad was.

"I suppose places where the ancestors, angels, deities reside, these must all be dimensions too. And devils, evil, they have their place as well." Sheila leaned back in her chair and sighed, trying but not really able to take it all in. She didn't even know where that information she had just spit out had come from, but it seemed true.

"You know, you don't have the right sister. Jasmin, she's who you want. I'll tell her she has to get here." Sheila began to heave herself out of the chair matter-of-factly. She was so glad to be done with this.

"You run from everything. You're afraid. You don't even know what it is to be brave. You sacrifice and suffer, throw tantrums and hurt. But in your entire life, you have never really stood up. You've never gotten off your knees. You'll never look God in the face, if you are ashamed of yourself.

"My child tried to help you. But she never did what she had to do, what she should have done a long time ago—left you alone. Left you alone in this world to force you to deal with your weaknesses and fears. You never realized they were fake, illusions hiding the truth that you are the most powerful person you will ever meet.

"You have never escaped the third dimension. You have given every human and situation in the flesh world power over you. WAKE UP!!! Have you gotten so used to being a coward that you don't even realize when you're doing it anymore? An attitude of failure will serve you nothing. Strip yourself of this weakness and meet me as you are: powerful, beautiful, True.

"'Lift up your heads oh you gates, be lifted up you ancient doors, that the King of glory may come in. Who is this King of glory? The Lord strong and mighty, the Lord mighty in battle. Lift up your heads, o you gates; lift them up, you ancient doors, that the king of glory may come in. Who is he, this King of glory? The Lord almighty, he is the king of glory.' I'm gonna learn you what it means to be a child of God right quick."

Sheila was stuck halfway out of her chair. Her muscles were telling her to leave. Something deep inside her was pulling her back. Both voices held the greatest peril. Lift up your heads, you ancient gates—she recognized the 24th Psalm. It was what she recited when she was feeling downhearted.

She sat back in the chair and looked up in utter despair, eyes red and dry with invisible tears.

"You're just a liar, granddad!" she sobbed. "If you had been here," she pointed to her heart, "If you had really been *here* you would have realized I have failed at everything I have ever done. All I am is fear. It echoes in my dreams! I was even a disappointment to my mother. I could see it in her eyes. I loved her but I failed her. God loves me but he's failed with me.

"I'm barely staying alive. I'm weak and alone. God's pity and mercy keep me alive. I think about all the times I've failed...I just want to die. I would trade my life with my mother's in an instant, and it would be a *relief*...You don't want me. I'm worthless. The only thing I'm good at is this bullshit job and I even quit that!

"Now you're telling me the balance of this dimension depends on me! Then we're doomed, grandfather. No! I can't do it. You'll see. In the end I'll fail you. I'll damn you! Just leave me be. Let me live out my meager life in peace and an ordinary happiness. I don't want to see you in Hell. I already know I'll be there, because in my life I've hated God...you can't know what you're saying. You can't."

Sheila rose and stood in front of the mirror.

"It was nice, what you said," a wistful smile crossed her lips, temporarily uplifting a face pained and tortured. "But we both know it's a lie."

She turned away and headed for the door. As she opened it she hesitated.

"Never speak to me again. Your words are cruel." She shut the door behind her and resolved to destroy that mirror, consequences be damned.

Shaking like a leaf, she collected her things and fled to her car. Inside it she grabbed and shook her steering wheel like it stole something.

"Jesus Christ you've done it now!" She screamed and railed at the top of her lungs. "I tried but it's too impossible. God, that's it. Stay out of my life. I'm telling you for the absolute last time. I'm not evil, but I'm weak. Leave me alone. Leave me alone. Leave me alone!" She ended in an enraged but hoarse whisper. A big part of her expected to be hit my lightning any minute. She could barely get out the words.

Had she just damned God? Had she just excommunicated her grandfather? Disrespected her mother's shrine? Turned away from every spiritual principle and tenet she had ever known?

Yes. She started her car and crept home. Looking for lightning all the way. There was certainly no going back now.

Back home, her cowardly creeping continued as she slipped into bed, trying to be as quiet and small as possible. But as soon as she got in, Raines' arms encircled her tight and he, still half asleep, began kissing her neck and snuggling. She froze with rage. She felt an overwhelming urge to beat him to a pulp. How dare he touch her? How dare he kiss her and imprison her?

She struggled against his grip, trying to wriggle free. "I'm not playing dammit. Let me go!"

Raines woke with bleary eyes and released his hold.

"What? What's wrong?" Raines sat up trying to get his bearings. But before he could get an answer Sheila fled crying out of the room.

When he found her, she was downstairs, locked in her study.

"Sheila," He knocked on the door. "Sheila what's wrong? What happened?" He could hear her crying through the door. Knocking turned to pounding. "Sheila, open the door!" A commanding urgency filled his voice. What was going on with her? He was filled with worry. He didn't really get hunches, but now he felt something was very wrong. "Sheila! Don't make me knock down this door woman!"

He was about to charge the door when suddenly it opened and she appeared in the opening. She looked...well, he had never seen anyone looking like that in his life.

144

"Am I weak or strong?" Her voice was mangled.

"What?"

"Tell me! Am I weak or strong? Do I have a chance to be something more than a failure?"

Raines dropped to his knees, put his hands on her hips and looked up at her. Her eyes had a look of pure need.

"You are strong. At your best you are pure joy. You amaze me every day. There's no one else like you, not because everyone is like a snowflake, but because you are so amazing. Whoever told you you were weak was a liar. Whatever made you think that was wrong. You are strong. *You are strong.*"

Sheila's eyes sang with relief.

"*Baby girl.*" Sheila heard a voice she couldn't have heard. She fainted dead away.

Moments later she woke to Raines stuffing her in the back seat of his jeep.

"Don't take me to the hospital. Don't take me to the hospital. I swear I'll kill you," she croaked.

Raines threw a leveling look at her.

"What's wrong with me…what's wrong with me they can't fix." Her voice sank dangerously low. She tried to sit up and only managed to lift her head a bit. She saw Raines standing there in the freezing cold in his briefs. Her head fell back. She was exhausted beyond belief.

"Don't take me to the hospital. I swear I'm fine…please." Before she could finish, she was fast asleep.

CHAPTER TWENTY-TWO
DISTRACTIONS

Raines stood there, not feeling the cold a bit. Was his wife going crazy? He thought about whether to take her to the emergency room or the psych ward. *Women on the Edge.* Tonight she had seemed more tragic, mad, more on the edge than anything he could ever have put on canvas. And he was more afraid and uncertain than he had ever been before.

He sighed. He supposed there was nothing the hospital could do. He carried her from the car back upstairs to their bed and tucked her in. Getting in to lay beside her, he lay there on his side looking at her for a long time.

"God let my baby be ok." He let out a short prayer. He couldn't remember the last time he had prayed. She lived and breathed by the spirit, but that wasn't his thing. He hadn't been raised that way. But at a time like this, perhaps praying was the only thing he could do. Finally, he went to sleep.

That night she dreamed the dream she had dreamed a million times before. She lay helpless and trapped, being stabbed by some faceless man who seemed to take pleasure in it.

Later that night she woke up, staring up at a dark ceiling. The white mist that she had sworn she saw before, but which was never there when she got the courage to turn on the lights, filled the room now. It seemed to shimmer. She was too tired to even dredge up feelings of fear or wonderment.

She thought about what Raines had said before she fainted. He sounded so sincere. Boy, she had everyone fooled. She turned to face him. God had blessed her enough to put people in her path who thought so much of her, more than she could ever be.

She kissed him. Sleeping lips woke up soon enough and he snaked his arms around her and slowly held her tighter.

"I love you," she managed between kisses. "Make love to me," she asked meekly.

He drew back for a moment and looked at her. She had so much explaining to do, but she probably never would. She was a mystery. As crazy as she had made him tonight, she only had to utter those words, I love you—not make love to me, though that certainly didn't hurt—to make him forget everything. But it seemed this time he couldn't forget. He was still scared. He felt the beginnings of tears sting his eyes. He closed them and buried his face in her neck.

"Baby, tell me what's wrong? I have to know. I have a right to know." His voice sounded hurt, like a fresh wound.

Sheila held his face in her hands.

"You asked me who told me I was weak, what situation led me to believe that. *I* told myself. And my entire life led me to believe it was true. Someone tried to tell me tonight that I wasn't that. They *lied* to me. Because I *know*. I'm just me, nothing special." She shrugged her shoulders. "That's ok. Being ordinary me is pretty damn lucky. Maybe the most special thing about me is *you*. And I love you for making me feel so valued."

She wore the smile of someone who had settled, of someone who thought that next to last was the best they would ever do and got happy about it. He recognized it from his family. And before he met her, he had seen it in himself. It broke his heart.

"Oh baby," he drew her in and held her tight. "You are *soo* special. You don't even know. I'm gonna try to prove it to you. Every day."

"Then make love to me!" She smiled an innocent smile. He broke out in a broad grin, "Okay." But somewhere inside, he was crying for her.

That night they made love. Yet when it was over, both were more confused than they had been before. Sheila maintained a calm placid surface tightly covering her more disturbing emotions. She felt pretty special to have him. She knew that was the best thing about her, that this was the best things would ever get. And that was good enough for her.

Raines lay in the bed, trying to sleep, but he couldn't find any peace. He felt ashamed of what he had just done. He had never before felt like he had made love to a woman when he shouldn't have. But he had felt such a need to connect with her. And he hadn't known what else to do to make her feel better. He felt inadequate and insensitive.

He had had no idea she felt weak. Suddenly he felt like he didn't know Sheila at all. She was the strongest woman he had ever known, after her mother Cathy, of course. He wondered if that was it, if growing up under the most powerful woman in the world had made the second most powerful woman feel like the weakest.

And had he just made things worse? Sheila always said when a woman had sex she gave up some of her power of creation to the man. Had he been robbing her of her power all these years, never knowing how desperately she needed to realize her own strength?

He was disgusted with himself and even the twenty-minute shower he got up to take couldn't completely wash away those sensations. Even whispering 'I love you' into her ears didn't make him stop feeling like there was one person too many in their bed. He probably should have left. But they needed each other in the most unhealthy way right now, and he just couldn't go. So, he lay there and tried to pretend tonight had never really happened. It almost worked.

148

CHAPTER TWENTY-THREE
THE GALLERY

That weekend was strange, Sheila had to admit. Something inside her just didn't feel right. And things between her and Raines were certainly off. She'd have rather had him giving her grief than that sad curious look he had. And he wouldn't let her touch him. He always backed off. That had *never* happened before. All this made for an awkward train ride up to New York.

She had gone into work that morning. It had been a real relief to get out of the house, away from Raines. She and Jerry hashed out a facilitation she had done the day before and had another meeting that he sat in on late morning. This one was a check-up on the African American program manager and one of her associates, a white man who a few months earlier had alleged reverse racism.

That had gone pretty smoothly. She had broken their wills so sufficiently in their initial round of mediations that they still acted like biddable children around her. Most importantly, Lilly, the manager, had stopped referring to Lee as "white boy" and Lee had stopped thinking the company would tolerate an atmosphere where all whites were given preferential treatment.

So the three-month check-in was almost a breeze. They had both lived up to the pledges they had signed, without any browbeating from her along the way, which was unusual. So the pledges were filed away and they started off fresh in a way. They toasted to their mutual success and happiness at the end of the meeting with sparkling cider.

All in all, her workday was a success. And finally, not for lack of trying, there was nothing else she could do to delay getting to Union Station. She hopped a cab and boarded the train, wincing to remember they had gotten the sleeper car. Neither of them seemed up to that right now. She wondered when now would be over.

Luckily, she had brought her needlepoint. She sat there patiently working on a Zen pattern of interlocking squares in blue, stopping occasionally to look up and make the most pleasant and detached conversation she could muster. She tried to feel content. She had all but forgotten the whole of last night. But deep inside a troubling thought roamed across her spirit, wondering if she was sinking past the point of return.

It was certainly a relief to step out of her world and worries and into Raines' reality—the world of artists. She had always enjoyed being in his world; it was license to be a weird combination of deep and flighty that she greatly appreciated.

They checked into his hotel—always the same hotel since his first New York City showing. He was superstitious about it, of course. She stayed behind as he went to the gallery to do one last check of the hangings and placement of his works before the show. Alone in the hotel she just sat quietly in the corner until he came home. She supposed she must have been thinking about something all that time, but she couldn't say what.

He came back and they got dressed, then it was time for her to do her thing. She led him squarely in front of a full-length mirror and told him what a king he was, how proud of him she was, how fantastic his work was, and how much everyone would love him and his opening tonight. She promised him he would sell out, that every word from his mouth would be perfect and that tonight he would live a charmed life, in which he was capable of easily handling any and every thing.

Until now she had always ended with a prayer, but tonight she omitted that. She had decided she wasn't praying anymore. There was nothing it could do for her, now that she had settled on the only kind of life she could have. So, they went directly to the limo and rode to the gallery.

And, as had become their custom early on, as the limo idled in front of the gallery, she gave him a blowjob in the back. He was such a nervous sort; it was the only way she had found to get him calm enough to handle these openings and the criticisms that went along with them. This time she could barely get him to consent to it, but there was only so much protesting a man could do when his wife was unzipping his pants. So of course, she had her way.

A contented Sheila and very relaxed Raines finally emerged from the car and entered his gallery. Tonight, it was *his* gallery—that's one of the things she had told him as he stood in front of the hotel mirror earlier.

They walked in to applause. She looked up at him, her face the perfect picture of pride and joy. She was so happy for him. He really was a jewel. And what he had done with his *Women on the Edge* series was amazing to her. Immediately they were surrounded by people who thought themselves his close friends. Some of them were. They all claimed to feel the same way.

"Mr. Montoya, you've done it again!" Mr. Jiles, a silly fish-faced white man who prided himself on funding poor ethnic artists, shook Raines' hand vigorously. He had tried to "help" Raines for years. Despite the fact Raines had told him many times he came from a wealthy Mexican family and didn't need his money, Jiles couldn't seem to get it in his head that "Chicano" was not synonymous with "poor".

"Jiles, thank you! I can always count on you, can't I?" Raines extracted his hand and gave one of his blessing smiles. Sheila had often asked him how he had learned to give such smiles, like a king looking on one of his subjects. You never knew if you were insulted or lucky after receiving such smiles.

"Raines, congratulations. This is such good work. Truly amazing." Charles shook his hand and looked feverish.

Sheila had dubbed him "the believer". He was Raines' disciple. He believed in the power of his work with a passion. It made them both uncomfortable at times, but on opening night, he was worth a thousand ringers if a one. They listened to him go on for a few moments about how important this collection was and how he had surpassed his expectations once again. It was gratifying. She could see Raines feeding off of it, drawing confidence and happiness from every word. That was the only reason she let him come around. In her opinion such men were dangerous. But Raines needed him.

Now with people pressed about them, "not even the decency to form a receiving line!" she often joked, Sheila began to pitch in.

"Jonathan! So good to see you again." She steered Raines toward the gallery owner, who looked relieved to see her. Raines must have really been insufferable at his last opening without her. "Now let's walk over to the piece *I* inspired and you give me your honest but embellished opinion. Nothing less! I won't have it." She weaved the three of them through the gallery to a piece in the far corner, the farthest from the door she could find. This succeeded in losing two thirds of the crowd. And what was left was manageable, mostly people they actually wanted to see.

"Why this isn't the piece! Oh, I see, its over there." She let a sly look creep over her face as she looked at Raines. They walked over to "Hilarity", the piece she had unblocked him with over the news of her quitting her job. "Hilarity" featured a woman standing on the edge of a building, looking like she was about to jump, with a most peculiar look on her face. It seemed some mix of relief, paralyzing fear, annoyance, and excitement, perhaps even joy. She wondered if she were looking at herself. And if so, what did the jump symbolize?

"Raines, what does it mean?" She looked up at him inquiringly.

He almost balked. She never asked him probing

questions at their openings. There were enough people doing that already and usually she ran interference. He looked around to see the crowd gathering around him again, anxious for his interpretation. She was supposed to be keeping them away from him, not drawing them in. Raines squeezed his hand on her arm and gave her a very unforgiving look, for which she repaid him with an unchanging face, that same questioning smile. Well, there was just no dealing with the woman. He turned to face the painting.

"She wants to escape, even though she knows the escape will be more painful than facing herself. And she wonders if facing herself could be the best thing after all. But for her, not having to answer that question is the whole point of jumping. We don't know what she'll decide. To step back from the edge or to continue tipping forward. She has been in the process of abandoning her life for a long time. So actually, getting to the point of it, not just nearing it, brings a kind of delirious joy and relief. But there's still a chance she won't. Small though. A small chance. I named it 'Hilarity' because that's what my wife put over the title I had given it with a sticky pad while I wasn't looking. Sly thing." Maybe there was a bit of bitterness in those last words. "But it somehow seemed appropriate titling, brings a bit of a three-ring circus atmosphere to the work. And all that just adds to the wildness of so many contrasting emotions swirling about inside her, with her wanting to feel none of it. 'Hilarity.'"

CHAPTER TWENTY-FOUR
HOTEP

Applause, oohs, and 'how trues' filled the room. The crowd dispersed throughout the gallery to repeat what he had said as if reliving a miracle, using it to take a fresh look at the other paintings.

"I'd like to buy that." A quiet but somehow thunderous voice came from behind them. Raines and Sheila turned to find Jonathan greeting the man who went with the voice. "Hotep, I didn't know you were here. Great you could make it. I told you it would be worth your while." Jonathan, the gallery owner, looked ecstatic. This guy must be a real VIP.

Hotep was a truly beautiful man, Sheila thought, though she couldn't quite put her finger on what it was that was so powerful about him. He stood about six feet tall, had a medium build, chestnut brown complexion and a well-manicured mustache. His eyes seemed to be opal black and sparkling at the same time. All in all, a decent looking man, but it seemed that when she had laid eyes on him, she heard singing.

"Mr. and Mrs. Montoya. Truly a pleasure." Hotep shook their hands in turn. "As I was saying, I'd like to buy this piece, and perhaps a couple others from this collection. It's had a powerful effect on me." Sheila didn't really hear what he said. It seemed as though a voice was saying "remember". She couldn't think of what she should be remembering.

His look did not waver from Sheila the entire time he spoke. It was a passive, inquisitive, furtive gaze. Raines noticed. If Sheila hadn't been so captivated, she would have noticed the dark clouds that were gathering in his expression.

He was a terribly jealous man.

"'Hilarity' is not for sale. This piece is very special for us and we want to keep it."

Jonathan frowned. "Every piece on these walls is for sale. That's what we agreed on. Of course you'll have to wait until we get lithographs and prints of the pieces you want done before you can take possession of them, but I'll be happy to make the sale with you this evening, perhaps after things have died down a bit?" Jonathan's face was pleasant, with just a hint of pleading around the edges.

Hotep took a long look at Raines. Weighing. "No, I'm afraid not. Perhaps another time, Mr. Montoya." He stuck out his hand.

"Mmmm." Raines looked at him. He was good at not giving an inch. Hotep, unsurprised, withdrew his hand and walked away. Jonathan trailed after him, stopping long enough to give Raines a look pretty close to hellfire.

"Did you hear the singing?" Sheila asked absent-mindedly. Then she caught a hold of herself. Had she actually said that out loud? Time for some damage control. "Oh, goodness me that man was rude! Could you believe him? What kind of man names himself Hotep in this day and age anyway? He has delusions of grandeur, and we are better off without him in our circle. Humph! But seriously, can you arrange with Jonathan for us to keep 'Hilarity'? That would be so fabulous! I do like this piece. I don't know why, but it seems to call to me." Sheila was backpedaling fast, hoping it did the trick. She looked up at him innocently, adoringly, with just a hint of desperation around the edges.

Raines looked at her, unmoved. It was a hard look. "Never disrespect me like that again. Did I marry a giddy teenager who lacks control, giving out her affections to whomever she pleases? You were mooning over him. I will not have it!" As quiet a voice as he used right now so as not to be overheard, it seemed to her he was yelling. There was definitely thunder in his voice. She stepped back, staggering from the force of his anger. This was the part of him so few others ever had a chance to see. It was why she knew he wasn't perfect. Raines turned around to face the painting. Voice quiet as ever, "'Hilarity' is for sale." With that he walked away, into a den of sycophants who cared nothing for him, where he could hide from who he was and what he was feeling.

Sheila walked towards the back of the gallery into Jonathan's office and shut the door behind her. She crumpled and burned in shame. She had embarrassed her husband, with the whole world—with his whole world—looking on. And it hadn't been a mistake or misunderstanding. She had stood there like dizzy teenager under the gaze of the football captain! Oh, she hated herself right now. She would pull out her hair, but she had spent quite a while on her 'do and messing it up wouldn't help anything.

She looked at herself in a full-length mirror on the door. She certainly looked like she felt—defeated. She pulled out her compact to fix up her face. She had to get back out there and help her husband, whether he wanted her by his side right now or not. That was where she belonged. That was her lot. She couldn't mess that up. Not anymore than she already had anyway.

Stepping back to take stock of herself in the mirror again, she found she looked a lot more presentable. She drew herself up to look queenly and serene. Letting out a deep breath, she opened the door to join Raines. Jonathan and Hotep were just coming in. They stood in the doorframe frozen for a moment, equally surprised.

Sheila spoke first. She wasn't going to make the same mistake again. "Gentlemen. Excuse me." Without another word or a backwards look she passed them, on Jonathan's side, and walked over to join her husband. She slipped her hand under his arm and smiled at the group he was talking to. Raines covered her hand on his forearm with his and pressed gently. His fingers brushed back and forth across her

156

knuckles. Her smile brightened.

"If you will excuse me, I have to talk to my lovely wife privately for a moment." Even as the words were coming out of his mouth already he was walking away, towards some less inhabited nook of the room. When he finally looked down at her, it was a look of relief.

"I'm sorry. I didn't mean to speak to you that way. I'm glad you came back. It's been murder out here without you. And knowing I hurt you…"

Sheila put her hand on his lips to silence him. "I always mean to honor you. Whenever I don't, you need to let me know. You have my true apology. Knowing I have hurt you, it's wounded me. I'm sorry. And knowing I'm already forgiven, I'm filled with love for you. You make me feel lucky." Damn, after all that repair work on her face in the mirror, she could feel tears springing up again. But of course he was there to wipe them away and kiss her cheeks.

"How do I look? Do I look ok?" He wiped underneath her eyes a little more.

"There, that's good. Now come on, you can't leave me alone with these barracudas. I'm not saying that's why I married you, but it's one of the reasons I'm glad I did. Ready?" He smiled at her. They turned to re-enter the craziness that was a gallery opening.

CHAPTER TWENTY-FIVE
ROMONA

For the rest of the night Sheila swatted away the obvious fakes. Some of their closer friends often joked about it and would retell to roomfuls of people how she dealt with particular characters. She was always worried that sooner or later, the person they were talking about would be in the room. But apparently, she had a knack for finding a person's weak spot and revealing it in a way that only she and the person knew what she was saying. And they always understood her secret threat, that she would out their weakness if they didn't behave.

She didn't *want* to be known as a cruel person, but she had to admit she enjoyed it. Her favorites to swat away from Raines were the women. An art groupie was much more sophisticated than a music groupie. They were usually rich, bored wives of wealthy men looking for an exciting distraction, or profanely powerful twenty-something women who never let anything—especially something so trivial as a wife—get in their way. Whichever kind of art groupie they were, Raines seemed to tick all of their desired boxes, and they couldn't get enough.

They would slither up to Raines, wearing some low-cut top-shelf killer dress, sometimes inserting themselves in-between the two of them so that they could touch her husband! Pressing their bodies right up against him, telling him the European galleries they had been to and how his work was so much better than so-and-so's.

She had to give it to them: these women were emboldened, and Raines would bend over backwards before he would offend a woman. He might quite honestly accidentally find himself in bed with one of them, wondering how he had got there. Well, she wouldn't go that far. He loved her much too much for that. Since they had started seeing each other exclusively he had never even had dinner with another woman that was not family alone. Some kind of Latin honor thing, she supposed.

But she often worried about where his charm and good manners would land him without her "guidance." She wondered how he had handled himself at the opening in LA without her. She made a mental note to check up on his behavior that night with some friends who had been there. Just to make sure.

Tonight was no different for the "vamps" as she called them. One such woman, Romona, was there in full force. Of all the regulars who hung about Raines, she was the woman Sheila worried about most. She had never been able to intimidate Romona. That concerned her.

"Honey, it's like I told you in Cali, I'm gonna see your name in lights! I'll be able to say I knew you when. Don't forget the little people now!" She chided him and joked as if she had known him all his life.

"And look, your wife is here this time." Romona's eyes passed over her with a dismissive look and locked back in on Raines. "Well doesn't *everyone* want to be near you now? Shine baby shine!" Sure enough, she slipped between the two of them and was up in Raines' face. How did she manage to press her whole body against his at once? That's what Sheila wanted to know.

Raines was giving her, and the people who had gathered around to hear any more pearls of wisdom he might dispense, one of his warming smiles. He exuded confidence. But he was running his fingers through his hair. As unflappable as he tended to behave, that was a sure sign that he was uncomfortable. Time for Sheila to rescue her man.

She thought about tripping Romona, then making a big fuss over her and calling an ambulance, telling her she had better watch her step or next time she might really get hurt. Actually, she fantasized about that. But it was much too severe, plus people would see and it wasn't her style for anyone but the intended to know what she meant.

She also fantasized that she was so gorgeous that Romona looked like day-old bread next to her. But in truth, Romona was, regrettably, one of the more beautiful women she had ever seen, full of poise and elegance as well. More than she herself possessed. So after much thought, she had finally decided to let her husband rescue himself; to see if he could. If he couldn't, then she would probably have to go with the tripping option.

"Well, don't you two look cozy?"

"Mm, hmm. Raines is my boy. Right baby?"

Had she just called him baby?! Breathe in, breathe out. Sheila's face remained serene.

"Why don't you sell her 'Hilarity,' dear? She is certainly leaning towards an inevitable conclusion." A bit aggressive for Sheila's taste, but what the Hell. Raines' hands were wringing his hair now. But no matter where he moved, Romona magically seemed to stay connected to him. If Sheila didn't despise her, she would certainly have asked for tips.

Romona laughed. "I *am* hopeless, Raines, will you save me?" She leaned into him, teeth shining in a killer smile. She was good.

Sheila took a moment to take in the irony. She had just grinned like a wide-eyed fool to a perfect stranger and now she was hot as fire over this woman drooling over Raines. She couldn't make up her mind whether to be ashamed of herself so she could still be justified at being mad at him, or whether to just call the whole thing a wash. In any event, it was time to put this woman to bed, in her own bed and alone.

Sheila had taken a position where she was more or less facing them, Raines and Romona looking like the lovely couple they weren't. Now she leaned towards Raines, who

160

instinctively leaned down to her. She whispered in a voice everyone she wanted to hear could hear. "I want our children to be artists." She withdrew to her previous position.

She had shocked Raines into a joyful stupor. He beamed at her with chagrin, pride, surprise, and love. She reached out her hand and grabbed his. "Come on you, let's work the room," and led him off to another corner of the room. Romona couldn't trump that one. She was so tempted to look back at the vamp, but that would have ruined the whole thing. Besides, now Raines was so wrapped around her she probably couldn't have managed to turn around if she tried.

The rest of the evening passed without incident. Serendipitous glances showed Romona working the room, but never approaching Raines again. Sheila whispered in Raines' ear, in a voice for only him, "Should I beat the heifer? I could you know." As usual, he gave her the disapproving look he had mastered whenever she got jealous. Somehow, she was supposed to know he wouldn't cheat even though gorgeous, determined women surrounded him. She supposed she did, but not by much sometimes.

The thought of having children had put Raines in such a good mood that he was the best she had ever seen him at an opening. Relaxed, funny, deep, sexy, with just a hint of brooding. He was at his most excellent when he was being loving. That had always been the case.

The gallery sold eight of his paintings that night. And not just to women he had made swoon, but to some serious collectors. Though no more was seen of Hotep that night, Sheila continued to be bothered with the thought that she should remember something about him. Those faint feelings were plunged in shame as soon as they were borne.

CHAPTER TWENTY-SIX
PANDORA'S BOX

At about three the next morning they finally found their way back to their hotel. The gallery opening ran until about midnight. Then Raines' friends dragged them to a bar for continued conversation over some harder liquor. And now at last they were peeling off second-hand smoke and alcohol-saturated clothing and taking turns in the shower.

Raines never slept on his openings. He was always too wired. Sheila tried to hang in as best she could, but she quickly turned into an overly emotional kid when she was severely tired. That morning they lay on the bed and Raines rubbed her feet while he excitedly talked about last night, repeating witty things he had said and mistakes he made, as if she hadn't been there every moment with him.

She lazed, sleepily enjoying her foot rub and letting his words wash over her. Whenever she closed her eyes, she saw Hotep's face, very close to hers, smiling and dazzling. She shook herself awake as long as she could. Eventually exhaustion delivered her into a wonderful sleep filled with her having sex with a man she had never known until the night before. Hotep's face always seemed to be in hers, grinning up close with a thousand teeth. She wished she knew what she was supposed to be remembering. His face hypnotized her. She woke up worn out, unable to figure out why.

Sheila had opened a can of worms. Mentioning children in front of Romona had been the perfect trump card. In offering him a family, the one thing Romona could not, Sheila had succeeded in making her totally irrelevant without having to get her hands dirty at all. But the victory had cost her. She had avoided the issue with Raines until now with great success.

Raines wanted sons and daughters. He thought it was the point of getting married. But she had never been comfortable with the thought of raising a tribe. She had never felt ready.

As she let the hot water in the shower work on rubbing out some of her body's soreness, another thing she wondered was what color their children would be. As near as she could guesstimate, she was 1/4th white, 5/8th black and 1/8 Native American. Raines would tell you in a heartbeat he was 100% Spaniard by way of Mexico. She believed him too, as proud as he was. If she had children with him, they wouldn't be black, they'd be 4/8th Latino, 1/8th white, 5/16th black and 1/16th Native American. What was that? How could she pass on her black heritage to a child who was less than 30% black? The thought of raising non-black children troubled her. She didn't know how to do it. She wondered if he thought he would be soiling his Latin blood with children by her.

She supposed she wanted to have children. But children that were as black as she was. Blacker, actually. Who would they be if they weren't all the way black or all the way Spanish? Who was she since she wasn't all the way black herself? But she had never had to acknowledge the other parts or her ethnicity. How would society treat them? How did people raise children anyway?

Sheila let out a growl in the shower and shook herself. She was talking herself in circles. As she stepped out of the shower and dried off under the heat lamps, though, one thought stuck with her. How could a motherless woman raise children?

Raines was asleep. He had somehow spread out to take up a whole bed as soon as she got out of it. She shoved him over and got back in. He curled around her as soon as she lay down. They *were* married, Sheila thought. She supposed they had to have children sometime. Years of married sex wearing condoms, plus their courtship, was a long time for a man, she conceded. She had thrown her lot in with him now, so why not? It was all very reasonable except for the fact that she just didn't want to.

Normally, she would pray and meditate on the subject, but from now on she had to rely on her own understanding and be damned for it. She had made that decision and there was no going back from it. So, she had reasoned it out to herself to wait a while and see how she felt about it later. She could hold Raines off until she made up her mind. Stirring, Raines rubbed her arm and kissed her neck. "I can't wait to have a little girl just like you," he muttered, half asleep. The words hammered in her head like an anvil dropping in a tomb.

PART SEVEN
CONFESSIONS AND
DESPAIRS

CHAPTER TWENTY-SEVEN
HAPPY RAINES

Raines rested his head in the crook of Sheila's neck and drifted dreaming in that space between sleep and wakefulness. It had been a perfect day. Sheila had consented to be the mother of his children. He knew she had said it to swat away Romona—he was no idiot. And it had worked too. He never seemed to be able to get that woman to leave him alone on his own.

But nevertheless, she had said it. And you don't say something unless you've been thinking about it. He had been waiting a long time for her to be ready, standing up against the unbearable pressures of his family. For the millionth time he felt a flare of anger that they had not shown up for the funeral. When your wife's mother died, it was time to put disagreements aside. Maybe this would please them.

Sons and daughters. Carrying on the tribe, even if they were only half Spanish. That stuff didn't matter to him, only a little anyway. He was in love with the thought of sons and daughters. And he would be a better father than his had ever been to him.

As much as he wanted Sheila to bear his children, he wanted her to be a mother to them even more. She was so special, and he always felt a deep sense of privilege at the prospect of raising children with her. She didn't yet know she had meant what she said last night, but he knew that all of his patience had paid off and the time was close at hand to be a real family. He fell asleep to that thought. In the deep recesses of his mind a part of him wondered how a woman who had never seemed to notice another man since they met could have been driven to the point of distraction by a quite average stranger in public with him. It constrained his joy only slightly.

CHAPTER TWENTY-EIGHT
LITTLE FIRES

Jerry was waiting for her with a grim expression on his face. Everything about the situation was wrong. First, she was usually one of the first people in the office, aside from the lawyers who she suspected never left. Jerry usually came in at nine sharp. It was 8:15. Second, Jerry never looked grim. He always appeared either deep in thought, grinning slyly, or with a totally blank expression, belying the fact that he knew exactly what was going on and what he was doing.

As she walked past his desk, he rose with papers in his hands.

"Come in. Shut the door," she said in a resigned voice. 'Lord, what next?' she thought, then edited her thoughts to take God out of the question. She opened the door to her office and threw her things on the couch, crossed the room and sank into her chair. Jerry was almost on her heels.

"You were gone…I didn't know what to do. I couldn't get you on your cell phone." Whatever it was, she now had no doubt it was worse than she had thought.

"John came here the same afternoon you left. He made me give him all the materials for the presentation. He said he was doing it on his own and didn't need to bother you with it. He wanted me to open the mediation files for all of the case results. Said he needed them, but wouldn't say for what. I told him I couldn't release that information. He threatened me with losing my job. I told him the files were locked and only you had the keys. He called me incompetent at the top of his lungs for the whole office to hear. Rick came by and tried to intercede. Those two got in a shoving match. John was yelling that he would have him fired. Rick said firing him wouldn't fix his problem.

"Anyway, John stormed off. I locked your office before I went to lunch. When I came back your door was open. Every single hard copy file is gone. They're in his office. The files are gone from my area too. He walked right past me ignoring me just like always, as if nothing's happened. After that I didn't know what to do. I backed up both our computers and our locked files on the shared drive and stored them off site. I don't know what to do about the stuff he already took. And I have no idea why he did it in the first place. I couldn't reach you. Maybe I overreacted." Jerry's face was full of pleading. He was clearly more afraid of her reaction than he was of John's tantrum.

"I have found that everyone shows their true colors eventually. I took away his options. Now he has no choice but to go crazy and act a fool. It's in his nature." Sheila pondered as she swiveled in her chair. It surprised her that she was not even shocked by what Jerry had told her.

"Jerry, go home. There's nothing more you can do here. Handwrite your letter of resignation. I'll authorize you to telecommute for the last two weeks. I'll be lost without you here of course, but we all must do what we can do. And no more. No more." Sheila's voice was resigned, but firm.

Jerry looked at her as if it pained him to leave. Slowly, he rose and left—left her office, left his work area, left the building. He just walked straight out, stopping only to grab his jacket and bag from behind his desk. In that moment, Sheila knew as she could have never known otherwise, that she could trust him. In a difficult time, he had submitted to her judgment, without equivocation. That made her responsible for him.

She shook herself out of her thoughts and got up to close her door. Walking over to her bookcase she pulled a small stepladder from the side and set it up. Climbing it, she peered over the top of her bookcase at Shiva, Hindu god of transition, who destroys the old to make way for the new.

The urge on her to pray was so heavy she was sweating in tension. But she would not relent. She did talk to Shiva, though.

"You and me, we've been through a lot. A lot just here in this office. But I guess it's nothing personal. You destroy what you must, when you must." Sheila had started off indignant and ended up defeated. She sat on the top step of the ladder and leaned forward.

"What am I supposed to do now? If it's meant to be should I fight or let it pass?" Sheila caught herself asking God and listening for the answer. She climbed off the ladder and backed away. "Oh no you don't!" she cried, shaking her head at no one she could see. "Don't you try and answer me." Now she was good and mad. Her deciding she wasn't going to have anything to do with God meant God was not supposed to have anything to do with her. Those were the rules. Her rules.

She had a sudden impulse to take everything spiritual she had in the office and trash it. She looked at the stepladder to start with Shiva, but shook with fear at the thought of throwing the statue away. She wanted to have God leave her alone, not damn her to Hell.

Then she was on her knees with hands clasped together. "Lord, this is the last time I'm gonna talk to you. And it is to say…Please, just leave me alone. I don't hate you. I'm not trying to be evil. I just can't do what you've laid out for me. I…I don't want anything to do with you. Loose me and let me be."

Her hands fell to the floor. It was with a heavy, deeply saddened heart that she rose from her knees. She felt so weary. She was only twenty-eight and she felt as if she had lived a thousand trying years since that day in Carderock Falls.

And now, in addition to all she had to deal with, her boss had gone crazy. She could always count on him to act a fool when she needed it least. It helped ease her fear that she

170

had completely overreacted by quitting. She sighed and walked toward her desk. She pressed memory 5 on her phone and leaned on her desk as she listened to the phone ring.

"Peace my sista," a warm masculine voice greeted her. Caller ID took away the possibility of surprising a person these days.

"Haile! It is so good to hear your voice." Sheila thought guiltily about how many messages he had left for her in the last month. She was embarrassed to have never spoken with him before now.

"How are you daughter?" Haile was like her adopted father most times.

Sheila took a deep breath, "I need your help…"

CHAPTER TWENTY-NINE
JASMIN

One hour later the entire contents of her office were packed, in the back of Haile's van, and on their way to her home. She sat in a chair, surveying her barren office. No more fruit would it bear, she thought. It's a good thing she had quit. She had played her last card.

Producing a small telephone book from her attaché case, she flipped through until she found Ed's information. Ed Cloury, CEO and CFO of her company. She turned on her computer and prepared an email to him. They had met clandestinely two years ago at an airplane gate waiting for the same plane. He was flying first class of course.

They had hit it off, before he had even known she worked for him. When he found out she had already saved him over a million dollars in litigation costs, he loved her. Now it was time for her to bank on his warm feeling for her, and his keen intelligence and business sense.

She put a subject of 'Fond Farewell' to the email and started typing before she had a chance to talk herself out of it. She reminisced over some of the fun times they had had at conferences and luncheons. About how he had given her her very first ride in first class when they met. She lay out, point-by-point, all of the things she had done for the company, not too arrogantly she hoped, and commented that she hoped she had been of some use. Sheila expressed a sincere desire to see him at the upcoming conference, which would be her last in his employ. Subtly planted in there, she raised her concern that the right replacement be found to take the company forward in her capacity, and her faith that he and John would make the perfect choice.

She pondered over her last words. 'Ever since my

mother's tragic death I have been lost. I hope I can find myself this way. Give Sarah my love.'

She ran a spell check and hit send before she could talk herself out of it.

God. It felt like forever since she had thought about Ma. But it was true; she was lost. There hadn't been any point to her life in a long time, it seemed. Living a life of escapism through Raines and workaholism, alienated from friends and family, running from God and desperately fleeing fate. Before she knew it, tears were running down her face as she wished desperately that her mom were there.

She woke up with the pattern of her wristwatch imprinted on her face. She shook herself to life and held her head. It was killing her. She looked at her watch. 10:37. Sheila collected the bags she had walked in with hours earlier and prepared to leave. She had earned the rest of the day off. On the way home, she resolved, she would call her sisters. She felt weighed down at every turn, feeling that she could not go one more step. She had gotten used to the feeling.

"Hello, hello." Jasmin's voice was warm and clear on the other end of the line.

Sheila had called but was now paralyzed. This had been a bad idea.

"I have caller ID you know." Jasmin's voice was patient. "And besides, I knew you were going to call today. God told me."

Such a very bad idea.

Jasmin paused. Sheila knew she would not say another word until Sheila did. Jas was very, very patient.

"My life as I knew it is over…"

For the ride home they talked. Sheila spelled out all of her problems with Raines. The guy at the gallery, the unintended mention of children, and of course her boss' latest mania. They chatted away.

"Hotep, eh? Well, I would be interested in this mysterious fellow, but I don't want to poach on your territory."

"You better stop!" Sheila heard Jasmin's laughter. "I am in such trouble for that, just leave it alone. Tell me what I'm supposed to do with Raines though! He thinks I want his children. How do I get out of it?"

"Sheila, are you married to the man or just playing house? If you don't want that man, I mean *really* want him, honey I will take him, and chile I'd be in a long line for that man too, I'll tell you that."

"Of course I want him, I just…"

"Oh I see, you're still a child, you haven't grown up yet. You're one of those women who needs to stay single and unchanged their whole lives. How's that working out for you?" Full of teasing, Jasmin giggled on the other end.

"I'm not being immature if I don't want to have children. Let's not be silly here."

"But why? Why don't you want to have kids? You're the light of the world. You always said you would have ten or twelve when we were young. What happened?"

"I'm so much less than Ma. How could I? And now? With her not here there's no chance." Tears quietly leaked from her eyes.

There was a long pause on the line.

"I knew you would call today. I want you to know how much I love you, and that I'm going through what you are. Have you had the dream yet?" Black tradition said you couldn't have peace until you dreamed of the loved one who had passed away.

"No." Sheila said dejectedly. "I've not been remembering my dreamtime," she lied.

"I did. She was smiling at me from a place very far away, yet I could see every detail. You were seated at her right side. She was standing and had her hand on your shoulder. You were sad. You didn't even notice she was there. She told me not to cry when I could be dancing." Jasmin's voice was choked up with tears.

"I haven't even listened to music since then. Too afraid. But in the end, you and I, all of us, we have to dance, to feel and express that joy she put inside us. I don't want to spend a lifetime crying. For now is fine, but without joy forever I can't breathe. I'm not her daughter unless I'm dancing." Jas let out a big sigh. Sheila could hear her blowing her nose and worshipping God. Suddenly she felt lonely.

"And as for you sister. None of us will be Ma. But we can be like Ma. We can be, we should be. That's why she came here. Now you married that man, and if you can have his children you are blessed. Besides. Ma wasn't a good Ma until she was one. So there!"

Sheila could almost see her sticking her tongue out.

"And if you don't tell him how you feel and work it out together, I will. You have forty-eight hours to act before I preempt you." Jasmin was very matter-of-fact. Sheila had no doubt she meant every word.

"I can't believe you would intervene in my marriage like that!"

"What marriage? Long as you don't want to have his kids, you just playing, and I can meddle in *that* anytime I want to. His family don't even like you no way, so you better have some kids. Be the only Montoya besides him you'll ever get to love you."

"Ohhhhh, let's not even go there. It is too early in the day for all that. Look, I will tell him tonight, so you don't have to 'intercede' for me. I gotta go. And I heard everything you said. I love you too."

"Have you told God that lately?"

"Look, if you're going to act like that, I'm not gonna call you." Sheila was annoyed. Actually, she was a whole

175

ball of emotions. She had been sitting in the driveway at home for a while now. Haile's van was in front of her. That meant he was inside. She didn't know what she had thought, that she could count on him to rescue her then silently fade into the background.

"Uh, I gotta run, Jas."

"Oh don't you hang up on me when I'm talking God to you!" Jasmin looked at her cell phone flashing 'call ended.' "Unbelievable."

Sheila slid out of her dark blue Audi and smiled as she closed the door. Fond memories of picking this car out with Ma, Raines brooding at home because she hadn't gone with him, washed over her. Ma was her best friend; of course they had gone together. Well, Raines didn't have any competition now. She headed inside.

Classical music played softly throughout the house. Sheila hung up her coat, threw her bag in her office and looked for Raines. She found him on the back porch silently sipping some coffee. Kissing him on the neck, she went back inside to make herself some tea, and to put on a warm jacket before joining him with her own cup outside. They sat there quietly for while. She had forgotten about this rich part of their relationship. The quiet communion they regularly shared. It felt like forever since she had been quiet and still.

Nestling her head in his shoulder she let out a long sigh.

"Looong day." She wrapped her arms around him.

"I heard. Haile filled me in." He hugged her closer. "I'm glad you came home. Talk to me."

"Haile!" Sheila straightened up, "Where is he?" She had forgotten all about him.

"Left. His son picked him up. They had a gig, he said. Be by to get the van later. I still have to unload."

"Oh," Sheila snuggled back into their embrace.

"So tell me, do you need me to go kill John? I mean, I knew you were crazy, had no idea about him though. Stole

176

your stuff. He has no honor." Raines' body grew rigid as he finished speaking.

Sheila looked at him.

"First of all. I am not now, nor have I ever been, crazy. Second, where have you been all these years I have been talking about the things this man has done. Third, he's not crazy, just typical. We can't all be pillars of virtue like yourself you know." She poked at him and they both broke out their best smiles for each other. She loved that he always gave her his best. Her alone.

"Raines."

"Mmmm?"

"It's December and we're sitting on the porch like it's summer. I'm freezing!"

She buried her face in his jacket as he picked her up and carried her inside.

"Wanna take a nap with me? I have been up all night. I need some sleep."

"Nap? You just drank a cup of coffee!"

"Oh yeah. Guess we have to figure out something else to do." He broke out in a grin from ear to ear. Sheila wriggled out of his arms and raced him up the stairs. He caught her.

Later, they lay in their bed looking up at the ceiling.

"Yeah, I wasn't sleepy. Now I can sleep." They fell asleep with the sun streaming in on them.

CHAPTER THIRTY
HOME LIFE

"So," Raines managed to get out between mouthfuls of food, "what does this mean for the rest of the week?"

"I don't know. I have no idea. He said he was going to do the presentation without me. I'd like to see that." Sheila buttered a roll. She still had a stockpile that her Great Aunt Ruth had brought up from the country. "I just can't believe it, but I guess its true. I mean, you know I've put 110% in that job since day one. I transformed that place. This is the thanks I get. Ma always said 'never let them see just how hard you can work; they'll expect it all the time and never value it for what it's worth.' When will I learn? It's a good thing I quit, 'cause this sure would make me."

"I know you've given a lot to that place. But I also know the work you do makes you so happy. I gave up on making a housewife of you a long time ago. But with you going freelance I'm getting a little closer!" Raines flashed a gleeful smile.

"Well, I was thinking about a little break. Get away from everything. But Jerry. He wants to go with me. I'm responsible for him. Besides. I wouldn't know what to do myself." Sheila leaned back from the table and put her feet in Raines' lap.

"Run the Institute." Raines was careful not to make eye contact and stared at his plate.

Sheila recoiled and sat upright.

"You haven't even been there since...since everything happened. Cathy was so passionate about that place. I can't believe you want to just leave it to Massad to run. She left it to you, not Jasmin or Corinne, and I'm sure it's not just because you are the one who lives here. She

178

wanted you to run it. She believed you were her spiritual heir."

Raines steeled himself and went on.

"Maybe you hate God right now. Maybe you don't know what you're feeling. But the woman I married is a woman of God, a spiritualist, one of the faithful.

"Now," he pulled his chair closer to her, "I'm none of the things you are, but I respect those qualities in you. I admire them, and I know you need them to survive. We haven't had any family devotion time since Cathy passed. Not one prayer, no worship, no church. I'm not even sure you've been in your shrine room either.

"I want you to be happy. I want to make you happy. But I know I can't if you stop believing. Sheila, the best thing about you is your faith. It's what breathes life into you, the source of your passion. And what keeps you sane. It allows you to bring the best into our relationship. Making it better. You are always teaching me something, making me want to be better.

"I like the time we spend together praying and worshipping. I guess it makes me a better man, a better husband. I know you miss Ma, don't talk to any of your friends anymore, spend all your time at work, and if we weren't having sex, I'm not sure how much time you'd really be spending with me.

"Are we just going to pretend you didn't just have a fit here and pass out a few days ago? That for the first time since I've known you, you disrespected me in public, over some quite average nobody?

"What can I do? You can't enjoy living like this. You like joy and certainty in your life. You are a task master that I have rarely seen shirk from anything. I love you, but lately I feel like you've been faking it. And I will not live like that."

What could Sheila say to that, she wondered as she sat back in her chair and crossed her arms.

"I'm sorry I've been ruining the marriage for you

but…"

"Wait a minute. Have you been listening to what I've been saying? I'm concerned about you, first and foremost."

"That's not what I heard. I heard you picking on me and saying you don't like how my weaknesses affect your experience. I can't stand that 'to the manor born' high-handedness of yours. You and your whole family act like you're perfect and everybody else better be perfect too.

"Whoa, whoa. Just slow down a minute. There's no need to bring my family into this. And I am not sorry for the fact that I come from a well-bred background. I never said I was perfect and I'm not trying to make you perfect either."

"Where *were* they? Hmm? My mom dies and not so much as a phone call from the royal family. Nothing. Now I'm mired in grief and you act like an auditor, laying out all the pluses and minuses of my life. Well, I'm sorry I've changed. That's life dear. I know you want us to have a tempered aristocratic marriage with everything just so, but life is messy. You know that."

"That is not what I want! Don't confuse me with my family."

"You are your family dear. You can't run from that. Face up."

"You are way out of line. If I wanted a real marriage that would have made the family proud I could have had that. I'm my own man."

Sheila sank back into her seat, totally deflated.

"Well, it took a long time for that to come out. If you wanted a *real* marriage. I have to hear about that bitch Sophia in every talk with your family. But you, you had been honorable enough not to mention her up to now. I know I'm the 'light of the world' and I seduced you away from everything you had ever known with my strange ways. I just don't feel much like shining these days. I'm sorry." Sheila's voice was one of total defeat. "Your family thinks I used voodoo to ensnare you. Maybe the spell is broken."

180

Raines kneeled before her in her chair.

"I'm *in love* with you. Who you are has made my life better than I ever knew it could be. Made me better than I ever thought I could be. If I let you go, I'd be the biggest idiot that ever was! Why did you even marry me? I said all that because…because I feel guilty that I can't be a spiritual source of strength to you now. Obviously being just a good husband isn't enough. Your pain is too deep. I'm not so stupid I can't see that. I want to help you. I don't know what to do. I don't understand God, so I don't know what to say, how to support you now.

"I know my catechism, service responses, rosary, all the saints backwards and forward. You've made me see that's nothing if that's where it ends. But I never went further. I relied on you to be the saved one among us, spoon-feeding me righteousness. I didn't take any personal responsibility for my spiritual growth. Now I need skills I don't have to help you.

"And I want to help you. I may dream of everything perfect and nothing out of place, but like you said, this is life. You've done so much for me. Let me do something for you besides put a roof over your head and be good for sex. Let me help your soul. Let's make it about more than fun, compatibility, mental stimulation and an emotional connection.

"Mrs. Sheila Montoya, will you worship with me? Can you teach me how?"

Sheila made the biggest eye roll she ever had. She was dumbfounded. "I just said everything I did: I tried my best to insult you, your family name, your background, and your motives. And that's what you have to say to me?" She threw her hands in the air. "I guess I'm stuck with a really amazing guy…Did you really think it was just the money and sex for me?"

"The other night. You were so upset. You didn't want to talk to me. I guess because, what do I know about your spiritual struggle right now? You just wanted me to make love to you. I felt like that was all I had to offer. It felt like the most dishonorable thing I had ever done to you. It's been eating away at me.

"You swallowed whatever you were going through to be there for my opening, you made me sane. And I brought up Sophia, so let me say this. I have not thought of her since we wed except to know how cruel a man I would have become had I married any woman but you. And that my life with her would have been very shallow. It was no contest.

"The only regret our marriage has brought me is my family. They disappoint me. The only person more upset than you that they didn't come is me. I bought them tickets. They wouldn't use them. I don't want to go back to who I was before I met you. I don't want to return to the world I lived in. And I see now I can't be a good husband to you and stay as I am. So, I have to move forward. Become more of the man I always thought you should have married, a faithful person. Maybe I should enroll in the Institute. I could learn all about God and the metaphysics you're always prattling on about. A new challenge for me. I could do a whole series about my spiritual transformation. Wow."

Raines looked excited and curious and sincere all at the same time. A minute earlier Sheila had known she had married the right man. Now a whole new set of problems was cropping up. She squeezed her eyes shut and rubbed the bridge of her nose. Her head was pounding.

"What's wrong? Isn't this what you wanted? Did I do something wrong?"

Sheila stared at him for a long time. And thought. She tried to wiggle out of it but in the end she realized it just wasn't in her nature to lie to him. She loved what they had and who he was too much. Taking a deep breath, she started.

"Thursday I talked to my grandfather…"

CHAPTER THIRTY-ONE
EQUALLY YOKED

"I said I wanted to learn. And you never do anything by halves." Raines wrung his hands through his hair and paced the kitchen. "I don't even understand most of what you said, much less know what to make of it." Raines caught himself, "But I believe you. And I believe in you."

"How can you believe me? This is not your universe. I wouldn't even believe it if it hadn't happened to me!"

"I've never seen a polar bear in real life, but enough folks I respect who ought to know tell me they're real, so I know they exist." She stuck her tongue out at him. "But that's beside the point. I just want to recap here. Your mother was a kind of secret superhero saving the world from—from what exactly? Help me out here."

"Damned if I know! Something about entities from other dimensions being regulated about when and how they can enter this one. I mean I know that there are different dimensions and that energies exist in different ways and consciousnesses. But that's about all. When we were young we used to have a problem with imps from the fifth dimension. Every being from that dimension's middle name is chaos. They used to hide Ma's pantyhose and the telephone books in made-up beds. It was crazy."

Raines gave her an incredulous look. "Who are you?!"

"Hey! Remember the polar bears." Sheila leaned back. She felt tension pouring out of her. It felt good to just get it all out.

"My head hurts." Raines finally stopped his pacing and sat down on a couch. He motioned her over and she lay her head in his lap. He smoothed her hair. "Whatever you need that I can do, I'm here. As absolutely unbelievable as all this is." Raines leaned his head back and stared at the ceiling. "Being a good husband is hard enough. Who knew it was nothing compared to the challenges of a spiritual relationship?"

He looked down at Sheila. Exhausted, she was snoring softly and fast asleep.

Raines sat absent-mindedly stroking her hair. Thinking. He never knew that he had not truly been her partner until he had spoken the words today. All these years, he had taken it for granted that he was satisfying her. And he was, as long as her mother was around to meet her spiritual needs. He had completely neglected those. He didn't even really know what her spiritual needs were.

Of course she was not herself. Not only had she lost her mother and best friend, she had lost her spiritual partner, and there was no close counterpart. These last weeks he had been as loving and supportive as he ever had been. All the while her most crucial needs had gone unmet. Now she had laid out to him the most fantastical unheard-of story, beyond all imagination. That had taken a lot of trust and courage on her part. She never ceased to amaze him. Now it was his turn to step up to the plate.

She had told him she didn't want anything more to do with God. With absolute certainty she had said that she was incapable and unwilling. She had said that she wanted to live a life with God on the sideline. That had stunned him as much as her story. He cursed his stupidity. This was the toughest thing she had ever experienced. Without any spiritual support, of course she was doubting God.

Now was not the time for him to be learning on the job. Raines picked up Sheila and carried her to bed. Then he did something he hadn't done since he was a child. He got on his knees and prayed.

"Lord," he strained at the newness of his feelings and actions, "help me to be…" He didn't know what to ask for.

He wasn't sure of anything. "Lord just help me. Help me to be a better husband. Help me to be a better servant," the words could barely get out of his mouth. He had never been anyone's servant. Not even God's. "Help me help my wife. Teach me. Show me what to do…Amen."

Raines sat there on his knees after his prayers for a good five or ten minutes.

"Well?" He looked upwards and stretched out his hands. "I'm waiting." Sheila always seemed to get her answers right away. Lacking any such speed in his response, he did the only thing he knew. Walking over to the bookcase in Sheila's shrine room, a place he had been only a handful of times over the years, he picked up a Bible. Sitting down on the floor he thought to try something he had seen her do many times. Closing his eyes and touching the Bible to his heart he recited, "Speak Oh Lord so thy servant can hear," three times then opened it. He read for a while. And everything he read, every understanding, was totally new. God answers prayers, he thought.

"Sheeeeeeeilaaaaa," he whispered as he rubbed her back and gently rocked her in the bed.

"Mmmm," she opened her eyes to a darkened room. What a day. "What?" she turned over and stretched.

"Didn't you tell me the metabolism is perfectly balanced between 2-6am?"

"Yeah," she mumbled. This did not sound good.

"It's 2 o'clock," he said in a sing-songy voice. "Get up and do some thinking or something."

She sat up cross-legged in the bed, staring at him. He looked like a kid at Christmas.

"So, um, I was trying to pray before. I'm pretty sure it was awful. But God answered me anyway!" Raines bounced and gestured as he talked. "I read Exodus. Moses didn't want to do what God asked either. He complained the whole way. But God sent Aaron to help him.

"We're nothing until God makes us something. So of course you're not able as you are. Who would be? The whole situation is crazy anyway! But if God told you to do it, I think He'll make you able. I always knew you were special. I had no idea you were this special though. I still have no real clue what's going on. But I'd like to help. Whatever you do, I'm here."

Raines looked as committed as she had ever seen him. She stared at him in complete shock.

"What did you do?! What happened when I fell asleep? You've been reading the Bible? Why?"

"I told you, I want to be a spiritual partner to you. God is helping me to be that through this," He lifted up a Bible that had been resting on the bed. She recognized it as one from the shrine room.

"You went in my shrine room?" Sheila fell backwards on the bed and held her head. "Am I in the Twilight Zone? I married a wonderful, magnificent, but thoroughly unenlightened man. Who are you? Most people always *want* to do something, but they never actually do it. I was appreciating the sentiment of what you said earlier. I didn't think you meant it.

"Oh God." She shook her head back and forth, trying to shake out the grogginess and wake to a different reality.

"Thought you weren't on speaking terms with the Lord? Hmm?"

She lobbed a pillow in his direction half-heartedly. "I can't take it! Go back to the way you were!"

"Well, it has been an amazing day. Maybe we should just sleep. There's always tomorrow."

Sheila eyed him suspiciously. There was way too much joy in his voice.

"Well...ok. I need a shower, then I can sleep." Sheila

got up and moved toward the bathroom. He caught her by the wrist and spun her around. Wrapping his arms around her he gave an earth-shattering kiss.

"I love you, you know." He smiled and gave her a big hug.

"Yeah." Sheila shook her head as she closed the bathroom door behind her. "I know."

In the shower she just stood there.

"Please Lord, just leave me alone."

CHAPTER THIRTY-TWO
HAILE

Sheila sat at the kitchen island and stared blearily at Haile. She used to be an early bird, but now at 5:30am she couldn't think of one good reason why folks should be up at that hour.

"You might not know this, but I'm not so much of an early morning person anymore." She sipped her tea.

"I haven't seen you in a long time. Besides, this was the only time I could get my van back."

"Right, Raines still has to unload it."

"No. It's cleared out."

"Oh."

Sheila sat back and took Haile in. For a man who was the closest thing she had to a father, she felt like a stranger to him now. She didn't know what to say.

"My dear, I can see you are troubled. Your aura is so disturbed. Why don't you come to the house: let us do some work on you." Haile reached his hand across the table and clasped hers.

"At the funeral I didn't give a tribute. But you have to know what I had with your mother was too personal for me to ever be able to express. It was pure love. And I've always felt that you were my daughter. I held you when you were a baby. You fell asleep to the sound of my heartbeat.

"I remember taking you to the park when you were a child, taking pictures of you smiling so wide I thought your face might break." Sheila smiled fondly at the remembrance. "You were such a cute kid, and you've turned into a beautiful woman. I don't know that I've been the best father figure, but you've delighted my heart as a daughter. You are your mother's dreams come true. Cathy doesn't want you to suffer like this. Let me help you."

"Everyone wants to help me. Haile, I don't even know what's wrong with me, so how can you begin to help me?" Sheila stood up and walked over to face the back windows.

"You cry just about every day. You sneak and do it. In the middle of the night you turn on the tub faucet and weep into a pillow so no one will know. You work to exhaustion just to keep from remembering that she's gone. You can't pray or talk to God because it's too much like feeling. And to really feel anything is a reminder of how alone you are without her." Haile turned her around to face him. "Have I got it about right?"

"How could you possibly know all that?" It was all Sheila could do to keep from breaking into tears.

"Believe it or not, your husband is no fool. He knows you get up and cry every morning and just about every night. You've always been ambitious, but you've been living at your office. A place you're quitting in mere weeks. You haven't called one friend in the last month. Not one. You didn't call me until you needed something. And you haven't been to the Institute since she passed."

Sheila drew away from him. "Well if a guilt trip is helping me, then I've been getting a lot of help from everyone!" She paced the kitchen. "So I cry and work and don't want to talk to anyone. So what? I lost my mom," the tears she had been fighting to hold back leapt forth, "and nothing is normal. Nothing ever will be."

"Shh, it's gonna be alright." Haile held her and rocked her back and forth.

"Everyone treated me like I was supposed to be fine as soon as she was in the ground. It's the stupidest thing I've ever heard. So, I went back to work. And I kept going. I'm doing the best I can," Sheila sobbed.

"*I know you are. I just need you to do a little bit better.*"

Sheila jumped out of her skin. And halfway across the room. She curled up into a ball and shut her eyes as tight as she could. She was shaking like a leaf.

"Sheila! Sheila, what's wrong?" Haile bent down over her.

"Go away, leave me alone. Just go." She was rocking herself furiously in her ball on the floor. "I just want to be left alone."

"Raines," Haile yelled up the stairs. "Raines!" He turned back to Sheila.

"What just happened?" Haile reached to touch her and she swatted his hand away, shrinking into herself even more. Still shaking, she pressed her fists against her temples.

"She won't leave me alone. She won't leave me alone!"

Raines came bounding down the stairs and took in the situation.

"What did you do?" He muttered to Haile as he rushed to Sheila, kneeling in front of her.

"All the time. Everyday. I can't take it. Leave me alone. It's your fault. I can't be up this early! She won't leave me alone. Raines! Take me home."

"I'm here, Sheila. You are home. What's going on?"

Sheila looked up at him, at Haile just behind him, and went limp. Suddenly she felt exhausted. Too tired to fight a losing battle, anyway.

"I'm losing my mind. I hear her speaking to me. I'm so sick of it." Sheila sank further down onto the floor with complete surrender.

"Who?" they echoed in unison.

"Ma." She was so tired she could barely keep her eyes open or focus on anything. "Raines, take me home." Sheila remembered thinking how cold the floor was before she fell asleep on the spot.

Raines picked her up and faced Haile.

"Did you know about this?"

190

"I knew she was grieving pretty bad, but I had no idea." Haile stroked his beard, deep in thought.

"What did you do?" Raines was furious. But he wasn't sure where to direct that feeling. He had left his wife with Haile and came back to find a woman out of her mind. But nothing about anything had been as expected lately. He hated this instability. Not knowing what to expect, all of these challenges to his regimented life were unhinging him. He desperately wanted someone to unload on. He couldn't be sure Haile was to blame, though.

"You'll have to let yourself out, Haile. I'll let you know how she's doing. This is the last straw. I'm insisting on some counseling now." He let out a big sigh and started up the stairs.

Laying her down on the bed, he did some pacing of his own as he watched her sleep. Finally, he settled into a chair facing her and went through his thoughts. Maybe he would go to the Institute. He could use some counseling of his own. Raines took a shower, changed into some clothes, and left a note on Sheila's nightstand saying he loved her and he'd be back by the afternoon. Then he headed out to a place he had never been to without Sheila. A place he had never gone to except to humor her. He prayed it held some salvation; some clarity to help him keep his life together.

As Haile shut the door behind him, thoughts stormed through his mind. Cathy was speaking to Sheila. It unsettled him. Of all the spirits that got caught in the third dimension, unable to transcend after death, he would never have thought Cathy would be one of them. Driving away that morning, he turned the question over and over in his mind. "Cathy, what are you still doing here?"

CHAPTER THIRTY-THREE
A DAY OFF

Sheila sat on the couch in the den buried under a comforter, sucking on a raspberry popsicle. The TV was blaring with some movie she had turned on a while ago. She wiggled her feet under the comforter and closed her eyes.

A day off. She hadn't not gone into work since she had gone back after the funeral. Even the weekends were spent working herself into a frenzy there. The weekend she had taken off for Raines' opening had been a departure from that. Since that Thursday night, nothing had been normal. She supposed nothing had been normal for a long time.

Now she was at home, Raines was gone, and there was absolutely nothing to do. She couldn't think what she had done with her weekends without work from the office. Oh yeah, she had spent them having fun. Now she was chilling in her own home and for the life of her couldn't figure out how to have fun.

Normally she might spend a day off, with her mom of course, perhaps helping her at the Institute, perhaps running around town in search of a rare book or visiting a holy person. She always loved her time with Ma. Right now, she was choosing not to remember the times they fought or disagreed. Everything was always rosy. Then she would come home, full of light and love and knock Raines' socks off in bed and make him a meal to remember. That's why he never complained about the time she spent with her mom.

That morning when she woke up again, she had found herself alone. Nevertheless, she still turned on the faucet to cover up the sounds of her morning weep. Then she got dressed and went out to the car. At the end of the driveway, she suddenly couldn't think of a single reason to go in to work. So, she had backed up to the door, changed into some sweats, scrounged up breakfast, and had been laying on the couch for the last few hours.

This was the most bored she had been in a long time. It was the longest she had been at home and not asleep since Ma's death. Sheila jumped out of the covers and walked around the house. She was bored out of her mind. Walking upstairs she reached for the note Raines had left.

'S, gone to Institute. Back by 2. Stay Black, Raines'

She giggled. He could still make her laugh. But the laugh was empty. She was lonely, bored and restless. She wondered if this was what a life without God would feel like. Going through all the motions, but empty at the core. She sat on the edge of the bed and swung her feet. She couldn't nap anymore; she couldn't rest anymore. She couldn't do anymore.

Falling back on the bed, she stared at the ceiling and thought. Life had been horrible since Ma died. And she had been acting just as horrible, it seemed, since then. She had the same cruel nightmare every night. Her husband had been wonderful and infuriating in equal measure. Her job was an emotional jumble between her crazy boss, her great assistant, and the sweet escape from her feelings that her work provided. Her friends would do anything for her, but to be honest she had hardly thought of them and had no idea how they were right now. That night at Ma's house and all that her grandfather had said were the impossible icing on top. She was at a turning point in her life. What was she going to do next? Could she really live without God? After all this time? She saw her mom's smiling face and remembered her laughing. It drove her to tears.

No one was home. She wailed up a storm, for the first time in forever feeling totally free to grieve. When she thought she couldn't weep anymore, her tears kept flowing, and her sobs kept sounding. Her eyes and throat were sore and swollen. But she couldn't stop crying. She wondered how much water she could possibly have left. How much could the world have left for her weeping?

Sheila lay limp on the bed with a mound of used tissues next to her head. It took all the energy she had simply to breathe. The room was filled with a smoky white mist now. She was too exhausted to be frightened. Hardly alive enough to even notice or question it. She had seen it so many nights before, opening her eyes after being stabbed in her dreams. This mist that had a light of its own and played tricks on her mind. And she heard voices. Voices she couldn't possibly be hearing.

Now, finally, she was too tired to try and stay sane. So she slept, not caring about anything that happened next. Somewhere in her heart, she was still weeping. Still carrying on.

PART EIGHT
CURSED WITH A CURSE

CHAPTER THIRTY-FOUR
THE LABYRINTH

Raines pulled up to the side entrance of the main building. A tall man in all-white garb stood inside the door and watched him. Stepping out of the car and towards the door, Raines tried to remember what Cathy had taught him, but couldn't. When he reached the door, he stopped and peered inside at Massad. He never understood why this man gave him the creeps. Cathy was such a good judge of character. But this man had never seemed quite right to him. It was more than that, though. Massad was the kind of man to whom he would never choose to expose his weaknesses.

Massad was a prophet, like Cathy and like Sheila. Psychic. He had stopped trying to deny it was coincidence or trickery early in his relationship with Sheila. It had unnerved him that she could go straight to the heart of his emotional and spiritual truths as a matter of fact. So he knew, as he stood there, that this man he didn't trust knew what was going on in his heart and soul. That made him furious. But he had no idea where else to go. Like a beggar, he stood there waiting to be let in.

Raines wished he had met anyone here but Massad. He had met many here, some confused, some unbalanced and searching for something, but mostly people of strong faith that he respected. It almost radiated off of them. 'Good vibes,' he called them. Sheila and Cathy had called them positive auras, or something like that. It all added up to the same thing. Good people. Massad, though, had never struck him as one of that number. As psychic as Sheila and Cathy were, he always wondered why they never seemed to pick up on it. Maybe it was all in his head.

Massad looked him up and down in thought. Raines

had gotten some faith. A great deal of sudden faith. What he didn't understand was why. He knew Sheila was buckling under. Why was Raines blossoming? One was nothing without the other. Massad's thoughts were tickled by resentment, jealousy. Why had Cathy showed this man such favor? He was not even one of the faithful. Or at least he had not been before today. This troubled Massad. Profoundly.

Breathing in deeply several times, Massad drew up his chi until his aura was bursting forth from him. He opened the door. They clasped hands and looked into each other's eyes, each surveying.

"Good Morning, Massad. I was surprised to find you in so early."

"Morning prayers have to be said. Did you know Cathy was usually here well before sunrise every day?" Massad turned as he spoke and lead Raines toward a long hallway.

'Not every day,' Raines thought. He held his tongue. Being confrontational would not help his cause today.

Massad ushered him into a channeling room, one elevated chair surrounded by several pillows. Massad took a seat in the chair and gestured Raines to take a seat, on one of the pillows. A power-establishing play that was not lost on Raines in the least. He sat, looking as regal as he could, which was certainly saying something.

"How bad is she? When should I come?"

Without making a single outward sign of reaction, Raines broiled with anger inside. He suddenly realized he could not trust this man. It was more than a simple feeling this time. He knew. Besides that, he would not tolerate anyone disparaging his wife.

"I did not come to discuss my wife. And you are not welcome in my home. What Sheila decides on that matter is her own choice." So much for holding his tongue. "I'd like to walk the labyrinth and spend some time in the medicine wheel."

"You certainly didn't need my permission or to display your lack of manners to do that." Massad used his energy to form a cloud of rust orange light to his right.

"Cathy's labyrinth and medicine wheel. Not the public ones." Raines felt a heat rising in the room. He must really be angry with this man.

Massad let out a rich long laugh. He settled his eyes on Raines and took stock of him again. He stood up and walked over to Raines, who rose to meet him.

"I'd like to see if you could."

Massad led Raines out of the building and onto the Institute grounds. No matter how many times he came to accompany or collect Sheila, he could not help but be filled with awe at what Cathy had made happen, solely by what seemed to him to be sheer force of will. 2.7 acres of beautiful land tucked away on the edge of Northern Virginia. A meeting place for holy men and women of virtually every faith. Seekers of wisdom from so many corners of the world, from novices to near-gurus. A landscape filled with beauty and power. None of which he understood.

What he had stood still long enough for Sheila to teach him were the ways of the labyrinth and the medicine wheel. The movement involved captured his attention. Walking the pattern of the labyrinth allowed him to go deeper inside himself in a way he was comfortable with, in a way that often surprised and enriched him.

The medicine wheel, and the first moon fire ceremonies they had often participated in, were just plain fun to him. It reminded him of the ways of Mexican Indians, as he imagined them. Experiencing others, sitting around the fire, growing as a man through acceptance, release and attraction. Stopping behind Massad's path for a moment, he realized he had learned a lot more from Sheila about a personal relationship with God than he had thought. Still not nearly enough.

Picking up the pace to settle in a few steps behind

Massad, he found himself climbing a steep hill he had never before approached. Often, he had watched Cathy, Sheila and select others climb this hill for sacred rituals and spiritual practices. Sheila was always saying non-believers killed miracles, whenever he wanted to come. He stopped short as he remembered the other thing she sometimes said. 'The things that happen in this place, you can not see.' He wondered what she meant, now more than ever. Massad had laughed at him. He didn't think he could do it. Given all that had happened to him in the last day, he wondered what more could happen.

They reached the crest of the hill and Raines saw what he could only describe as God's garden. It was the beginning of December and in a large oval stretch of land, surrounded on three sides with trees and dense brush and on the fourth side facing this hill, things were blooming! He could sense a quiet feeling of joy that encompassed the area. Though he knew nothing, he was beginning to understand.

"Well, here you are." Massad withdrew behind Raines and sat on tree stump. "Yell out when you need me." A barely suppressed smirk settled across his face.

Raines hardly noticed. What help could he possibly need in such a joyous place? Moving forward, he started down the hill. Slipping on a wet patch, he fell several feet to nearly the bottom of the hill. It was steeper than it seemed. He refused to look back at Massad, sitting coyly at the summit.

Brushing himself off, he moved forward into the garden and took it in at eye level: it was no less majestic. About twenty feet to his left was the labyrinth. One day Cathy had told him how she had built it by hand. Just her and a few hundred pounds of rocks she had collected over the years from sacred places. Forty feet ahead was what he could already tell was a huge and elaborate medicine wheel. He could sense it was amazing.

Raines stood there, reflecting on what to do. He had

come looking for help, but one glance at Massad reminded him he could ask this man for nothing. He had stupidly gotten into a pissing match that had planted him squarely in a place where he was pretty sure he had no business being. He turned around to see Massad staring intensely, as if he were trying to burn holes through him. Raines' mind flitted to his earlier days when episodic violence had been such a big part of his identity. Just then he felt a sadness that the cruelty had been let out of him since courting Sheila. He would have loved to beat Massad senseless. Turning back around, Raines headed toward the medicine wheel.

The medicine wheel spanned about fifty feet. It was circular and divided into four sections. Raines tried to remember what East, West, South, and North were supposed to symbolize. He thought he remembered east was healing. He should start there, and as had been drilled into his head from Cathy and Sheila, 'go clockwise!'

Halfway to the wheel he had trouble breathing. The air was getting very thick. His legs seemed to be getting heavier and heavier and he had trouble moving forward. Coughing and gasping for a full chest of air, Raines took a knee for a short break. Leaning forward, he found himself on all fours fighting for air. When he tried to raise his head he found he couldn't. He sensed a light hovering ahead in the wheel, just out of his reach.

Soon he was flat on the ground prostrate and only getting the smallest stream of air in. Making a huge effort, he finally got a full breath in.

"Massad!" The yell took everything out of him.

Immediately he felt himself covered with a cloth. He thought it was green. Then another cloth came on top of that. He could breathe!

"Stand up." Massad's voice penetrated his joy at free-flowing air.

Steadying himself, Raines stood up slowly. Only a dull light reached him through the coverings.

200

"Please turn around and walk forward."

He turned and moved forward at a slow pace. He found himself moving from a steady jog to a dead run, soon scrambling up the hill. When he was on the other side of the hill, he tore the covers off. The air had become stale beneath them. He sat on the ground and gulped down some air. Massad was standing directly in front of him, looking completely unruffled.

"What happened," Raines demanded.

"You were not worthy to go any farther. I'm surprised you got that far."

"Not worthy of what?"

Massad stepped very close to him and stared into his eyes.

"There's no way you deserve that woman. What made you think you could come so close to the presence of God? What training do you have? What awareness? What single focus, self-control and love? You don't even know what you're doing. Did you even pray and give thanks to God before you entered this sacred space? Was your heart mind and body filled with a worship of God as you approached? Did you ask Him for help as the way ahead got harder?" He wouldn't tell Raines that he hadn't been able to walk Cathy's private medicine wheel either; that rescuing Raines had been the closest he had been able to get.

Massad stepped back and quite clearly sneered at him. "Not worthy of what?" mimicking Raines. "Unbelievable." Massad regained a more placid air and went on. "Don't touch the covers and don't look back. Walk straight ahead and leave this place."

Raines, now sweating in the cold, couldn't think of anything to do but obey.

'Thanks a lot God,' he thought, 'you have made a fool out of me in front of a man I can not stand. I feel like an idiot.' He wiped his face and neck with his scarf. 'I can see why Sheila's mad at you.'

Massad led Raines back to the main building and into Cathy's former office. A quick look around saw many changes. Presumably Massad had made himself comfortable here.

"You should bathe. There's a full bathroom there," motioning to a door in the room. "I'll find you a second set of clothes and lay them out in here for you. Take your time." Massad left quickly and, as usual, without a backwards glance.

A few minutes later Raines found himself disrobed and in the shower with the shower head on pulsate. His body seemed tighter than it should be, as if all of him were clinched. He couldn't remember being this exhausted in a long time. For better or worse, he had always found himself with almost boundless energy. Now he leaned against the shower walls letting the water pound away some of the tightness between his shoulder blades.

Stepping back into the office he found some clothes folded in a chair near the bathroom and changed into them. Walking around the building, he ran into many people who knew him. Everyone wished him well. Many took a moment to pray for him. All of them asked after Sheila. All of the love in the place overwhelmed him and he found himself openly crying. It was a strange feeling. He felt accepted here. Free to express himself. People he had met only briefly welcomed him now with such sincerity. And he could see they all really loved Sheila.

This was what he had come for, though he hadn't known it when he headed out this morning. A place where he could unload and experience his own grief over Cathy's death. He had been so busy being there for Sheila and keeping up with his gallery opening demands, he had pushed his own feelings to the side. Now, he was surrounded by five or six men of God. Men who had known loss, knew how to pray, knew God, and expected nothing more from him than he do what he felt. He finally had enough space, peace, and freedom to weep for a woman who had changed his life in so many ways. He finally found out how much he missed Cathy. It hurt. In some crazy way it felt good to finally feel the pain.

The only time he had ever really worshipped was with Sheila. She had always encouraged him to worship with men at the Institute. She said there was something powerful and sacred about men worshipping with men and women worshipping with women. He had never understood. Now he felt that power. He didn't know a lot of things, but he felt the power of God these men carried with them and he was glad to be there.

Eventually, he emerged from the hallway feeling refreshed and somehow more whole, though sadder. Fishing his watch out of a plastic bag he had placed his things in after changing, he was shocked at the time. 4:14. He had arrived shortly before seven this morning and in his note he told Sheila he would be back by two. He hated breaking his word. Searching again in his bag he produced his cell phone and unlocked it on his way down the hall. "Call Home," he spoke into his headset. It rang and turned over to the voicemail.

"Sheila, hey. I know I'm late. I'm sorry. It won't happen again. I'm on my way home now, but it's rush hour, so…let me know if you need anything. Call me: I want to talk to you. I love you. I prayed for you today. And everyone here is praying for you. I need to talk to you about what happened here. You will be upset. Possibly angry. Bye baby."

He reached the door where he had parked his car and stopped. His jeep was covered with white flowers. He leaned against the wall and closed his eyes. "Thank you God." Walking outside, he gathered up many of the flowers and laid them in the back seat. He headed home a better man than he had been when he came.

Weaving his way home through the rush hour traffic, it was dark when he pulled into their garage. He was disappointed to find Sheila asleep, sprawled out with a pile of tissues on the bed. He wondered if she would ever return to the way she was. He had the feeling that there was no going back to those more carefree days. He added it to everything else he was feeling.

He sat on the edge of the bed and took off his shoes. He felt a tiredness that seemed like it wouldn't go away. Stripping down to a tee shirt and boxers he discarded the disgusting tissues, and climbed into bed. He rubbed Sheila's back and rocked her for a while. She moaned and nestled against him. As Raines fell asleep, he wondered if he would ever wake up.

Massad sat in Cathy's former chair in her office late that night at the Institute. He sat back from the papers he had been studying for the last two hours. Since Cathy's death, the Institute had been hemorrhaging money. She *was* the Institute. Now, in so many ways, the entire Institute was grieving and he could not hold it together. Or rather, he hadn't wanted to. It wasn't his money anyway. The place was Sheila's now. She had not even spoken to him since the funeral. Not a single thank-you for his caretaking of her mother's prize possession. Not for the first time he thought about how richly Sheila deserved everything that was coming to her. She and Cathy both had treated him as a lap dog. All that was about to change. Before long it would be his money; his Institute. And changes would be made.

He mused over the day's events. Raines' little show had certainly been a surprise. He would be dangerous one day. But not yet. Every day he would regret he came here. The thought of being brought low in that valley would taint his worship experience until there was no love and surrender in his way. Then he would be approachable. And the not-so-little 'gift' he had given him was just a bonus. Massad had

204

revenge to exact upon Cathy's lineage. Raines was going to help him more than he could ever imagine. He was delighted at the thought. The irony of it lifted up his heart as he completed his midnight incantations and closed down the building. For Massad, the best was by far yet to come. And he couldn't wait.

CHAPTER THIRTY-FIVE
TAINTED

Sheila woke with a start. She felt…something she hadn't sensed in a long time. She felt contaminated, awash in negative energy. Reaching for the book on her nightstand, she used it to poke Raines' shoulder.

"Raines, Raines," she kept poking as she called his name.

"Mmmm?" Raines rolled over and opened his eyes. "What?"

"What did you do?" Her voice was exacting.

Raines sat up and looked at her. "What?"

"I can't explain it. What did you do to come home so unclean? What happened?" Raines reached for her, "No. Don't touch me. Just tell me."

"So I'm unclean?" Raines felt some irksome annoyance and disbelief verging on anger. But overwhelming those feelings was a sense that she might be right. He let out a big sigh and withdrew his hand from near hers. "I see you listened to my voicemail."

"No. I just feel filthy."

"I uh, well…I got into it with Massad. Um…the next thing I knew I was in the clearing with your mom's medicine wheel and uh, things didn't go well. Massad had to get me out. I guess you were right all these years about me not being able to go there." Raines tried to flash his most pitiful smile but Sheila was unmoved. Nothing was worse than her being mad at him for a good reason.

"What else?" Sheila was probing for the answer. She knew she hadn't heard it yet.

"Well, nothing. I took a shower in your mother's office, changed into some other clothes. Spoke to some people. Some men prayed for me: that was great. I called you and left a message. And drove home. Some of Cathy's students covered the car with flowers. I put some in the back seat. I got home and fell asleep. I'm really sorry. I definitely know I was wrong. Something's definitely wrong when Massad has to help me."

Sheila fell back on the bed and held her head. She held up her hand to interrupt him. "You are an idiot," she said exasperated. "And you still haven't told me."

"What?!" Raines said throwing up his hands. "Maybe if you told me what to say I could say it."

"How did you come, between this morning and now, to be burning with hate?"

Raines reacted as if an unexpected blow had hit him. Hate? It couldn't be possible. But somehow as soon as she said it he knew it was true. He could sense a gnawing feeling. He recognized it.

"I see you know what I'm talking about now," she commented at seeing recognition creep across his face. Stepping off the bed, she dug out some Florida water from her nightstand and doused herself with it. It stung and smelled of rubbing alcohol and citrus.

"Now, you're going to start from the beginning and tell me *everything* that happened."

Sheila was hot with anger. She could not believe Massad. Yet, she was also overwhelmed with weakness. Halfway through dressing in a frenzy and filled with the singular thought that she had to confront Massad; that he would be held accountable for his cruelty, she just stopped. Collapsing in a chair she realized that she had nothing. She was powerless to face him, to deal with any spiritual challenges. She had disavowed her relationship with God.

And using God's tools without His indwelling, without being guided by Him, was pure witchcraft. She wouldn't have it. And even if she wanted to, for the last month she had not maintained any of her practices. Massad might easily overpower her.

Damn! She hadn't anticipated this. Her decision was supposed to make her free, not imprison her. She didn't need to feel any weaker than she already was.

She had to defend her husband and the Institute. But to what end? She wasn't going to take over the place. She wasn't prepared for the ramifications of firing him, though that's what her gut told her to do. And surely, her husband could defend himself. But even as she had the thought, she knew the truth. Massad had led Raines like a lamb to the slaughter. That valley might as well have been a place of death for Raines. He wasn't equipped. Massad was charged to value life above some machismo contest. But Massad had planted a small, growing seed of hate in Raines. She felt it radiate from him like a vile stench.

Because of that, she knew that Massad held malice and manipulation in his heart. He was trying to destroy Raines. Or use him. But again, to what end? Just questions and dead ends.

Pushing herself out of her seat, she took off the clothes she had just thrown on. She had experienced so much pain and frustration in the last few days, she wore the emotions like an old housecoat.

Stepping out of her walk-in closet, she faced Raines. She blinked. She had almost forgotten he was here. Contaminated, needing help. Could she really not help him? Where was all the energy for her emotional catastrophes and being a good wife supposed to come from? A thought of how ruined her life was since Ma died ran across her consciousness.

Breathing in deeply, she drew up what she knew had to be the last of her strength and focus. "Raines, the taint inside you, that little piece of hate, it's infected all of you. I can't fix it. You need a light-bearer for that. I gave it up. I can't just step into it again. That's not how it works. So, for a while you'll have to contain it. Pray, read your Bible, ask God for help. Most importantly don't dwell on negative, weak, or suspect thoughts.

"I can't do anything about Massad either. I'm sorry, I'm helpless. I'll call my sisters. I'll try and get them to come. They can deal with it. In the meantime, I'll sleep down the hall."

She looked at him with a forlorn and longing expression. She reached out and moved to touch him. Like encountering a pulse or wave of electricity, she was repelled back. She wondered at how sensitive she was to this. It didn't seem to make sense. Surely Massad wouldn't have left such an obvious indicator of his work for her to sense, and she shouldn't be able to sense much of anything in her current state, much less something so detailed and tiny.

Shaking herself out of her thoughts she looked at Raines, he looked as pitiful as a puppy let in from the rain. "You hang in there. It'll be alright," she lied. Turning, she closed the bedroom door behind her. Leaning on the other side of the door, she wondered if things would ever return to the way they had been. But she already knew the answer to that.

The morning brought a harsh winter light into the guest bedroom down the hall. Sheila covered her face with the pillow and moaned. She had forgotten to close the curtains last night. Gradually she sat up and dangled her feet over the end of the bed. She hated sleeping alone. Raines worked a lot at night, but he was by her side for at least a couple of hours most nights. She hadn't seemed to notice his absence weeks ago when he had gone to LA for his exhibit. It was as if she had been absent herself for that time.

She didn't like this room. She had threatened to sleep here several times over the course of their marriage. They had had some explosive fights; fights about silly things now that she thought about it. She had gotten outraged about his lack of a spiritual consciousness. Shoving herself out of bed, she sighed. She supposed they'd be fighting a lot less now.

She stood looking around the room. She had no idea what to do next. Deep under the surface, she had a gnawing desire to meditate, to find her center in God's peace. Instead, she paced. She had told Raines she would do something. But she knew she could do nothing. So how would she keep her word? She wanted to call her sisters. That would be the best thing. But then she'd have to explain. They could take one look at her and see. She weighed that fear against the darkness she had felt broiling in Raines last night. She knew what she had to do. But it would not be without a price.

Sinking down at the foot of her bed, Sheila took it all in. She was making a major decision without her mother. She was grappling with a deeply spiritual and dangerous matter and didn't have her to turn to. She had been at a dead run away from anything to do with God since her grandfather had spoken to her. But God was faster, and the thing she had run from had overtaken her. It seemed as if she had been going backwards, in order to end up in a mess like this.

The thought of her mom brought her as much sadness today as it had the day before. It seemed like it was only yesterday that she and her mom had been laughing over something silly. But yesterday seemed so out of reach. The loss was so present, but her life—the griefless joy of those memories—was beyond her. How did people live like this, she wondered?

Last week driving to work she had passed an awful accident. A man had been bleeding in the passenger seat of a gray Lexus while firefighters pried open the door. Two bodies were in stretchers on the ground covered with white sheets. She prayed for the rescue of the surviving passenger, for the comfort of the families of the deceased and for the transcendence of their spirits.

She had prayed hard and in earnest. But as she looked at those bodies laid out, glimpsed only for a moment as she drove past, she had wished *she* were dead. That they could have swapped places. Surely those who had died had wanted to live, as much as she wanted to die. It was an outrageous and flitting thought, only lasting a second. Like a wistful wish to win the lottery. Nothing you really meant. But still...

But she was alive and had to give up fantasies of her peaceful end, of any end. Life had just ratcheted up a notch, and she could no longer glaze over its essence, as she had done at work.

She had to keep her word to Raines. She had to call on her sisters. Before she knew what she had done she found herself on her knees, hands clasped in prayer. Jumping up she shook her head and headed to the bathroom in the hallway for a shower; a fresh start. She still felt like something was gaining on her.

Raines was in a bad mood. He hated sleeping alone. A married man shouldn't have to, he mulled. He thought about how much he had missed Sheila last night, even though now more than ever he saw how little he understood her world. Now that she was acting stranger and more fragile, he loved her more. He felt she needed him, really for the first time.

He didn't want to fail her. He walked into the adjoining bathroom and looked at himself in the mirror. He didn't *look* like a cursed man. But as soon as she had said it last night, he knew that it was true. For the first time, he had no control over what would happen next in his life. He felt Sheila needed him, and more than ever he depended on her. How could either one of them succeed?

Walking to the guest bedroom, he heard Sheila showering in the hall. He grabbed his Bible and sat down on the carpeted floor next to the bathroom door. He was reading Exodus. He had discovered for the first time that the Bible was something more than his parents' salvation. It could be his. *And* it was a pretty exciting story. He had always admired Sheila's passionate synthesis of so many different faiths, but he knew that could never be him. He needed to stick with one thing, and hope that could make him a man who could really stand next to her in all she did. Besides, his parents would never allow it.

He was reading God's instructions to Moses on how to build a special tabernacle where he could commune with God. It was full of jewels, the finest weavings and overlays. Raines' mind ignited at the visual picture. He read more deeply, trying to commit the descriptions to memory. In the back of his mind, in the midst of all his artist's musings, he was aware of a deep truth. If he had been cursed with a hateful seed, meditating on God could help.

Tearing off a piece of paper from his notebook he scribbled a note and left it on the floor in front of the bathroom door. He flew downstairs, pulled out a blank canvas and started sketching. Sheila emerged wrapped in towels from the bathroom and bent down to pick up a piece of paper she had trampled. "Painting God's tabernacle," it read. She folded the note and went to call her sisters.

PART NINE
HERE SPEAKS THE COMFORTER

CHAPTER THIRTY-SIX
SISTERS

Sheila waited at the flight arrival section of the Dulles International Airport in her car. Jasmin and Corinne had arranged for arrivals at almost the same time. And, as usual, Sheila had gotten here too early. She had driven around and idled so long she thought she might be tagged as a security threat soon.

They emerged together, pushing their bags in a cart ahead of them. As she might have imagined, Corinne was prattling away, while Jasmin held a placid resigned look. Sheila put on her hat, pressed the button to open the trunk, and stood outside next to the car. As soon as Jasmin saw her, she ran from Corinne towards her and gave her a big hug. It was so good to see her sisters. Sheila felt as if she almost melted in that embrace. All she could feel flowing from Jasmin was love. No judgement, no expectation, just love.

Jasmin drew back and put her hand on Sheila's stomach. "Pregnant yet?" she smirked, "'Cause you know I'm gonna tell on you if you ain't."

"Corinne!" Sheila brushed Jasmin off to hug Corinne. "It is so good to see you," Sheila glanced back at Jasmin, "both of you." She smiled that same beaming smile she had had since childhood. One of total happiness.

"Ooh, in the car," Jasmin cried, "it's freezing!"

"Come on desert flower," Sheila opened the doors and shooed them in, then threw the bags in the back, closed the trunk, and headed home.

The way home brought what seemed like a happiness and peace Sheila just couldn't join in on. She tried, but Jasmin and Corinne were enclosed in a bubble she couldn't break into. She wondered if it was because of God.

Moving into her right lane before the exit home, Corinne put her hand on Sheila's shoulder, "Take us to Ma's."

"What?" Sheila answered, petrified, as if the wind had been knocked out of her. "I mean, you must want to get settled first. Especially after such a long trip. You can have a nice bath and long nap. A good meal and…"

"Maman en premier," Corinne interrupted.

Sheila took several deep breaths. It was hard to get the air in. She took the beltway exit towards her home.

"No. No," Sheila muttered in a very final tone.

Silence filled the car for the next few miles. Sheila turned up the radio. The heat was getting unbearable for her. She thought she might crawl out of her skin and go running from the car at any moment.

Jasmin leaned forward and spoke in her ear with a very quiet voice. "God will never leave you. Whenever you stop running, you'll know that." She leaned back, held her palms open at chest height and began to pray aloud,

"Mother Father God, bless us in this place. Dearest Lord God, You are most wonderful to us. We praise You for all things. We worship You even as You have taken our mother from us, because You gave our mother to us. Holy Spirit, come now and bring with You all power, majesty, and directness in Your infilling. Allow and enable us to do what You have truly brought us here to do and nothing else. Open up our hearts and spirits and minds. Let us each receive You fully and no other.

"Lord God, we Your children have lost our way, and our sister is lost. We beg, pray and request of You now in full faith and credit that You restore her in Your sight and hide her in Your presence, that no harm may come to her. Pluck out her fear, for indeed she is full of all that is not You. Soothingly align her to Your will, more gently and truly than You have ever done before. Bring us together as again as sisters and children of the light. That we may be responsible for each other and that You may fully and freely work through us for the resurrection of her spirit right now, Lord.

"God and master creator, we don't know what has happened, but You do! Bring a resolution to her pain through perfect peace. Your perfect peace. Your perfect peace reigns over all and causes us every one to tremble and confess. Sovereign Lord, most merciful, benevolent, and true, descend now, even to our lowly place, with Your forgiveness and compassionate teaching to bring us upright into Your presence.

"Cover us with Your Son's blood and let us be redeemed in Christ. Even as we fail, we beg in awe and fear for a renewed spirit and Christ-mind that we may overcome our flesh and all the trappings of this third dimension, that we may ascend. Loose the chains of our humanhood. Give us true eyes, oh God, that we may look first at ourselves and see all within us that You would have removed. Give us the courage to release all that we are and embrace all that You would have us be.

"We praise You, oh God, for the answering of our prayers before they were even uttered from our lips. We submit to You, oh God, for the perfect plan that You will work through us and are working through us even now. We fear You, oh God, for the miracles in our path that You have already declared, and the angels and hosts that surround us and work for our good even now. We love You, oh God, for we know You are the one Truth. We cry out to You, Lord God, to always love us as You said you would. So be it and so it is."

Jasmin opened her eyes and looked up. Halfway through her prayer she had felt the car stop and Sheila's door open and close, but she had not stopped praying. Corinne had grabbed her hands and let up a good wail that hadn't stopped even now, but she had not stopped praying. Now, looking out the car window, she saw Sheila in a field across the street from the shoulder where she had left the car. She was just standing there. Before she could sink into worrying, God's peace came into her. She knew God was in charge.

She pulled her hands out of Corinne's grip. That woman could squeeze the blood out of a turnip if she got carried away. Massaging her fingers to get the circulation going, she spoke. "Corinne, go get your sister."

"Oh she's *my* sister when she acts up," Corinne retorted as she searched through the glove box for tissues and cleaned up her face in the mirror. She peered across the road at Sheila. Finally, she opened the door and stepped out.

Sheila missed her Ma. She thought about how all this turmoil had been caused by the singular act of her death. She pondered on how every one of her present troubles had either been entirely caused or greatly exacerbated by one loose piece of ground her mother had stepped on that day over a month ago. A single step taken more carefully could have saved her all this misery, every single stitch.

When Jasmin had started to pray, she had boiled over with sadness. Jasmin was praying for *her*? As if she were some lost orphan with no hope and no sense. Never mind that she was just that. They prayed on her head as if she had been given up to the sea.

To keep from begging them to stop—even she had the sense not to interrupt a prayer—she had pulled over and hauled tail out of the car as fast as she could. Then she had run across the road to the middle of a field where she suddenly couldn't think of a thing to do, except think about how blisteringly cold it was. But as long as she didn't have to hear them, as long as she didn't have to see them, knowing that they were praying for her, she was ok. The beasts that were inside her could feel peace. Well, not peace, but rest. And she could live. Going on as she had been. Bringing her sisters to save her husband had been too high a price. It had cost her herself.

"Ça va?" Corinne's voice called out from the edge of the field.

Sheila turned around and ambled over to her sister, kicking and staring at the ground the whole way.

Corinne handed her the gloves she had left in the car when she had run out. Sheila put them on and sighed.

"Home?" Sheila peered up at Corinne with a weariness beyond years.

"Oui." Corinne put her arm around her and they walked back to the car. It was so cold, Sheila wondered if her tears were freezing on her cheeks.

CHAPTER THIRTY-SEVEN
EXORCISED

Raines sat on the couch in his studio staring at his canvas. He had been trying to paint for a while now. He hadn't known he could produce such trash. His Bible lay next to a drink he had started on earlier. He picked it up as he took a drink from the bottle next to him. He hadn't drunk whiskey straight from the bottle in a long time. It felt liberating. He was searching the Bible for people who had been possessed, to try and understand what was happening to him. But none of it made any sense to him, and it certainly didn't tell him how to get out of the situation, because Jesus didn't just happen to be walking by for him to call on.

Raines paced his basement studio, stopping to look at the clock. Sheila should be home soon with her sisters. About time. The hatred inside him was unbearable, now that he was conscious of it. He found himself doing things he hadn't since his wilder days. He had gotten cut off by a Lexus the other day and almost burst a vein in the car from angry cussing. He had gotten drunk last night and called his parents. He couldn't be sure, but he was almost positive he cussed out his father and called him worthless. He had snapped at Sheila. Worst of all, she just had taken it silently. Never a comment, never a harsh word for all the wrong he was doing. That angered him. She was supposed to care about him, especially at times like this. He kicked the hell out of a paint can he had lying on the floor. Black paint splattered the carpet, walls, and some of the ceiling.

"Oh Christ," Raines grabbed his bottle, jacket and headed out the back door. Maybe the cold air would bleed out some of his anger.

They swept into the house like a hurricane. Raines could hear them stomping about upstairs, screaming, like sisters gone too long without seeing each other were bound to. He had a headache. Reaching for his whiskey bottle, he noticed it was empty, and sat up instead. His head was killing him. It wasn't even dark yet outside and he had drunk an entire bottle of whiskey. He had meant to clean the house some before they got back. He couldn't remember what had gotten in the way of that.

He walked to the bathroom in the basement and splashed some water on his face. Sometimes he looked in the mirror and it seemed a different face was looking back at him. Not today: that same miserable, slightly drunk guy named Raines was peering at him. He took off his tee shirt, spattered with paint from his third attempt in as many days to depict Moses' tabernacle. He was beginning to think it was impossible. Why did God always ask for the impossible? On top of the basement hamper, Sheila had placed a few clean outfits for him. He picked a nice fleece pullover to put on, gathered his hair back into a ponytail, and headed upstairs.

"My beautiful sisters!" Raines put on his best smile and went to hug Jasmin and Corinne. They both drew back from him. The room got quiet. Where was all that noise he had heard earlier? Raines' arms fell to his side. 'oh yeah', he thought, 'I'm cursed. Dammit.'

"Well, it's good to see you. I'll be downstairs, ladies." He headed back towards the basement, then paused, turning to the kitchen. He picked out a decent bottle of red wine, a corkscrew, and a wine glass. Then he resumed his trip downstairs.

Jasmin stared absently at the stairs Raines had just descended. "Almost forgot. Almost forgot." Jasmin and Corinne shared a look Sheila couldn't seem to break into.

"My dear, at least you don't exaggerate," Corinne commented.

"Yeah," Jasmin agreed, "let's get to work."

Sheila helped them with their bags upstairs into their rooms. Then they made it clear they wanted to go into her shrine room and cleanse and center their energies before working on Raines. She was filled with dread. As they headed to the room, every step was weighed down more and more with fear. They got to the front of the door and all that was left was for her to put her hand on the knob, turn it and push. Her fingers hesitated just above the knob. She turned toward her sisters and stared them in the face.

"I can't go in with you." She started to walk away towards the steps. Maybe she'd share a drink with Raines until they were done. She felt Jasmin's first and second fingers pressing into her neck. They were pressing on the energy point that tapped into a person's obedience to the Will of God. She had seen her mother do this only a few times. It burned. It seemed to freeze her in her tracks. She blazed with a kind of angry shame.

She heard Jasmin's voice in her ear. It seemed to be coming from inside her own head. "You will stay here until we are finished with you." The fingers released and suddenly she could move again. She leaned against the wall and slid down it until she was sitting on the floor. She wasn't going anywhere. She didn't even *want* to anymore. Corinne and Jasmin were already in the shrine room. With her forefinger on the carpet she drew countless circles within circles.

Inside Sheila's shrine room, Jasmin opened her eyes and laid her hands on Corinne's shoulders. They both sat cross-legged facing each other. Night had fallen and settled in outside. It had taken them time to cleanse the physical and spiritual space of the room. Offerings had lain rancid on some of the shrines. Worse yet, the energy was of death and defeat. They had choked on it. After dealing with that, they made new offerings of things they had brought with them—

things they could be sure were of a clean spirit—and had settled in to work on themselves.

For an hour they had chanted. For an hour they had sung, then repeated affirmations, some over a hundred times. Finally they had meditated for about an hour. Now, Corinne's eyes opened and she placed her hands on Jasmin's shoulders. Staring at each other, they built up the energy and intent between them until they were of one accord and one light instead of two minds and two flames.

"My peace rests upon you, sister," Jasmin recited, "and I declare you as the head." Corinne was the eldest after all.

Corinne's gaze became Divine in Jasmin's eyes, and she knew that her spiritual allegiance and obedience had just been sealed.

"God's glory rests upon you, sister, and I declare we are one body in Christ." Corinne's voice grew quiet but somehow thunderous, "Let us now rise up from this place and bring not peace but a sword." Corinne withdrew her hands and stood up. Jasmin followed.

Sheila was sitting somewhat listlessly on the carpet outside the door. Jasmin looked at her and her heart ached.

"Stay focused, sister," Corinne continued to the stairs. They headed to the basement, towards Raines.

Raines was filled with fear at the sound of quiet footsteps descending the stairs toward him after the sound of a door opening and closing. Corinne emerged from the stairs, and she looked ready to slay demons. Jasmin behind her looked just as foreboding.

He had started working on God's tabernacle again since their return. It hadn't felt like that much time had passed. Again, he was unhappy with his efforts. The colors were still too intense, too violent. Before they had been too soft. He was at his wit's end, but still captivated.

Then they had come down here, reeking of grim judgement. Corinne walked right up to him and stood directly in front of him, peering into his face. Jasmin stood closely behind and to her right. Fear almost took his breath away. Instead he summoned up all the Montoya courage he could and stood straight, looking ahead.

"I don't know," his voice strained and cracked, "what I'm supposed to..." Corinne's look told him to shut up. He closed his mouth and tried to think of something.

Jasmin looked at Raines closely from behind Corinne. She had felt blackness and negativity oozing from him when they had first entered the house. Now, up close and with her spiritual focus on, she saw what she could only describe as black tendrils coming from him, lashing out in every direction. Right now, every tendril was gathered, to strike out at Corinne, trying to ensnare her. She was taking the brunt of the spiritual attack so Jasmin could do just as she was doing, look and see. All of the black arms came from a tight knot in his stomach. She peered more closely, trying to see what was at the center.

Suddenly tentacles struck out at Jasmin's head and neck. A moment of blindness overtook her. She must have stuck her head too far around from Corinne and been noticed. Struggling, she concentrated on removing her right thumb from over the opening of the bottle of Florida water, stretching her arm out toward Raines, and upturning the bottle over his feet.

Attacks of negativity resulted in an inability to do even the simplest things for your own spiritual survival. It became impossible to preserve the Christ-presence within. It had been incredibly painful and difficult even to sprinkle Raines with the Florida water, designed to scatter some of his negative energy so she could escape from it.

As soon as the Florida water hit his feet, Raines stepped back. Corinne rushed ahead with him step-for-step, and Jasmin felt freed from whatever had been dragging her down. In that moment of movement, she saw something. The tight black center had loosened for a moment and she had seen a rust-orange light. She had to pursue it now before that knot tightened back around it completely. She stepped forward and, before she could become paralyzed from the attacking black arms, pointed the first two fingers of her right hand against his stomach and pressed at the point of the small but now blinding orange light.

She sunk to her knees in distress. She felt the spirit being choked out of her by this attack. Yet she would not allow her connection to extinguish. She visualized a white light from her heart center flowing through her arm to her fingers and from her fingers to the center of the orange light inside the pit of Raines' belly. The light in her heart center was connected to the Source.

She felt Corinne standing behind her to her right. Corinne's energy was flowing into her, linking with hers and surrounding the orange light. Two is better than one, their mother always used to say. With reinforcement, she felt able to unclench her jaw. Jasmin began to recite *The Judgement Call*.

"In the Name of the I Am that I Am, we invoke the presence of Jesus Christ. They Shall Not Pass. They Shall Not Pass. They Shall Not Pass." Behind her she heard Corinne chanting. It sounded like a Vishnu one for driving out demons. Interesting choice, she thought. She was not sure they were dealing with a demon. Not sure at all.

The room began to get hot and she felt their incantations and chants amplifying. The tide of energy was shifting as she observed the black tentacles becoming less focused and their white light begin not just to surround the orange light but to penetrate it. She heard a high-pitched keening that began to get louder and louder.

"Open the door!" Jasmin screamed, "Let it get out!"

Corinne formed her hands in a sign for dispersing hexes and backed toward the door, turning and opening it as quickly as she could before hastening back to her sister's side. The white light overflowed into the orange light and

Jasmin and Corinne both knew what was coming. The last hoorah. All the black arms melded into one spear and with viper-like speed pierced Jasmin in her side. Moments before, Corinne had formed her hand in a Hindu sign of protection and placed it at Jasmin's side. It blunted the effect.

As Corinne continued *The Judgement Call* behind her, she formed her own white light into an arm. It reached into the pit, closed around the orange light and slowly pulled it out. Holding it directly in front of her she inspected it for a moment. Struggling to stand up she upturned her bottle of Florida water on the imprisoned orange light. The piercing shriek was almost unbearably loud now.

"Go back to your master and never return," she spat, "right now." A loud pop sounded in the room as the white hand crushed the orange light completely. Everything that was dark and negative rapidly dispersed and fled the room, leaving a stale haziness. Jasmin and Corinne sank to the floor, leaning against each other. Silent tears of exhaustion and release flowed from their eyes. Jasmin sprinkled Florida water over their heads and they rubbed it on their faces, necks and hands. It stung.

After a few moments of purging and cleansing, Jasmin and Corinne stood, exhausted but stable. They took in the room. Everything that could be overturned was. And paint spills streaked the floor. Jasmin picked up a painting on the floor. It looked like some kind of inner sanctum. Something was written over it in black paint. It looked liked Sanskrit but she couldn't be sure. It reeked. She walked with it to the open door, flung it out as far as she could and slammed the door behind her. Turning, she approached her brother-in-law on the coach. His elbows were resting on his knees as he sat. His head was in his hands and he was crying, trying as best he could not to sob. Corinne was sitting to his right and as drained as she was. She was directing all the energy she had into a healing ray flowing into him.

Jasmin stooped in front of him. "Look at me Raines."

His shoulders began to heave and she gently pulled his hands away and lifted up his face to meet her gaze. "You are a strong man, Raines. And you did an amazing job. I'm proud to know you're in my family." She smiled at him. And she meant every word. That was the key to Jasmin's entire existence. She never said anything she didn't mean. And because everyone who cared about her knew that, it freed them up to do the same.

"I'm sorry," Raines spoke clearly as he wiped the tears from his face.

Jasmin massaged his shaking hands as she peered into his face. "Please go upstairs and wait for us in the shrine room with the door closed. You can rest. You've had a big day. God bless you and keep you beloved." She released his hands and stood up, stepping back so he could have room to leave.

Raines looked at them both, rubbed the back of his neck, rose and left without a word. Jasmin crashed on the couch with her sister and they looked at each other. Jasmin could see Corinne was as bewildered as she.

"When was the last time you ever!?" Their look finished the sentence for both of them. Corinne leaned her head back on the couch and rubbed the bridge of her nose. "Can you believe Ma used to deal with this kind of thing all the time?"

Jasmin leaned forward and stared hard into space. "All these years, keeping Massad bound by her side to isolate and contain him. What a dark master he must be, to employ a taint like that."

Corinne shook herself and leaned forward with her sister. "I can't see how Raines held on all this time. Obviously Sheila wasn't doing anything. I never knew he had it in him. I'm not sure I could have done any better."

"Do you see how weak we must be," Jasmin seemed not to have heard her, "how much weaker we must be than Mama? It took the two of us in our full power to deal with his taint. Not him but just his taint. And all these years she had bound an evil one to her." Jasmin shook her head and wiped away a few tears that had sprung up. "We're just shadows of her."

"We got the job done," Corinne retorted dismissively. "And now we have some more work to do. Girl, we have got to clear out the house of this stale funk. And in case you forgot, our sister is up there and she's just about lost her spirit. Clearly Massad is not going anywhere until we go get him. So focus on right now." Corinne stood in front of her and clapped her hands in front of Jasmin's face three times.

Jasmin stood up. "I'm here. Let's do this."

Picking up the tools they had brought down with them and had laid at the foot of the steps, they began a spiritual cleanse of every square inch of the house, room by room.

"You see the time, Corinne," Jasmin urged at about quarter after eleven. They had to get done before the witching hour.

"We'll have enough time." Corinne reflected on the last several hours they had spent in this house. They had just entered the master bedroom. It was the last room they had to clear before dealing with their sister. She was dimly aware of pushing her body and mind to the point of exhaustion. It was becoming a harder and harder task to stay focused and keep the mind and body bound to the spirit's will. She felt these three parts were about to fly apart at the seams and leave the Will of God as only a passing fancy. Aware of Jasmin's chanting in the background she joined in and felt buoyed by that. Energy surged into her and she eventually felt electrified by the love of God again.

Shortly before 11:30, they had finished with the master bedroom. They stood in the doorway facing each other. Their eyes were swimming and they had to admit they were positively dead on their feet. In unison they recited, "My peace rests upon this space. God's peace rests upon this house. Elohim, Elohim, Elohim."

Jasmin peered out of the bedroom doorway. She saw Sheila sitting on the floor beside a closed shrine door, much the same as when they had left her hours ago. Jasmin leaned her head against the frame of the door and sighed. She couldn't believe they had more to do. She wanted to cry. She had reached and passed her breaking point long ago.

"Come on God, just a little more grace," she pleaded.

Corinne began reciting scripture, "Lift up your heads, O you gates; be lifted up, you ancient doors, that the King of glory may come in. Who is this King of glory? The Lord strong and mighty, the Lord mighty in battle. Lift up your heads, O you gates; lift them up, you ancient doors, that the King of glory may come in, Who is He, the King of glory? The Lord Almighty, He is the King of glory." They rubbed their hands together briskly at their heart centers.

"I'm braced now." Jasmin looked at her sister and saw a light in her eyes that she hoped was reflected in her own. Together they headed toward Sheila.

Jasmin knelt down and rested her hand on Sheila's shoulder. Sheila looked up at her with a face full of a shy kind of shame. It nearly broke Jasmin's heart.

"Please lay on your stomach dear." Sheila nodded slowly and moved to lie on the carpet. She cradled her head on top of her hands, facing away from her sisters, and sighed.

From the middle of her back they began working on restoring her energy flow. They rubbed in different directions as they worked, Jasmin focusing on the heart center and Corinne on the sacral and root chakras. They looked up from their work a few times at each other in surprise. Her spiritual energy flow was completely shut down. Not a trickle was flowing from one light point to the next. She had fallen completely into the third dimension, with no activation of her spiritual core at all. Silently they continued their work.

Over the next twenty minutes, Corinne and Jasmin worked tirelessly on their sister, directing seemingly every

228

drop of light-filled energy they had into their sister's body. Working to unblock her spiritual pathways and restore her God-connection. At 5 to midnight, they stopped, sealing her off to preserve the work they had done. A small, barely perceivable, but still existent stream of energy flowed from the silver cord that entered the top of Sheila's head and coursed through her body, moving from her tailbone to a grounding cord in the earth.

Together, they rolled their sister over onto her back. Jasmin rubbed her hands over Sheila's face and positioned her face directly over hers, breathing into her face. "God's grace cover you love. Peace and joy in your soul, beloved."

Sheila smiled in her sister's face and let out a big yawn. "You just don't understand, Jas." Sheila sat up and rubbed her eyes. She shivered. "It's cold!" Looking out the window she was confronted with a pitch-black sky. She turned suddenly to Jasmin. "Raines…I felt you fix it. I can't thank you enough. I can't let anything happen to him. 'I am my beloved's and my beloved is mine.'" She hadn't meant to recite scripture, but habits were hard to break. She had that scripture inscribed in Hebrew on the inside of both of their wedding rings. The Song of Songs was a sexy book of the bible, and Raines hadn't minded at all. It denoted ownership over each other's hearts, over each other's everything. They fought, and often she was irritated with him. But she just didn't function without him.

These last few days had been Hell. She had tried being in his presence, but the psychic disruption was too much for her. Unable to help him spiritually, she had overcompensated in other areas; cooking his favorite meals, washing and ironing his clothes, even the sweats and t-shirts. It had been the closest to a housewife she thought she would ever come. He was hers and she had to take care of him. They had chosen each other as family, and that meant everything to her. He was the one she had chosen.

Corinne could see the worry on Sheila's face. "He's

fine," Corinne gestured toward the shrine room, "He's in there."

Sheila looked at the shrine room door hesitantly. "Oh," she mouthed.

Corinne grabbed her left wrist gently and cuffed it. "Go on in there and talk to him. It's about time."

Sheila suddenly looked cornered. She stared down at her wrist encircled by Corinne's hand. She recognized this move. It was another way to entreat a spirit's obedience, even when the body wasn't willing.

Sheila turned to Jas, "I don't want to," she pleaded quietly.

Jasmin leaned forward and patted her hand sympathetically. "But you will, dear," she whispered in her ear as she stood up and straightened out her clothes. "In the meantime, Corinne and I," she announced, "are going to rustle up some grub. We have worked hard. We have worked alone, save the grace of God." As she looked at Sheila, something in her expression seemed very troubled. "And we are absolutely starving."

Corinne stood up and leaned against the wall near Jasmin. "We'll go on down as soon as we see you go in."

Sheila looked at them. They were both staring her down. She was calculating how much energy she had to expend in this battle. Slowly she turned around, let out a deep breath and reached out to turn the knob to her shrine room. Staring down at the floor, she kept walking forward and softly shut the door behind her. Taking care not to look around, she saw Raines asleep curled up in the middle of the room. She tried not to notice the entire room was glowing, and so was he.

She walked over to a bench sitting underneath a window, sat down and clutched at one of the pillows there. Staring out at the back yard, she tried to find a spiritless peace that could fight off all the Godliness she was confronted with in this place. She tried not to cry.

230

CHAPTER THIRTY-EIGHT
RECOVERY

Downstairs, Corinne and Jasmin raided the kitchen with a vengeance, and shortly had some pan-fried trout sandwiched between bread with a few other ingredients. After a short burst of talking about food when they had been preparing it, they had fallen into a deep silence. As they ate their sandwiches, Corinne looked over at Jasmin, "Have you ever…"

"No," she answered morosely. "I would not have the thought it possible if I had not seen it. Not in *this* house," she shuddered.

"You know," Corinne reflected as she munched more on her sandwich, "I was pretty mad at God after Ma died. Righteous and flaming mad. But I never turned away. It just wasn't in me. Now, to see Sheila like this—how can we ever prevail against Massad as we are?" Corinne threw her sandwich on her plate. "If we can't save the Institute, to me, it'll feel like killing Ma all over again!" She stood up and pointed toward the alter room upstairs. "And it's her fault!" she cried. "And I guarantee you she knows it too. I guarantee she knows that it is because of her that everything Ma stood for will fall apart around us. Before our very eyes." Corinne paced around the kitchen island. "And she does nothing! Rubs out God's name from her life like moving a piece of furniture. Just replacing it with nothing.

"Of the three of us, I've always thought she was the strongest, the one most like Ma. And spiritually, I've always been the weakest. I know this. But I had other gifts. I just wasn't a prophet. Anything I have, for the sake of the family, I give it, with *joy*. But that woman upstairs, she knows exactly what we need and won't give it. We kill ourselves doing a job she could have handled while she sits helpless in some agnostic stupor. How can she be so selfish? How can she damn the family like this? Even if she hated God, can't she just love us enough to get over it? Even a little? I know this: mother would rip her to shreds for it, and the problem and behavior would be corrected. I just don't know what we can do to fix it."

"Shhh," Jasmin put her finger up to her lips. "Please be still, Corinne. What has your speech done but enflamed us to fear and a doomed hysteria? Everything you say may be true, but I won't have you drive me to a desperate madness." Jasmin's voice grew resolute and firm. "We need prayer and divine intervention. There's nothing else for it." Tears sprang from her face. "I don't know what to do. But there's nothing else for it." Jasmin took both of their plates and dumped half-eaten sandwiches in the trash, "Enough of this bread of sorrow," she muttered.

Placing the plates in the sink, she washed her hands and called over her shoulder to Corinne. "What we need is to shower, pray, and sleep finally." Turning off the tap she shook off her hands and turned around. She walked over and gave Corinne a big hug. She visualized the pink light of hope flowing into Corinne's heart. Discouragement would kill them as sure as any outside enemy. And if they were not for each other, then who would be? Why should anyone else be?

"Thanks J," Corinne replied sheepishly.

Jasmin put her arm around her and smiled an agelessly tired smile. "Come on then." They took their showers, knelt beside each other to pray, and crawled into bed, sinking into sleep before worry could overtake them again.

Raines woke up and found himself curled in a ball on

the shrine room floor. He snuggled more into a pillow and blanket. He realized they hadn't been there when he had sat down on the floor earlier. Looking around, he saw Sheila sitting on a bench leaning against the window, tracing a sideways figure eight onto the pane. She was shivering.

Raines tried to spring to his feet, but found he simply didn't have the energy. Slowly he sat up, got on his feet and straightened up. Walking over to Sheila, he sat on the bench with her and wrapped his blanket around the both of them. He was overflowing with a thousand emotions. Without meaning to and before he realized what he was doing, he was hugging her desperately and crying against her shoulder. She just rocked him, hugging him back just as fiercely.

"I love you so much," they both seemed to say at once. Untangling his arms from around her, he held her face and kissed her. Sheila sank against his chest, "Take me to bed."

Raines sat down with her on the edge of their bed. Suddenly, Raines pulled himself away from her and shook himself. "What's wrong?" she uttered.

"I…," he looked flustered, "I can't control my feelings. I don't know what's going on inside me. I've never felt so much love before." His head delved back into his hands and he growled.

Sheila smiled a regretful kind of smile. Divine love—he was filled with unconditional love from the work her sisters had done. She was so out of sorts lately, it was like he was talking about something she knew about but had never experienced. She ran her hands over his hair. "That's God's Love. True love."

Sheila felt a sudden need to share in some of that love Raines was floating in that seemed so out of her grasp. 'The fruits of the Spirit are love,' she thought. He had it now because he was seeking God. She didn't because she had turned away. Sheila lay back on the bed and pulled him toward her.

His eyes searched her face. They hadn't touched at all in the last week since he had been poisoned at the Institute. And before that, the last time they had made love, he had felt as if he had been taking advantage of her tender state. But, in the end, she was his wife. And he missed her. He needed her.

"I love you, Sheila," he whispered before he kissed her. Sheila couldn't think.

She felt a hand reaching away from her to the second drawer of his nightstand where they kept the condoms. "Don't," she muttered, pulling his hand back to her face. He paused for a moment, hands outlining her jaw line. "Are you sure?"

Sheila nodded with a quiet smile on her face. Stars swam over Raines' eyes. Just the idea of being with her this way, truly being man and wife for the first time in his opinion, nearly overwhelmed him. He was awash in a wondrous passion for experiencing his wife.

Raines took a moment to place a pillow behind her head. Then he did something he had never done before; he stopped to pray. "Jesus Christ, thank you for my soul, thank you for my wife. I praise your name. Thank you!"

As he said these words aloud, he smiled and looked into Sheila's face. He could see something inside her shut down. As if he had literally flipped a switch from on to off. Gathering Sheila up tightly in his arms, he just held her.

"What'd you have to go and pray for? Why'd you have to bring God into it?"

Raines looked at her and smiled, "God was already in it!" he said jovially. "Anytime you want to…well…anytime we have a chance to have a child, it must be the work of the Lord," he laughed. Sheila's mood darkened and Raines scrambled to backpedal. He cradled her face with his hands, "God's in everything, and I just felt like acknowledging Him right then. I was just so happy," he stared off into space, "I did what came naturally and thanked Him." Raines looked at her with a bit of a pleading expression. "You're still not talking to God?" Sheila squirmed underneath him and looked away. As she made to get up, Raines smiled, "Wait, Sheila," he wanted to find just the right words, "when we make love, I always feel like you're giving something to me. Let me give something to you tonight. If you had some of God's love for you, I know you would love Him back. And maybe then you could do what He's asked of you."

"Oh Raines…" it was all too much. Tears leaked from her eyes.

"Shhh." Raines pulled her into a deep kiss, and her ability to think or object ceased.

As they made love, Raines felt like an ocean of light was exploding inside him. He tried to find a way to describe how he was feeling, now finally and truly making love to his wife, possibly creating a new life, and finally being a source of spiritual support for her. 'She's really my wife and I'm truly her husband,' he affirmed in his mind.

"Raines, Raines."

He didn't want to answer her. He was afraid she was going to ask him to stop. He wasn't sure he'd be able to. They were well past that point.

"What," he answered, preparing himself for the worst.

"I love you. Thank you," Sheila managed to get out between gulps of air.

Between the intense pleasure and abandon that was spreading through him, the thought of just how much he loved his wife came over him. 'Thank you, God,' he said silently. Sheila wrapped around him so tight he could never have escaped if he wanted to. He kissed her and wrapped his arms around her even tighter, tension mounting all the while. Burying his head in her neck, he cried out. Sheila melted away in happiness.

Raines grabbed a pillow for himself, pulling the comforter up from the foot of their bed. He wrapped Sheila in the covers and lay down under them beside her. Sheila curled up beside him. Lifting her head on an elbow, she looked into his eyes.

"Let's not use condoms anymore, dear."

A huge smile crept over Raines sleepy face. "Yes boss." Raines clasped her hand and kissed the inside of her palm. "That's very alright, Mrs. Montoya." They lay kissing each other and smiling and giggling.

"Raines!" Sheila said in a surprised voice.

"Hmmm," Raines rubbed and kissed her shoulder.

"Do you think we made a baby?"

Raines held her face in his hands and kissed her. "Nothing would make me happier." He looked at her more seriously, "How would you feel about it?"

Sheila lay back and thought for a moment. "I'm really scared, but I think I'd like to have a baby with you," she smiled.

"There's my girl," Raines cooed as he settled back down beside her. "Love you so much," he mumbled before falling fast asleep.

PART TEN
THE END OF THE ROPE

CHAPTER THIRTY-NINE
LEAVING

Raines awoke to find every single muscle aching in his body. He was exhausted. Looking around, he found he was alone. As soon as he thought to miss her, she walked through the door.

"Look who's up," she chimed as she said on the bed beside him. "Good morning," she leaned down to kiss him.

"What time is it?" He rubbed his eyes.

"7:30."

"Why are you up and dressed? Look at you," Raines let out a low whistle, "You look gooood. Stand up, turn around, lemme see."

Sheila rose from the side of the bed and did a little spin.

"I am a lucky man. You're not going to work, are you?"

"New York. The conference starts today!" Sheila was a bit miffed that he had forgotten, but then, she had almost forgotten herself.

"You're not going, are you? Not after all John's done to you."

"It's a bit like my last official act. I've got contacts to schmooze, I want to be sure to get some face time with the president, and I want to see John offer our presentation like it's all his work—call it a morbid curiosity. Gotta go."

Raines sat up. "Sheila, I don't want you to go. I don't trust John. He's shown he's volatile. I can't let you be around someone like that."

That was as close to an order as Raines had ever given to her. She weighed her next words carefully in her mind.

"I can't let him to get the better of me. And I have to network for my budding consultant company. You know I have to work. When I stay at home all I seem to do is cry." She pulled a tissue from the bed and wiped her tearing eyes before her makeup got ruined.

Raines swung his legs over the side of the bed and thought carefully.

"There are a lot of reasons I feel you shouldn't go. On top of that I just don't *want* you to go. Will you ever give your husband the chance to protect his wife? Do I not have that right?" Raines' voice was quiet but commanding. "I feel…something is just *wrong* with this trip, and I don't want you to go." Raines reached out for her hand, "Please don't go."

Sheila let out a frustrated sigh and inspected the carpet on the floor by her feet. Is this what it was going to come down to, doing what she felt she had to and defying him, or being obedient and slowly dying?

"I can't submit to this, Raines. I can't stay here. I can't. *Here* is killing me, it's tearing me apart. And that's something you can't understand: every curse is different. You've escaped yours; I lie down to mine. And now I have to live with that. There's no hiding from it in your arms; it's my reality now. Everything you do, every move my sisters make, it upsets me, like someone walking on my grave. I need you all to leave me alone now, so I can get settled. I have to have a chance to live in some sort of peace, the peace of the world. At least this way I can have something to me besides my failures, besides my incompleteness." Sheila stared into space, "I can have a chance to make something of a life for myself, as just a normal woman. That's the best I can hope for now.

"I'm sorry, I can't let anything get in the way of that. I've made my decision. You've fought me at every turn. But you should just give it up. I can't afford your terms. God ought to be happy I'm not in league with the devil, but He's

239

not and I can't help that. I have to do what I can do, not get mired in what I can't. So that's that. I'm going to New York and I'll be back Thursday."

"You will not move from that spot." Jasmin stood at the door to their bedroom looking commanding, rumpled robe and all.

"Wha…"

"And you will not say another word," Jasmin advanced toward her determinedly, ablaze with anger. Raines, who was more intelligent than his wife usually gave him credit for, knew enough to get out of the way, taking cover at the far end of the bed.

"Who are you to tell God what God should and should not be happy with settling for? Who are you not to submit to your husband? Yes, I was listening at the door and heard it all. You have to do what you can do? And what in the world is it that you can do without God? Can you draw breath? Can you take a step, think a thought or say a solitary word? If you aren't doing the work the Lord has commanded, then you *are* in league with the devil. So no, God will *not* settle for that. You know that. You're not cursed—you've simply made a choice to rebuke God, and that's worse. I don't know what's going on in this house, but no sister of mine will continue to carry on like this. Not as long as I have breath in my body and Spirit within."

Sheila quietly took in her sister as she spoke. The words just washed over her, not even making a dent. She could overpower her sister without much effort. Spiritually, metaphysically, she had been the stronger of the two. This was the first time she had ever realized that. Had been. Seeing as how she couldn't abide by witchcraft, which was what use of metaphysical or spiritual practices without being tied into the Source amounted to, she now *had been* the stronger of the two, and had to sit here and take this assault. While she had let her spiritual discipline and skill slip since Ma passed, Jasmin had not missed a beat, and she used what

240

she knew, what Mother had taught them both, to root her to the spot as surely as if she had been tied and chained.

Sheila's rage at being lectured battled hard to overpower her shame, doubt, and ever-present fear. It finally won, and for the first time in her life, she used the tools of God without His in-dwelling. She loosed herself from her sister's bond and unleashed a wave of angry power in her direction. Jasmin looked horror-stricken and stepped back almost the instant Sheila stood up from the bed, eyes blazing. Raines could have sworn he had seen some sort of flash in the room. He didn't doubt anything these days, no matter how shocking. He also knew his wife well enough to know she could not stand a dressing-down, and guessed what was coming next.

"Don't you dare," Sheila's voice filled the room with anger, "Little sister. You are in no position to tell me anything. How dare you even try?"

Sheila was advancing on her sister, driving her backwards until Jasmin bumped into the wall and Sheila was almost on top of her it seemed.

"I will not tolerate your judgment, your sanctimonious know-it-all attitude, or your unbelievable assumption that you know anything about my situation and what I can and can't do! No one is going to tell me what to do anymore! No one! I have no Lord, no God, no Spirit. And you will not bring it up in my presence again. You know nothing about it. If you knew anything you would understand that I deserve your sympathy and tears, your support," she beat her fist against her chest. "But if I can't have that, I'll surely not have your damnation. Just, just leave it be. Go home and let me live my…"

Jasmin had an overwhelming headache. She couldn't even distinguish Sheila's words. Though she got their meaning unmistakably, Sheila was pounding each thought painstakingly into her head. Jasmin had never thought it would come to this. 'This is how people feel when they suffer heartbreak,' a feeble thought of her own came through her sister's bewitching mental assault. 'Broken, let down, facing a horrid reality they thought would never come. Yes, I have a broken heart right now,' Jasmin fainted dead away.

Sheila stopped mid-sentence and stepped back in shock. She took in the shape of her sister's body, lying crumpled on the floor. Heard the sounds of Raines springing from the bed, saw his form come into view. But she could make sense of none of it. She just knew she wanted it all to be over. 'This is how people must feel when they suffer from broken hearts,' she thought. She took in several deep breaths with slow exhalations. Slowly, Jasmin came around and Raines had her sitting with her back against the wall while he went to get some water and a damp cloth.

Sheila knelt down beside her sister, who sat frail and weeping. Taking Jasmin's head in both hands with her thumbs at her temples, Sheila put her mouth to Jasmin's third eye, prepared herself and took a long-drawn inhalation. She drew back into herself all the mental and spiritual assault she had just unleashed on her sister. Sheila stumbled back with a suddenly blinding headache. Rubbing her eyes, her sister finally came back into focus, and Raines, standing frozen at the door.

"I'm sorry," she said, her head was throbbing. She made her way to the bathroom and downed five or six aspirin in an attempt to tamp down the nonsensical pain. Not seeing what else she could do, Sheila kept on through the bathroom, down the stairs, to the front door to grab her case and travel bag. A waiting cab took her to Dulles Airport.

In no time, and with a finally dulled headache, she was in another cab, speeding through the New York City streets toward the conference center. But in every way besides her flesh, she was still trapped in the moment when she had attacked her sister. With tools their own mother had taught them, tools Sheila had used in the most ungodly way imaginable.

242

There was no going back. There was no way out. She didn't even see how she could go on. So when the cab pulled up in front of a swanky hotel, indistinguishable from all the rest, she had no idea what else to do but get out, check into her room, check her make-up, and head down to the conference, just as falsely and Godlessly as she had thought she would when she had planned it all out earlier.

CHAPTER FORTY
THE CONFERENCE

Sheila was pressing the flesh, as they called it. She had always been a great networker and mingler. But today, even by her own high standards, she was sterling. She had worked the ballroom and hallways with tender efficiency in the last two hours. She had seen just about everyone she had on her list. Everyone except the CEO, and of course, John. She was saving John for last. And hopefully she would see Ed at lunch or dinner to say her brief but well-thought-out piece. She had spotted John of course and he had noticed her. But by silent agreement, it seemed, they had both decided to leave their exchange for later. That was fine.

Finally, Sheila caught a glimpse of Ed Cloury. Well, not so much a glimpse of him as a receiving line forming away from the entrance to the banquet hall for their late lunch. She knew only one person could be responsible for that—it took a lot to keep these folks from their meals. Sheila calculated. Of course, ideally she wanted a moment alone with him. She weighed that desire against the likelihood of actually getting that moment at this jam-packed conference. In the moments it took her to think this over, she absent-mindedly went to the beverage table and poured herself a glass of water.

'It's so hot in here,' she thought, barely realizing it was her own guilt and not the temperature causing her to feel as if she were roasting. She took a second to drive those thoughts down deep where she couldn't recognize them. Instead, she focused on taking in the room again, just in time to see Ed heading towards her. She was prepared for him in the beat it took him to be standing before her.

"Mrs. Montoya!" He pressed a somewhat sincere kiss

on her cheek and gave her a once over. "My, don't you have a glow in your cheeks. I'd almost accuse you of being on vacation in our busiest time, but I know you're much too hard working for that. Please, join me for lunch." And with that, he took her on his arm and led her into the ballroom.

Though Sheila had braced herself, she had forgotten how overpowering Ed could be. 'Formidable', Ma had called him once. Before she knew it, he had pushed through the lunch line and entered the hall. It was named after some tree she didn't catch, perhaps maple. Sheila smiled and looked engaged. After she had gotten over the initial shock of his extremely high energy, she actually was interested in all he had to say.

"Sarah asked about you last week. She sends her love, of course. She wishes she could see you, but you know she can't stand these things. Your calls to her after we lost Johnny kept her going. It was so thoughtful of you to reach out to her directly. You're the only one in the company who did. She looks forward to your calls every other Tuesday morning. You don't call me, but I'm the boss, I get it. She's still waiting for me to give it all up and take her on that cruise around the world that I promised. That was forty-six years ago! Haha! Well, maybe one of these days. I might take a page out of your book and just chuck it all.

"Now what is all that about? Let me say my dear how sorry I am about your loss. And all of us at the head office want to express our sympathies to you. A person only has to know you but a little while to see how much you loved your mother and what a special relationship you had with her. You have really done her proud in the way you have carried on, I'm sure. I hope you know that. I've reviewed your work since you returned, stellar as ever, until last week anyway. What's happened there? And this time I *will* pause long enough for you to answer!"

They both laughed at that one. He pulled out a chair for her on the dais. Sheila had forgotten how much she liked this man. He was a bit rash and intolerant of fools, but in many ways, he was very much what she had wished her own father had been like.

"Well, it wasn't for lack of trying, but I think John wanted my tenure there to end a little sooner than I had planned. And I can't work without files, so I have been drawing a bit of vacation time. I was home trying to relax, and it was driving me crazy! I just don't know how not to work. But luckily my assistant has been unflagging in his support. I'm taking him with me, you know. He's very eager to get a leg up and learn more. I only hope I don't fall on my face. And that's my story, except it can't begin to convey my love for the company, my job here and all I've been a part of, or, quite honestly, my affection for you. So I can only hope my past actions and future endeavors will make those things evident and honor them."

"Oh my girl, never have I been more pleased with a practiced speech!"

"Oh you! I just wanted to have something nice to say for my departure. Don't you go teasing me over it."

"Never! Now, seriously, what do I need to do to get you to stay? You said it yourself: you can't stand not to work. Whatever you need, and not only because you're the daughter I never had, or because you've saved us millions and tons of bad press. You've actually made things better inside. People are happier. They feel safer and more secure because of the systems you've set in place, and because of your touchy-feely mediations. Never thought such a silly thing would work, but it has. So what'll it be, time off, a raise, fire John? Yes, I thought that last option would raise an eyebrow. Not so much fire as reassign to another office. He *hasn't* saved me millions."

"He hired me."

"I think we both know what that was about. And I must say, you don't appear to have given in to it, though sometimes its hard to tell. Oh yes, I know it all. The benefits of being king."

Sheila marveled at this man. Even Raines didn't know about the determined flirtation John had laid siege upon her with when she was first hired. Once, he had actually pinned her down on the couch in her office. She had gone home crying to her mom that night. Then for some reason, John had just stopped. She wondered after it, but never regretted the change, the change that in the back of her mind she always knew her mother had had something to do with, but had been to afraid to ask about.

"Ed, thank you for your condolences, and please thank your office as well. I won't say any more on that and avoid the risk of running my mascara. But really, I think its time for me to leave the company. I've got some things I need to deal with, and I need some space to do that. I'm actually excited about striking out on my own. I can't say what it means to me that you are willing to pull out all the stops for me to stay. It makes me feel valued. Thank you. I won't be staying, though."

Sheila was really shaken. She doubted everything now. Should she stay? He was offering to move John, and give her anything else she wanted. She wanted to ask God what to do, but instead of feeling torn about that, she was too ashamed to even consider it. So instead of feeling conflicted, she just felt confused. And that was a sensation she was used to.

"You sound resolved, but you don't look it. First chink in your armor I believe I've ever seen. Hmmm...That offer's good until we hire your replacement. And in the time you've got left on the job, I want a report into my office, not John's, on where everything stands, including your recommendations about how your position should be carried out in the future, and what we should be looking for in a replacement. Now that should give you something to do, even if John has all your files. I know you have copies of all the important records. Sounds like your office is a hostile place, so work from home and email me the information if you like." Mark was beaming. Just the thought of productive work sent him reeling in joy. Here was a man who was fit to lead.

"Yes sir." she said with a little salute.

"Now give me a bunch of your business cards so I can pedal your wares to my colleagues."

They both laughed and chatted on through lunch. When they parted at the doors of the banquet hall, she felt a little refreshed, having accomplished all she had hoped to and more in her talk with him. That left only a few more things to do.

CHAPTER FORTY-ONE
THE CHASE

Raines lay in the bed thinking. His head was swimming with thoughts, yet somehow still calm. He had been napping on and off all day. He figured he needed, and had earned, a good rest. Sometime earlier Jasmin and Corrine had come in bearing a delicious breakfast on a tray. Raines thought that was nice. Jasmin sat on the edge of the bed while he ate and Corrine stood over him. They peered at him for a while and asked a few questions as to how he felt. Once they seemed satisfied, the mood lightened and they went from an atmosphere of two doctors and their patient to one of more relaxed family chatting. Jasmin had a knowing grin on her face and Corinne a chastising look on hers throughout— as if they knew exactly what Sheila and he had been up to last night. He wondered, how loud had they been?

He was full and having a rather good time until their conversation turned to Sheila. That's when the mixed emotions started. Here was the wife he loved, that he had just made love to, the future mother of his children, and she had just defied him! It was so unlike her. There had been plenty of times where she had gone on and done what she wanted to do despite his objections, but usually she turned him around so much that he would think it was his idea and only figure out afterwards that she had gotten the better of him.

Thinking about what she had told him only a week before and how the Godliest person he knew suddenly couldn't stand God really sent him on a head-trip. He didn't even want to think about what she had just done to her own sister. He was sure he didn't even understand the half of that.

And he didn't want to talk about any of that with either of them. He needed to talk about it with Sheila, but he guessed that that was not going to happen any time soon. So, he lay down and God forgive him, pretended to be sleepy so that they would leave. It wasn't a complete lie. He really had been tired.

Now, a couple of long naps later, he was in many ways in the same position he had been in with them—only he couldn't run away from himself, and he was no longer that sleepy.

He thought back to his memories of the night before. There had been…something…inside him. Something wrong, a curse taken form, just like Sheila had said. When Jas and Corrine had come down those stairs, the most painful and confusing moments of his life had started. He had tried to wrap his head around it a thousand different ways, but to no avail. It really was an exorcism—there was just no way around it. He hadn't known how bad off he had been until they had pulled that—*thing*—out of him and he could look over his attitude and behavior of the last week in hindsight. He had been as close to an abomination as he ever wanted to be. How Sheila had put up with him he didn't even know. Yet she had done it—and given him 4 square meals a day to boot. And completely yielded herself up to him the moment he was healed. And then turned around and defied him like it was going out of style! He was getting a headache just thinking about her.

One thing was for sure, it was a lot harder to deny what she had told him about her 'destiny' since his experience last night. It wasn't that he hadn't believed in the things that she and her mother had practiced and believed; he just didn't have any experience with them. Raines had to come to the cold truth that he had not thought most of the things Sheila and her mother had done were necessary— maybe he had never thought they were real at all.

But now, it was a lot harder to view what Sheila had told him as irrelevant and simply the rantings of an eccentric and unbalanced woman. Oh, she was unbalanced alright.

250

Now though, he was inclined to see that there was more to it than that—a lot more.

But last night had also been more than that. The start of a new chapter in their relationship. A change in him and his walk with the Lord, one that he hoped was still unfolding. He hadn't minded it at all. Maybe it had even been the start of a new life. All of these thoughts he wanted to share with his wife, his best friend. To admit to her he had never valued the spiritual side of her nearly as much as he should have, to talk about what she was going to do with her relationship with God now, to talk about how wonderful he felt about what they had done last night, to ask a billion questions about what Jas and Corrine had done to him and what he needed to do next, to ask about how he could let his love for the Lord grow. To give her the space to talk about what had happened between her and Jasmin earlier—if she wanted to. Most of all he just wanted to hold her tight for as long as it took for him to know that everything would be alright.

But she was in New York and he was lying in their bed in Maryland. And while he was no longer sleepy, that didn't mean his body wanted to cooperate either. He felt like all the strength and energy had been drained out of his limbs and had no idea when it would return. As much as he absolutely hated feeling powerless and out of control, he had gone through enough to be forced to admit that, just for a little while, he was going to just have to accept the way things were instead of bending them to his will.

Making a not so small effort to turn over onto his stomach he let out a huge sigh just as he heard a gentle rap on the door. "Come in Jas," he muttered through his pillow.

Jas came in with her coat on. Corrine followed behind with her jacket over her arm. And Raines pushed himself to sit up at the sight of this.

"We didn't want to disturb you. Lord knows you need your rest," Corrine rushed, "but Jasmine said it would be unthinkable to leave without saying goodbye."

Raines blinked as he took this in and put two and two together. "Oh, right. Sheila mentioned it was a quick trip." He felt kind of sad. He hadn't wanted to be alone just yet. "Um, listen…" he searched for words but found none to frame his awkward question any more gracefully, so he just blurted it out. "Am I ok? Is there something I need to do?"

Jasmin walked over and gave him a big hug. "Just keep being you and you will be fine," she beamed. "And I hope it goes without saying—you head for the hills the before you mix it up with Massad again, brother-in-law. You were meant for better things than to have to be rescued by two women," she said knowingly, putting her finger precisely on the fine point Raines had been trying to keep his ego from focusing on all day.

Raines paused, but by now he was used to being caught off guard by the insight of what Jasmin said, so it didn't take him too long to recover. "I'm glad you were here." It was all his ego would allow him to admit. "Let me see you out," he rushed to pull off the covers before he had a chance to realize two things. First, he hadn't the strength to jump out of bed, even though his mind thought otherwise. Second, he was stark naked.

Jasmin let out an "Oh My!" and a giggle at exactly the same time as Corrine growled an exasperated, "Oh really!" and just a second before Raines used the remainder of his strength to pull the covers back over himself and closed his eyes.

Jasmin pulled herself together and said slowly, "I think the best thing to do is leave now. Our cab is here and we'll just close the door behind us."

Raines peeked at them as they were walking out of the room. He thought he could hear Jas say, "That Sheila's a lucky gal," and Corrine respond, "I *guess*," begrudgingly. At least that did a little for his ego, which was very nearly crushed beyond recognition. He settled back into bed and took a look under the covers. Well, at least he had represented well. Sheila would howl with laughter when she found out about this.

Trying to focus his mind, Raines thought more seriously. He had to get himself to New York. He needed Sheila. Groping for the phone, he thought over his decision again. He really had no energy. Jasmin had said to rest. But he needed his wife. So, he had to get to New York.

He had been tired before. He had been exhausted before. Yet he had always gotten the job done. He called a cab to the airport and by guts alone managed to take a shower, pack an overnight bag and get himself downstairs. Just like always, Sheila had left every conceivable piece of information on her whereabouts on a few pieces of paper from her memo pad on the refrigerator. Raines stuffed them in a pocket and put on his coat just as a horn honked outside.

At a little after four, he had touched down at La Guardia and was in a cab in bumper-to-bumper traffic. It had only occurred to him when he was on the plane that he wasn't dressed to be able to blend in with her conference. And he would really get it if he embarrassed her by slumming around the lobby in any less than the best of business attire. Or even her room for that matter. Who knew if she were schmoozing some CFO or potential client up there? But he had to see her. So that concern became secondary.

CHAPTER FORTY-TWO
THE PRESENTATION

After lunch, Sheila was tired. But things were just getting started. She hopped between a few different panels for a couple of hours. If she never saw another black or dark blue suit it would be too soon. Really, she was just marking time until 4:30—the start of the plenary session she and John had been scheduled to present together. Now it was just John presenting, and she was overflowing with barely contained contempt for him. She needed a focal point on which she could pour out all her anger and frustration. And it was his misfortune to be so convenient.

So, she brought her focus to bear in sitting through parts of a few sessions between lunch and that appointed hour, made a few insightful comments during breaks to make her presence felt, and in general tried to be memorable in a sea of hundreds of others trying to do the same.

At a little after four, she felt as if she might drop. Running up to her room she took a cold washcloth to the back of her neck in an effort to break the unbearable heat that had been pressing down on her since she had left home. She shook it off, refusing to think about those recent events.

She had to laugh. As horrible as things were, she had to admit what her sister had uttered in her ear yesterday had been true. She couldn't escape God. Even in her most valiant and severe efforts to reject him, she was now more than ever intimately aware of just how miserable life could be without Him as the center. She didn't know how people lived like this—but one thing was for sure, she was going to find out. After all, Raines had basically lived without God his whole life and she had married him, so it stood to reason her life— although a lot more empty—just might be alright.

4:15. Sheila, clad in a soft pink two-piece with white trimming, made tracks to the main ballroom and grabbed a seat at the back of the crowd of dark suits, preparing herself for the last hoorah of life as a company girl. One look in the mirror had told her she couldn't take much more of this. She had to go home. Somehow make amends to her sister, check in on her husband, and who knows, maybe even make another unsuccessful attempt at "resting." But for the next hour, her agenda was John—figuring out what was in his head and making sure he felt the full brunt of her displeasure.

As the lights dimmed slightly, John stood up on the dais and suddenly two six-foot projections of his head appeared on screens to either side of him. He looked good, she had to admit—keen, tenacious, experienced, prepared. She wondered if she had looked as good today. A not so confident 'of course' echoed in her mind.

"If I could have your complete attention and a quiet focused room, I'll tell you perhaps the most amazing story you've ever heard." Sheila perked up and leaned forward.

"I'll tell you a story that can change your life, captivate you, thrill you, and shine a ray of hope into your lives." As the spotlight tightened on his face the crowd seemed to hush and wait on his every word.

"I am going to tell you how I can make work at the company more fulfilling, how you can give the best you never even knew you had on the job—and save MILLIONS doing it!"

The crowd laughed and applauded at his dramatic introduction. Sheila just broiled. Those were her words verbatim. Begrudgingly, she had to admit he hadn't delivered them half bad. What had she expected? It was abundantly clear he had no intention of falling flat on his face.

"Raise your hand if the work my department has done has made your work environment better." Nearly two-thirds of the hands around the room went up.

"Now, the rest of you are lawyers, and you have my

apologies that your workload has been lighter since we've made some changes." John made a grandiose bow as the crowd laughed again. Even Sheila chuckled. She didn't know he had it in him. And she had to admit; the sight of all those raised hands had stunned her. She knew that the "work my department has done" was largely her work. And until this moment she had had no idea just how impactful it had been.

"I'm going to let you into the inner sanctum," John's voice lowered, "share with you my secrets to success, blueprints for the future, and the power of now—all before dinner." The crowd erupted.

Damn, he was killing. Even Sheila as his strongest opponent could see that. What, had he been secretly going to comedy and elocution lessons?

"Now, wherever my assistant is, she needs to get over to the control booth and start the slides so we can get this presentation started. I know how seriously you all take your meals and I wouldn't dream of keeping you here past my appointed time, but we do have a lot to get through. So, anytime hon, and we can jump right into it."

A few more chuckles and some began to look in the back of the room at the raised booth holding a myriad of sound and video equipment. Sheila wondered who John had helping him, looking near the booth she didn't see his AA or executive secretary. She wasn't sure why he needed help anyway, as the presentation they had prepared basically ran itself. How drastically had he changed it that it needed hand holding to get through, she wondered?

"Mrs. Sheila Montoya, Mrs. Sheila Orly Montoya. If you are within the sound of my voice, please get it together, get up to the A/V booth and do your job."

John's lightheartedly barked orders brought a kind of embarrassed and hesitant laughter from the audience as more of them looked around. It took about two beats for his words to sink in, then she went a ghostly white and stone cold. A few people who knew her had spotted her and stared expectantly. She wanted to curl into a ball and vanish.

"Sheila? Hon, let's get this show on the road now…Anyone see her? Oh," He had his hands above his eyes squinting into the crowd. "That's her in the back with the pink? Earth calling Sheila, Earth calling Sheila." A few more, very few, embarrassed laughs sprinkled the hall.

Sheila felt compelled to slink from her chair to the A/V both on the other side of the hall, but what was that about? More slave mentality? Jumping when he said jump, no matter how humiliating and unreasonable the order? She was mad, as outraged as she had ever been. And, as she was rarely an indecisive woman at moments like this, she made up her mind on the only thing to be done. Standing up, she smoothed out her skirt, making sure to take her time. She gave John a little wave and, as coolly as a woman who was on fire could, walked nonchalantly out of the room.

In the elevator, she could barely hold back hot, angry, humiliated tears. She just crossed her arms and tapped her foot in a fury until she got to floor 25 and sped off to her room. All the bluster and hate she felt on the way up gave way to the humiliation and pain that overtook her once locked in her room and away from the world. She crumpled against an ottoman on the floor. She wondered if this was what Hell felt like, the gnashing of teeth and all. What had possessed him to pull such a stunt? He really wanted to hurt her. She thought ruefully about how right Raines had been in his objections this morning.

And, as she racked herself with tears, she took a desperate and biased inventory of her life, with everything in the negatives column. Marital disaster seemed on the way. She had just been professionally humiliated. Her sisters must hate her by now. She was the daughter of a dead mother who would be ashamed of what she had become. Sheila was a godless, joyless, directionless witch. What a life.

How long she lay propped up against that ottoman crying no one could say, especially her. But eventually her sobs became less violent and she began to realize a freezing cold had penetrated her. Looking up—her head was killing her and would hardly even turn properly—she took in the scene across the room.

The thin white curtains at her windows were whipping at the window, half the length of the wall, which was pivoted and half open. That opening seemed to glow white hot, and she wondered about it.

CHAPTER FORTY-THREE
COMPLICATIONS

Raines regretted dressing so casually all over again the moment he stepped into the hotel lobby, where the cover of GQ seemed to have exploded in on itself. By his watch it was about 5:30. Likely, Sheila would still be caught up in the conference. As charming and commanding as he could be, he wondered if anything could overcome the impression his jeans would make on Sheila if he walked up to her in the midst of a formal function with her colleagues.

He had seen a Burberry a couple blocks back that the cab had passed. He turned back toward the hotel's revolving entrance doors, deciding incurring her wrath about his casual wear was just not worth it, when something inside him simply said, "No."

"Oh Hell," he muttered, turning around and walking back toward the desk before his mind could start wondering where that voice had come from within him and why.

"Hi, I need to see Mrs. Sheila Montoya: she should have checked in this morning."

"Certainly sir." A pleasant looking woman typed into a computer on the other side of the desk. "Yes, she is checked in. If you would step down to the courtesy phone at the end of the desk I can ring you through to her room," she said, motioning to a phone about fifteen feet away.

"I need to *see* her. What room is she in?"

Raines saw her quickly take in his apparel before continuing, "I'm sorry sir, we don't give out the room number of any of our guests. I'm sure you understand, security reasons."

He regretted for a third time not dressing better. He leaned forward and tried to bleed just a hint of commanding into his tone, but perhaps it came out angry and fed up instead. "I'm *sure* there's something we can do."

"Perhaps I can be of assistance sir?" A passing manager stood beside the desk operator to face him.

"I hope so, I'm trying to see Sheila Montoya and need more than to be connected by phone to her room," Raines said, still directing his attention to the young woman.

"Sheila Montoya. I know Sheila, she stays here at least once a month on business. Who, may I ask, are you?"

"I'm her husband, Raines Montoya, and I very much need to see her," Raines said impatiently.

"You. You're her husband?" The manager looked a bit flustered.

"Yes," Raines responded, feeling suddenly challenged, "Want to see the marriage license?"

"No, no," the manager said, fumbling with his papers. "Sheila has reserved the room in both of your names. If I could just see some id."

After a highly irritated Raines had shown his id and been given a key to room 2505, the manager stood looking in the direction he had walked. That was *not* the man who had walked up claiming to be Mrs. Montoya's husband earlier.

On the way up in the elevator, Rains had an uneasy, anxious feeling that had nothing to do with the nervous man at the check-in desk.

CHAPTER FORTY-FOUR
JUMP

Sheila struggled awkwardly to her feet, breaking a heel in the process, kicking off her shoes as she made her way to the window filled with one thought: 'I can be out of this pain *now*.' She braced her arms at the edges of the open window, noticing that even with the pivoted glass in the middle, there was still enough space for her to stand up in the opening. 'I can end this now.' She rifled through her thoughts to find the reasons why she should go on living and found not one. Oh, yes. This was the answer! Just end it. And relief drained through her at the thought that this pain would shortly be gone.

She put a foot up at the bottom of the window but hadn't the strength to hoist herself up. Looking back, she grabbed her head with her hands, remembering from the jarring movement that her head was still killing her and hurt to move. She saw the ottoman that she had just cried a river on. With a sudden cool calm, she walked toward the ottoman, and began to push it towards the window.

But when she turned to face that direction, something, someone, was blocking her path. Any day before her mother had died, she would have cried for joy at the sight. Floating about a foot from the floor, a Chinese woman stood on a large lotus petal, holding a vase that was leaning forward just enough for water to flow out of it in one hand, while her other hand made a Vishnu sign for peace. It was Quan Yin, the Buddhist Goddess of Mercy, the deity she felt closest to in all of heaven and earth.

She just fell forward into her arms, despite all the prostrate, reverent obeisance she should have made. And in those arms, which quickly moved to enfold her, she found pure unconditional love.

"I want to die," Sheila muttered as she dropped her arms to her sides, completely supported by the Goddess' embrace. "How can I be what she wanted me to be without her?" Out of tears, her voice was weak and croaky. "Help me," she pleaded.

Moving away from her, Quan Yin motioned toward her with the left hand three times and slowly faded away into empty space. Sheila noticed the window no longer glowed. But it was still open. The ottoman was still halfway towards the window.

She understood. By Quan Yin removing the enchantment on the window, she had steadied her a bit emotionally. But she wasn't going to stop her, to force her to live. She had to make up her own mind what she was going to do.

Sheila walked toward the window, skirting around where the goddess had been. Again, she braced her hands on the edges of the window, leaning her head out and looking down. A long, straight drop. No way she would end up just horribly injured, that jump would kill her. She eased to lean against the wall beside the window, one hand still gripping the edge.

Now that she was a little less hysterical, the full weight of what she was considering brought itself to bear. She saw how wrong and unfair this would be on her sisters and husband, to all of her family. And what if she had gotten pregnant last night? That would be two lives she would take by jumping.

Her mind wandered back to her Summers as a child. She and her sisters were in Virginia with their cousins, living their best, inexhaustible lives. They played croquet on Grandma's lawn and threatened each other with their mallets. They ran around Great Aunt Jean's yard playing freeze tag until they were absolutely breathless. They scared each other witless playing Bloody Mary at night in the bathroom mirror.

262

Once they had even made small cuts in their hands and held them together to become blood brothers. It didn't occur to them that they were already related. They were her family, and she would go to Hell and back for them.

But deciding not to kill yourself solely on account of others was crazy. That couldn't be the only reason. There had to be some reason she should live for *her*. She just couldn't find that reason. Didn't she have to have a reason? You just couldn't decide to keep on living out of pure grit, could you?

No, she couldn't stay alive for other people or just out of spite. Her biggest fear had come to pass: circumstances had revealed that she was an utter failure. And, amidst all the hurt and pain of that—her grief, mistakes she made, and the humiliation of the moment—the thought of suicide was not only *not* repulsive, it was actually welcome and relieving.

Her hand flexed as she hoisted herself back toward the window.

"*Baby girl,*" came a voice that froze her in her tracks.

"Not again," she growled between her clenched teeth. "Not again!"

A hand touched her shoulder and she turned around, nearly stumbling out of the window in shock as what she saw registered in her head. But now she wanted to live, frantically grabbing the sides of the window and propelling herself away from it. Before her stood her mother!

"*Baby girl.*"

Thank God! It had all been a dream. Everything was back to normal. She stumbled toward her mother, meaning to embrace her forever. As she did, her mother glided away from her toward the door. Not walked, glided.

Damn, not the real thing, just an apparition. It hadn't been a dream. If anything, this was the dream. But still.

"If this is my dream, let me touch you!" Sheila cried out, "Hold me in your arms as you used to."

"*I should not be here, and I cannot be touched by you.*" Cathy's voice and manner seemed stiff. "*Even though I never taught you much of what you needed to know, I would have chosen you to replace me as the gatekeeper.*"

"Pick someone else! Can't you see it's undone me?"

"*From every generation, there is one. The decision was made before you were even born. There are no mistakes. But that's not why I came.*"

Sheila looked shamefully back to the open window.

"*That's not why I came either,*" Cathy said, moving towards her. She moved her hand towards Sheila's face, then withdrew it before it touched her. "*I wanted to tell you that I love you. I'll always love you. I'm so proud of you,*" tears streamed down her face and her voice trembled with emotion. "*And maybe I never told you, but you were always my hero, my strength. I've been trying to wake you up for a long time. Shouting at the top of my lungs. Trying to shake you awake—out of fear and into possibility. No matter what happens, I am always in your corner, I'll always believe in you.*"

Even as she said these words, she began to fade away, leaving a white mist where she had been. Sheila dropped to her knees. Her mommy believed in her. She rose and turned to face the window, walking determinedly towards it. She pushed the ottoman the rest of the way and used it to climb into the open window. Gripping the edges with her feet and arms, leaning out as far as she could, Sheila cried out at the top of her lungs, "I must live!!!"

She was wrong about not being able to live for someone else. She wanted to make it true, everything her mother had said to her. She wanted to grow strong and make her proud, to be someone who was worth her mother's love, to show herself and the world that her mom had not made a mistake in believing in her. It was enough of a reason to live. It *had* to be.

Very slowly, Sheila eased herself back in from the window to stand on the ottoman and then the floor. She slammed the window shut so fiercely that she almost shattered the glass, and the force of the air she displaced felt like a cold slap in the face. Waking her up. Awake at last.

She stood up and kneaded the muscles in the back of her neck, turning around to see Raines, frozen in the doorway, ashen as a ghost. Crossing the distance between them in a beat, Raines was holding her face in his hands. "Are you alright?" he asked frantically.

Sheila gripped his forearms and looked in his eyes, "Finally, I am," and fell into his arms.

"What were you *doing*?" he asked as he squeezed her.

"You wouldn't believe me if I told you," Sheila gave an exhausted laugh.

"Try me."

"I will. I'll tell you all about it. Raines," she moved back to look him in the eyes, "I'm so sorry for everything, but it's going to be alright. It's all going to be alright."

Raines pulled her head towards his chest as his heart sang with relief. "That's my girl." He murmured as he rocked her gently.

Minutes later they were in bed. Out cold.

Later that night, they finally woke up, and, over room service, talked until the sun rose. They exchanged equally earnest apologies over their behavior of late. Raines' eyes popped out more than once as Sheila recounted her experience that day, and he held her tight as she finally talked about her mom and all she had been feeling since she died. He rubbed her back through her tearful apology to Jasmin on her cell phone and smiled as he heard their conversation turn to one of laughter.

Then it was Sheila's turn to hold him, as he talked about all of his feelings in the last week since he had been cursed, then dried his tears over Cathy's passing, and yes, doubled over with laughter that the Montoya family jewels had been on display for her sisters.

"So you're back on God's side?" Raines asked as Sheila leaned against his chest, both of them sitting up to watch the sunrise.

"Yes," Sheila's voice seemed half resigned, and half at peace. "I mean, I'm still upset with Him, but I think I'll get over it. I want to get back to my old self and go even beyond that, to make her proud, and I think, in the end, everything will be alright."

"Sounds good. Sounds great," Raines held her snug around the waist, "So, what do we do now?"

Sheila nestled more into him and let out a long pensive sigh. "Well, I have a long list of things, but, to start, why don't we just go home and get some rest?"

Raines let out a sigh of his own. "Music to my ears. But can we wait awhile on that? I'm just too tired to go home right now," he laughed. And as the sun rose, they fell fast asleep again. As they drifted off, they didn't know it, but they were both thinking the same thing, 'Thank you God.'

Sheila had her nightmare again, lying stabbed and bleeding by an assassin she could not see. She woke up in a fright and for the first time in a week, Raines was there again to soothe her. When he said everything would be alright, she actually believed him. Somewhere inside her, past all her grief, pain, fear of failure, and uncertainty, she just knew it was true.

EPILOGUE
AWAKE

During their late checkout that afternoon, Raines coolly observed the twitchy desk manager as Sheila signed a few papers and handed in their key cards. He made a note to ask Sheila about it when they were on less of a high. By eight that night they were finally home, a place it seemed they hadn't been in a long time. Raines started a fire in the chimera on the patio while Sheila made some tea and put it in two travel mugs. They sat on the porch in their coats sipping tea for a long time.

"Great tea," Raines said, taking another swig.

"Yeah, I *thought* you'd like the whisky in it, you lush," Sheila elbowed him.

"Hey, good is good." Raines drained the cup.

Sheila unfolded her legs from underneath her and moved to the edge of the bench, dropping her head into her hands.

"What can I do," Raines asked as he pulled her into his lap.

"Oh, you're doing it. Now there are some things *I've* got to do." Sheila straightened up and slowly stood. Raines followed her inside.

"Brrrrrr. It's cold out there!" Sheila cried as she peeled out of her coat, hat and gloves. "Oh!" she gasped as Raines suddenly pulled her towards him, smothering her with kisses and holding her tight. "Oookaaay, I see you've got your sea legs back," she laughed.

"I want you," he murmured as he nuzzled her neck.

To be honest, sex had been the furthest thing from her mind. But now that he mentioned it…She shook that thought away and stamped her foot, "I told you, I've got stuff to do!"

He caressed the side of her face and gave her an intense kiss. "Don't take long," he growled as much as commanded. With what looked like considerable effort, he unwrapped his arms from her and headed out of the kitchen. She heard him stomping up the stairs like a spoiled kid having a tantrum.

Smiling and shaking her head, she walked towards her study. Flicking on the light, she sighed to see it wasn't as organized as she liked it, which meant there were one or two files and papers out of place. Ignoring that, she moved to sit down at her desk and turned on the banker's light.

Pulling out some of her nicer paper and selecting the fountain pen that was filled with purple ink, she sat thinking a few minutes, tapping the pen against her temple. For the next ten minutes she scribbled on her paper, then, being the neat freak that she was, carefully rewrote her notes on a fresh piece of paper.

Actually, they weren't notes so much as questions. Who had opened the window in her hotel room? What price had her mother paid to appear in her room instead of transitioning to the next level? Had Momma's death been natural? What was she going to do about Massad? How would she get her relationship with God back on track? What would she do about Ma's Institute? Who was Hotep to her? The last question was the biggest: what would it mean to fill her mom's shoes as gatekeeper?

Setting her pen down, she reread the neatly scripted words a few times, committing them to memory. Leaning back in her chair, she let it all sink in for a moment. Then she did something she hadn't in what seemed like forever. Slowly sliding down onto her knees, she clasped her hands together, leaning her head against the desk. She had a little talk with God. She got back on track.

Placing a hand on her desk and heaving herself up, she straightened out and headed out the door with an eye towards the steps upstairs. 'Now, about that husband of mine,' she thought, smiling. A woman's work was never done.

Made in the USA
Columbia, SC
05 September 2021